Readers love Kate McMurray

What's the Use of Wondering?

"This is a beautifully done, sweet, sexy, romantic, true love tale! Highly recommended to bring a smile to your face!"

—*Divine Magazine*

"…a sweet coming of age/transitioning to adulthood story."

—Jessie G Books

There Has to Be a Reason

"…a beautifully written story. Very realistic. Definitely a book I would recommend to others."

—Gay Book Reviews

"…I really enjoyed this. I had never read this author before but will definitely read more of her work."

—Night Owl Reviews

The Boy Next Door

"The story was unique and not something I've read over and over, which is refreshing!"

—Alpha Book Club

"I was completely captivated by this book."

—Inked Rainbow Reads

By Kate McMurray

Blind Items
The Boy Next Door
Devin December
Domestic Do-over
Four Corners
Kindling Fire with Snow
Out in the Field
The Stars that Tremble • The Silence of the Stars
A Walk in the Dark
What There Is
When the Planets Align

DREAMSPUN DESIRES
The Greek Tycoon's Green Card Groom

ELITE ATHLETES
Here Comes the Flood
Stick the Landing
Race for Redemption

THE RAINBOW LEAGUE
The Windup
Thrown a Curve
The Long Slide Home

WMU
There Has to Be a Reason
What's the Use of Wondering

Published by Dreamspinner Press
www.dreamspinnerpress.com

DOMESTIC DO-OVER

Kate McMurray

Published by
DREAMSPINNER PRESS

5032 Capital Circle SW, Suite 2, PMB# 279, Tallahassee, FL 32305-7886 USA
www.dreamspinnerpress.com

This is a work of fiction. Names, characters, places, and incidents either are the product of author imagination or are used fictitiously, and any resemblance to actual persons, living or dead, business establishments, events, or locales is entirely coincidental.

Mass Market Paperback ISBN: 978-1-64108-230-3
Trade Paperback ISBN: 978-1-64405-836-7
Digital ISBN: 978-1-64405-835-0
Library of Congress Control Number: 2020944413
Trade Paperback published February 2021
v. 1.0

Printed in the United States of America

This paper meets the requirements of
ANSI/NISO Z39.48-1992 (Permanence of Paper).

DOMESTIC DO-OVER

Kate McMurray

Chapter One

"Dream" Divorce! screamed the tabloid headline. It was the first thing Brandon saw when he got out of the subway. The story was punctuated by a photo of Brandon looking distressed.

He knew he should have taken a cab.

It was a windy, late-winter day in New York, and a recent dusting of snow danced like a cloud across the 14th Street sidewalk as Brandon walked west toward the Restoration Channel offices near Chelsea Market. He tried to focus on those snowflakes instead of his recent, well-publicized divorce, especially since so much of what was being printed in the tabloids was about eight miles from the truth.

And now he'd been summoned to the Restoration Channel offices, probably to negotiate the end of his contract, because his very popular house-flipping show, cohosted with his pretty wife, had been summarily canceled the minute the word *divorce* was first uttered in public.

Then again, maybe getting off TV would be good for him. He could reopen his old real estate agency and parlay some of his fame into a few clients to get started. He could return to obscurity and not worry about tabloid headlines or television contracts. He could give up trying to make his marriage look like a happy union instead of the fraud it was.

He walked into the reception area and was greeted by a woman who grinned widely when he appeared.

"Oh, Mr. Chase! It's so great to see you. I'm so sorry about the divorce."

He nodded.

"That Kayla was a real bitch, stepping out on you the way she did. I totally understand why you wanted to end things."

"That's not really—" But Brandon cut himself off. It wasn't worth getting into, especially not if the network was about to end his contract.

"Mr. Harwood is expecting you," the receptionist said. "I'll walk you back."

He followed the receptionist to the office of Garrett Harwood, the head of programming for the Restoration Channel, a network that aired mostly the kinds of programming people had on in the background when they stayed in hotels. Home renovation and fashion makeover shows were the network's bread and butter. The channel was incredibly popular, which was the main reason Brandon's divorce was such big news. His show, *Dream Home*, had been a massive hit for the network… which was probably why everything crashed down on him so hard when the paparazzi caught Kayla out to dinner with her boyfriend.

He steeled himself and walked into the office. "Hello, Mr. Harwood."

"Brandon! So good to see you. Please have a seat."

Brandon debated making small talk first but ultimately decided not to say anything, and instead just sat in the chair across the desk from Harwood.

"Let me cut to the chase," Harwood said.

Brandon's pulse kicked up a notch. Here it came. His time as a minor celebrity with a show on the Restoration Channel was coming to an end.

"I have an opportunity for you."

That was the last thing Brandon expected to hear. "You… what?"

Harwood grinned. "Here's the deal. While I don't regret canceling *Dream Home* because the show couldn't have continued under the circumstances, you still have a lot of goodwill with this company and remain incredibly popular with our viewership. Even the *Dream Home* reruns we've been airing on Tuesday nights are getting huge ratings. So we'd like to offer you a new show."

"Are you serious?" Brandon was so sure he was coming here today to get fired that he'd basically already planned out his retirement from television stardom. Part of him had been sad at the prospect of leaving the limelight, but another part was looking forward to it. So much of his life had been given over to maintaining his public image that he was kind of looking forward to just… living.

But no, Harwood wanted him to star in another TV show.

"Here's the premise," Harwood said. "Are you familiar with Victorian Flatbush?"

"That little area in Brooklyn with all the old mansions?"

"The same! Well, my daughter just bought a house there, so I was walking around the neighborhood. Some of those houses are gorgeous, but many are pretty run-down. There are, in fact, six for sale just in a four-block radius, all at bargain prices. Well, bargain for Brooklyn."

Brandon could see where this was going. "Wait, you want to do a show about flipping Victorian mansions in Brooklyn?"

"Exactly."

That would be a hard no from Brandon. Flipping houses in New York City was just too risky, an incredible financial investment that probably wouldn't pay off. Even if one could get the house cheap, the labor and materials cost more than in most other parts of the country. It was why he and Kayla had usually flipped houses in the distant suburbs. Not to mention those old houses often had all kinds of hidden problems and would have to be brought up to code, which could get *really* expensive. The odds of him turning a profit on a house like that were pretty small.

"I can see you're hesitating," Harwood said. "We could expand out of the neighborhood in the second season and work on brownstones, or make over houses in the outer parts of Brooklyn. But I think the New York angle is key. Show the world that the city is more than just big apartment buildings."

"The financial risk—"

"We'll up your per-episode salary from what you were getting on *Dream Home*, and the network will go in on every house you buy to help shoulder some of the risk. That's how invested we are in making this work."

That did change the equation. On *Dream Home*, although they'd received a salary, the financial risk of actually flipping the houses was entirely on Brandon and Kayla, meaning they'd often had to compromise to make a profit. Nothing dangerous; Brandon had always thought an important part of house flipping was to give buyers a place to live that was safe and welcoming. But it meant laminate instead of hardwood in some cases, or not removing load-bearing walls, or buying backsplash tiles on clearance instead of the more expensive ones they liked better—that sort of thing. Kayla had always had a good eye for a bargain and could tweak a design if it was more cost-effective to do so. After they had the requisite fight about the design on camera, of course.

They'd both had roles to play. On the show Brandon was the frugal one who wanted to keep the design practical and attractive to a wide range of buyers. Kayla liked things a little splashier and was willing to spend more on great design even if it meant narrowing the pool of potential homeowners. The reality was that Kayla wanted the profits more than anything and usually introduced something wild and then caved to show that they were willing to compromise.

That they were a loving couple working together on projects they were passionate about. That was the whole story of the show.

"We're calling the new show *Domestic Do-over*." Harwood held up his hands, miming a marquee. "It's good, right? I love alliteration."

Brandon almost laughed. Harwood was fairly new to the network. His predecessor had only retired about a year before, so Brandon hadn't worked with Harwood much. Brandon supposed *Domestic Do-over* was a pretty clever name for a show about home renovation.

"Okay," said Brandon. "What about Kayla?"

Harwood shook his head. "What about her? You're not working together anymore."

"No, but… I mean, she still has a contract and…."

"We're buying out the rest of it. This would be a show hosted just by you."

"I know, but—"

"Look, we gave this a lot of thought. We tried to keep *Hip Houses* on the air after John and Melinda got divorced, and no one wanted to watch it. Our viewers aren't here for our hosts' interpersonal drama. They like happy couples, not bitter exes. But what they *do* like is a good design challenge. These old houses are bound to have issues. They'll need electrical and plumbing upgrades, probably some structural work, all of that stuff. It adds a plot twist." Harwood lowered his voice a little, mimicking an announcer. "Is Brandon in over his head this time?"

Brandon pursed his lips. He wasn't pleased that Kayla was being left out. They'd been partners for a long time, and he wasn't sure he was interesting enough to carry a show by himself. Although, of course, a divorced couple wasn't good for the Restoration Channel brand.

"If it helps," said Harwood, "we've been talking with a local contractor who specializes in restoring old homes, and he's interested in coming on board. Great guy. Lots of sex appeal, but a little rough around the edges. I think the viewers will love him. We're committed to this project. We just need a host."

"In other words, you're doing the show with or without me."

"Well, yes. But we want you. You'd be a fantastic host. You know this market well, you know how to flip houses, and the audience loves you."

"I don't know. It's still a huge financial risk."

"Tell you what. We've got our eye on a house right now. It's been on the market for almost four months now, so the asking price is negotiable. Go take a look at it. I think you'll fall in love with it. If you don't, then that's fine. We can find another project for you."

"Or buy out the rest of my contract."

"Or that, but let's keep an open mind here. We've got you through the end of the year, right?"

"July."

"A few more months, then. Still, you know we love you. We want to keep you as part of the Restoration Channel family. We'll find something for you to do. But I think you'll see this house and love it on sight. Here, let me give you the information."

Harwood turned around and rifled through a folder on the credenza behind his desk. Turning back, he handed Brandon a piece of paper. It looked like the printout from a real estate website.

The photo of the house made it look haunted. Several windows were boarded up, the paint was clearly peeling badly, and the front door looked like it had been knocked off one of its hinges. According to the data on the paper, the house had been built in 1917. Five bedrooms, three bathrooms, about 3,000 square feet. The asking price really was a bargain, less than a million dollars in a neighborhood of $3 million homes, and if it had been on the market for four months, it was likely overpriced, even at that.

"All right, I'll go look at it."

"I knew I could intrigue you. We really want you for this project, but no pressure. If you're really done, we can negotiate the end of your contract the same way we did with Kayla."

"Then let me look at the house and sleep on it."

"Great!" Harwood stood, signaling that the meeting was over. "I look forward to hearing from you, Brandon."

THE HOUSE was on Argyle Road, a few blocks south of Prospect Park in Brooklyn. Brandon had known this neighborhood of old houses was here but had never been to it before. He walked down Church Avenue from the subway station until he got to the road he was looking for. Six-foot-tall brick pillars with stone flower boxes on top signaled the start of Argyle Road, so Brandon turned.

And was suddenly transported.

Church Avenue was a bustling thoroughfare clogged with buses and cars, with crowded sidewalks, people rushing between the shops or running toward the subway station. It wasn't pretty, as such. Although the neighborhood had historical significance, the section of Church Avenue between the subway station and Argyle Road was mostly big discount stores and bodegas, crumbling brick architecture, and the occasional empty storefront. Brandon had walked by a shop proclaiming "fresh fish" on a big neon sign, but it smelled like some of those fish had been sitting out in the sun for a few days.

Then he turned onto Argyle Road, and it was like he was in an entirely different universe. It was quieter, for one thing. There were fewer people, and trees everywhere. Before him was an entire street of large detached houses, well-maintained lawns, and vintage streetlights. It looked more like a wealthy suburb than Brooklyn.

The houses were amazing.

They were a mishmash of styles. A tall Tudor house sat across from a Queen Anne, which was down the block from a Greek Revival home with columns across the front, and there was even a Japanese-style place that looked like a pagoda. Some of the houses were breathtaking in their size and beauty, painted a variety of colors—navy blue, white, yellow, mint green—and some looked like they should have been condemned years ago. Albemarle Road, which intersected Argyle, had a row of landscaped islands through the middle, green space in a borough where space was a premium.

Brandon cursed. How dare this neighborhood try to charm him! He'd wanted to resist this so much. The brown street signs indicated he was now in a historic district—which meant getting permits for renovations from the city would be a unique challenge, yet another reason *not* to do this—but man, he'd love to live here.

Then he arrived at the house, and it did indeed look like something out of a horror movie. But he had the code to the lockbox, so he punched it in, took out the key, and let himself in.

The inside of the house was… pretty bleak, actually. The front door opened into a narrow hallway and a staircase. There was an archway to his right, which led to an empty living room. The brick around the fireplace looked like someone had already taken a sledgehammer to it, and the ancient wallpaper was peeling. The rest of the house was more of the same. The layout inside was boxy and compartmentalized, the hardwood floors on the first floor were stained and scarred, there were mouse droppings in the kitchen, and the beige carpeting that covered the entire second floor smelled like dog.

And yet.

Brandon could see what this house had once been. The metal grate over the fireplace was an ornate piece of ironwork. The swirls in the wood used for the bannister on the stairs to the second floor were unique—Brandon hadn't seen anything like it in a long time. The wallpaper was actually kind of neat in the places where it wasn't a peeling, discolored nightmare, and Brandon could imagine what the main living areas had once looked like. The crown moldings, the wainscoting on the second floor, the archways…. No one made houses like this anymore. The kitchen had clearly been renovated sometime in the late seventies, but even that had a certain kind of charm, from the orange tile someone had chosen to the boxy design of the cabinets.

Before he knew it, Brandon was mentally making over the space, deciding which walls he'd remove, trying to determine if the floors were salvageable, imagining what a modern kitchen could look like with a few touches—light fixtures, tiles—that would nod back at what this house had once looked like.

Shit.

Brandon wanted this project. He knew all the hazards. He'd have to pay for an exterminator to fumigate the bejesus out of the place first. The walls likely held asbestos, outdated electrical systems that would have to be brought up to code, and pipes that needed to be replaced. But the structure seemed sound. The floors creaked in a few places, but Brandon knew how to fix that. He could make this house into something spectacular and sell it for twice the current asking price.

He pulled out his phone and called Garrett Harwood. "I'm at the house," he said when Harwood answered the phone.

"And?"

"I love it. I'm in."

Chapter Two

Travis already had regrets.

It wasn't that he had any particular aspirations to be on television, but he'd gotten the phone call inviting him to consult on a TV show about restoring old mansions, and he'd been so excited to have the conversation that he'd said yes without thinking it through. A half-dozen meetings later, and somehow he'd agreed to be the project manager for a home renovation project that would air on the Restoration Channel.

He'd never watched the channel much. He did every now and then, but often the contractors did double duty as hosts of the show, and much of what they did was so staged that Travis found it awkward to watch. He doubted those guys even had their contractor licenses; what were they doing wielding sledgehammers?

But working on a mansion in Victorian Flatbush definitely tempted him. He'd walked by those houses dozens of times—he lived not far from the neighborhood—and he'd been itching to get his hands on some of the more dilapidated ones. So though he didn't care about being on TV, this was too good an opportunity to pass up.

As he walked up to the house now, he saw that even though filming wasn't supposed to start yet, workers were already setting up TV equipment in the tiny front yard.

Travis was supposed to meet with Brandon Chase, do a walk-through of the house, and get more information about how filming would go. He had no idea what to expect, especially since the whole place was already crawling with people.

Then Brandon Chase walked outside. Travis recognized him because he had watched a half-dozen episodes of *Dream Home* to find out what he was getting himself into. What he'd learned was that Brandon and his wife Kayla flipped houses, mostly in suburban and exurban New Jersey and upstate New York. Each episode showed one house. The flips were never straightforward, but then, house flips rarely were. They bought houses in terrible shape in order to maximize profits, and turned them into modern, neutral houses intended to appeal to a wide range of buyers. Although Brandon swung a sledgehammer around and got his hands dirty a couple of times an episode, the role of the hosts seemed to be mostly to do the cosmetic stuff like picking out tiles and paint colors. Their tastes had struck Travis as very bland. His friend Sandy might point out that this was bound to happen when they didn't have a homosexual handy.

Brandon was handsome and charismatic on television. He was tall, with broad shoulders, tousled blond hair, and greenish eyes that shone in the sunlight when they filmed talking-head interviews outside. Travis had thought him sexy in a made-for-TV kind of way, but now, in the real world, he had some regular-guy charm. He had on a lightweight jacket open over a plaid shirt and a pair of well-worn but nicely fitted jeans. So he was appealing—but also married, so Travis shoved that aside.

Travis walked up to him. "Hi, I'm Travis Rogers, your new project manager."

"Yes! Of course. Great to meet you." Brandon held out his hand. "Let me just find Virginia and then we can get started on the walk-through."

Brandon ran back into the house and returned with Virginia Frank, one of the show's producers. Travis had met her at the Restoration Channel offices the week before, when he was still considering whether to come on board. She was a tall woman with curly red hair, dressed to the nines and not like someone who'd enjoy getting dusty walking through a construction zone. Her emerald green suit was an odd contrast to the crumbling house.

She clapped her hands twice and said, "I'm so excited, guys. I want to start with just a brief explanation of how this is all going to work."

Travis felt a little awkward about being thrust into this situation right away. Virginia pointed to a set of four folding chairs set out on the porch. Before he sat, Travis said, "Is the porch structurally sound?"

"The wood is just a facade for a stone porch, actually," Brandon said. "I already checked."

Travis nodded and sat.

"So, here's the deal," Virginia said. "We will be shooting the first season over the course of about eight months. The plan is to have the renovations overlap some, but not so much that it becomes an undue financial burden. So we spend two months on this house, but then start our second house before we wrap up this one, and so on. It will be an hour-long show, one house per episode, and we'd like to shoot eight episodes, but will do six if that's all the houses we can manage to finish in eight months."

Travis tried to school his face. That was an awfully ambitious schedule. Judging just by the peeling paint and boarded-up windows on the outside of the house, a ton of work was probably needed inside. This was a three- to four-month job, easily. "You're saying this house has a two-month schedule?"

"We're hoping to have it done in sixty days, yes," said Brandon.

"That seems… optimistic."

"Time is money," said Virginia. "Two months to make an episode is a long time, and the longer we hang on to the house, the higher the odds we'll lose money on the project. So we need to turn these houses pretty fast. Not to mention we want to capitalize on Brandon's name and the public moment he's having."

Brandon moaned. "Do we really?"

Virginia sipped from a travel mug as she eyed Brandon. "I want this show on the air before your fifteen minutes are over."

Brandon sighed. "In a few months no one will remember who I am."

"Precisely. I mean, I suppose we could still trade on your family name, but I'd really prefer to bolster you on your own merits."

"Did something… happen?"

Brandon and Virginia both turned to Travis. Virginia tilted her head like a confused dog and said, "Brandon and Kayla got divorced. Kayla cheated on him. It was all over the tabloids."

Travis shrugged. He didn't pay attention to that stuff. He tried to read between the lines here, though. Did Virginia want to capitalize on Brandon's tabloid fame in order to attract viewers to this show? That seemed sleazy.

"Let's not relive it," Brandon said. He looked embarrassed, so maybe he wasn't on board with Virginia's plan. Something about this hooked Travis's attention. Something *had* happened here, and Travis was surprised to find he cared about what that was.

"Anyway," said Virginia, "Brandon runs the show. He does interviews directly with the camera and does the voiceover to explain what we're doing. But you, Travis, will have an on-camera role as well, as sort of the voice of the crew. We've hired two teams that will work in eight-hour shifts to get the project done, and your role will be to manage both teams. You don't necessarily have to be here the whole time. In fact, once we get the second house, you'll have to be over there too. We'll work out a schedule that works for everyone. We want you to give regular reports to Brandon on camera, and in particular, to report if we have issues with the house. We may ask you to weigh in on design decisions, and you probably have a good sense for what things will cost, right?"

"Sure," said Travis.

"So that's how we see your role. Brandon will be getting in there and helping with some tasks too. We want some footage of him installing floors and tiles and things."

Well, that was just what he needed. Travis rubbed his forehead to mask his reaction and said, "Is that safe?"

"I'm a licensed contractor," said Brandon, sounding a bit defensive. "Having me do some of the labor on *Dream Home* saved us some money. I'm not qualified to do the engineering or structural tasks, but I can paint and install floors, and I like doing the cosmetic stuff anyway. It's like putting my own stamp on a project."

"All right." Travis tried to picture Brandon working on a house. Travis had worked on dozens of projects just like this, full-gut renovations that were sweaty and labor intensive. He tried to picture Brandon doing something tedious like laying floor tiles wearing tight jeans and a T-shirt stretched over his torso, and… well, it was a nice image.

"We can discuss more as we walk through the house. Essentially, this will be a renovation project just like every other one you've worked on, but we'll be filming it. The camera crew will be much smaller than all this." Virginia gestured around her. "We're doing orientation today."

Travis looked around, worried about what he'd agreed to. "Can we take a look at the house?"

"Yes!" said Virginia. She stood. "Let's take a look."

As Travis feared, the house had a lot of major issues. On top of the bare minimum things like patching the floors—if they could be patched—and replacing the windows, there were mice and likely other pests that needed to be exterminated, the electrical and plumbing probably needed to be replaced, and to be competitive in the market, they'd need to upgrade the HVAC. But the house itself was quite charming. The woodwork, the old sconces in the hallway, the ceiling fan in the living room, and the curly maple banister were among Travis's favorite touches. But even all of those needed to be cleaned and refinished.

There was easily a hundred thousand dollars in repairs needed just on the first floor. "You really think you're going to get all this done in sixty days?" Travis asked.

"It will be a tall order," Brandon said, "but Virginia's right. We have to try, or we'll lose money. And you're probably only looking at repairs and upgrades. Wait until you hear about my design changes."

Oh boy, here it came. "What do you want to do?"

Brandon led Travis and Virginia into the kitchen. "It starts here. We gut everything. Nothing here is salvageable. The cabinets are falling apart, the appliances are ancient, and I would advise against opening the refrigerator because something clearly crawled in there to die." Brandon grimaced. "But we do new everything. New floors, new cabinets, new appliances. I have some sketches I can show you, but basically I want to take down the wall between the kitchen and dining room, and possibly even the wall between the dining room and living room to create one big, open entertainment space."

Travis nodded slowly. He didn't love the idea of removing walls, especially since that would call for even more structural work, but he could see how that would make the space more functional. "All right."

"Then we do white cabinets, since this is a pretty small space. Light and bright to make everything look bigger. Light tile backsplash, white counters. Maybe we do an island in a contrasting color."

And so it went. Travis could see why Brandon made for good TV—he was handsome and smart and clearly in his element. However, Brandon's design plan for the house involved making everything neutral and bland, removing all character from the house. As Brandon described the exact shade of white he wanted to paint the first-floor powder room, Travis finally interrupted him. "So your plan is to take a historic home and make the inside of it as generic and modern as possible."

"The space needs to be functional and appeal to enough buyers that we make a profit."

Travis crossed his arms and looked at the bathroom. The wallpaper, printed with marigolds, was hideous and clearly not original to the house—for that matter, this half bath was likely not original to the house either—but picking more interesting wallpaper or even just painting it a color that wasn't white would be a better choice to keep it in line with the original design of the home. "Wouldn't it be better to try to preserve as much as possible? Taking down that hallway wall would cause you to lose those beautiful sconces and the crown molding. I agree, get rid of the horrible linoleum in the kitchen, but the floors on most of the rest of the first floor are probably salvageable. Sand them down and stain them a color that's a little more updated, and they'll look great." Travis looked at the floor. "You can't just patch them because nobody makes planks in this width anymore, so it's kind of an all-or-nothing job. But even if you do end up replacing them, this isn't the sort of house you just put laminate in."

Brandon bristled. "I know."

"Not to mention the Landmarks Preservation Commission may not let you do your whole plan. I mean, they probably will as long as you maintain the exterior. I worked on a house in Park Slope last year in which we moved the kitchen to an entirely different floor and added an addition on the back, and the LPC was fine with it. But getting all this approved could hold you up for a bit."

"I've already submitted the plans. We're just waiting on a final ruling."

Well, there was that, at least. Travis reached out and touched one of the hall sconces, then pulled his hand away and dusted his fingers off on his jeans. "I'm just saying, if I were in the market for a historic house in a neighborhood like this, modern and generic is not the aesthetic I'd be looking for."

"Fair point. But the LPC doesn't care about paint colors, so we'll see what they come back with. They likely won't grant *all* the permits I applied for."

Travis nodded. He could sense Brandon's irritation. He'd overstepped his role. "Sorry. It's your show. Just saying."

"I'm anticipating a two-hundred-thousand-dollar renovation. Does that seem about right to you?"

"Yeah. Hard to say for sure without getting a look at what's inside the walls, but I think that's in the ballpark."

Virginia clapped her hands twice again. "So! Regardless of the permit situation, we're going to start filming on Monday. Travis, you'll do the walk-through with Brandon on camera and let him know if you have opinions on anything. Mostly just agree and estimate how much it will cost. Can you do that?"

"I can estimate the cost of labor and materials. But if you've got two crews working—"

"Assume a straight hourly cost for labor. So, like, painting the first floor will take six hours at blah blah dollars per hour…."

"Then yeah, sure, I can estimate costs."

"Great! You guys can talk on camera about how tricky it is to get permits from the Landmarks Preservation Commission and the kinds of issues you're likely to run into in an old house like this. The house is ours now, so you can start taking apart walls or ripping out carpeting, even, if you want to find things. I know Brandon has already talked to an asbestos abatement company, and we've got electricians, plumbers, and structural engineers on standby."

Travis nodded. "We'll need all of them. And an exterminator."

"But what do you think of the house?" Brandon asked. "That's the real question."

Brandon looked earnest and hopeful, as if Travis's opinion mattered here. But it didn't; Travis was contractually obligated to renovate the house as Brandon and the network saw fit. On the other hand, Travis *did* like the house and knew it had the potential to be a beautiful home. *If* Brandon didn't obliterate the house's character.

There was something here. Brandon clearly cared about the house, about this project. His taste was questionable, but he was knowledgeable about how home renovations worked. And there was a *lot* he wasn't saying. His whole demeanor was practiced for TV, but Travis sensed that there was a lot going on underneath the surface, and a part of him wanted to get at whatever that was.

"I love this house," said Brandon. "I can see potential everywhere. Don't you see it too?"

Travis took a deep breath and nodded, because he could. "Yes. But honestly? It's a huge job, but the house is charming and I'm excited to get started on it."

Virginia clapped her hands again. "And I'm excited to start filming!"

Chapter Three

THE VERDICT from the various city permit agencies was that they could do just about whatever they wanted inside the house as long as they preserved the outside and kept some of the original character of the home inside. The only thing they could really do outside was change the paint color, but that was okay with Brandon. He was mainly concerned with the inside.

Brandon couldn't help wondering a little how much his name had greased the wheels.

He took some of Travis's arguments about the house to heart. He still intended to tear down walls, but he could move the wall sconces Travis liked, preserve the curly maple bannister, keep the iron grate over the fireplace, keep the glass doorknobs on most of the doors, and things along those lines. He still wanted to do a modern kitchen, but maybe they could pick some antique-looking treatments for the bathrooms or do a feature wall in the living room with wallpaper that evoked the right era.

The initial filming was going okay. If the dailies were anything to go by, Travis came across a little stiff on camera, but Virginia insisted it worked. Part of the story would be that Brandon dreamed big, and Travis would have to tell him why he couldn't do everything he wanted. That was good, because Brandon worried about going over budget. Two hundred thousand dollars, his budget cap for the project, was an absurd amount of money, but he knew it would go fast.

In addition, Virginia insisted that viewers really liked when there was some kind of crisis in the house that had to be fixed. It added tension and kept people watching. So they were supposed to make a big deal out of any "surprises," even though the budget accounted for all the bad things they expected to find. Travis played along, putting a particularly dramatic inflection on "asbestos" as he explained for the camera that it was very likely everywhere in the house.

Brandon wasn't totally sure how to feel about Travis. On one hand, he seemed kind of grouchy, and he clearly wanted to fight Brandon's instincts to modernize the house so it would sell for top dollar, even though he'd gone along with the plan since their initial meeting. On the other hand, Travis Rogers was *smoking* hot. He had a lean but well-muscled body, likely formed from manual labor and not the gym. His light brown hair was a little shaggy, and he seemed to have his razor set for "scruffy beard," because he always looked about the same level of unshaven. So there was some art to the I-don't-care facade, but Brandon liked it.

Of course, the world still thought Brandon and Kayla's divorce was caused by Kayla cheating on him. The tabloids reported that Brandon was brokenhearted and lonely. Although he hadn't welcomed the shakeup to his life, "brokenhearted" was perhaps stretching things, though late at night, he might admit to being lonely. On the other hand, he didn't have time to be lonely, not with getting the new show off the ground. Most days he went home after filming, stuffed takeout leftovers in his face for dinner, and fell immediately asleep.

Now that Brandon was helming a show as a solo host—contrary to the usual Restoration Channel blueprint of having happy heterosexual couples host all their shows—he felt like he needed to appear asexual on screen. He owned a mirror, so he knew he was a decent-looking guy, and he needed to remain the sort of handsome, nonthreatening man Restoration's mostly female viewership liked to tune in to see. So even though his divorce was like a license to have sex with anyone he wanted without having to explain to the wife at home, even fantasizing about making a move on the project manager on his own home renovation show, with cameras everywhere, was an imbecilic idea. No matter how sexy Brandon thought Travis was.

Everything happened at light speed. Just a few weeks after Brandon reluctantly agreed to do this show, filming began with him doing a walk-through of the house, with Travis trailing behind him as he explained to the camera what he wanted to do. They'd already done computer renderings of Brandon's design plans, and set up time in a recording studio for voiceovers, so now this walk-through was just a matter of traveling through the house, pointing at walls while he explained the plan, and letting Travis weigh in with his opinions.

After going through the living and dining rooms, Brandon could tell Travis was holding back. He mostly took notes on a clipboard and pointed out potential issues, but he didn't offer many opinions. One of the things Brandon missed most about having Kayla around was that he had no one to really play off of, someone who would disagree with him. Kayla had always challenged him in a way that made their designs better.

And now they were in the kitchen, where Brandon was explaining to the camera that he planned to gut the whole space. The original kitchen was boxy and poorly laid out, but if they ripped everything out and took out a closet at the back of the house, they'd have a big blank slate to work with. Brandon tried to picture himself working in a kitchen this size, where he'd want the appliances to be, where the optimal prep space should go.

But this was not his house. He might have been charmed by it, but he was fixing it, not planning to keep it. He called on all of his knowledge about what was trendy, what was timeless, and what buyers had been looking for in his last few flips. He described his vision, and Travis nodded and wrote something. Then Brandon walked over to the wall between the kitchen and dining room and put his hand on it. "This wall will have to go."

Travis's shoulders rose. The gesture was almost imperceptible, but Brandon caught it and said, "Travis, if you have thoughts, please share them."

Travis looked up, his eyes wide. He glanced at the camera and said, "I still need to take a look to be sure, but I'm guessing some of these walls you want to take down are load-bearing. I'm pretty confident this one is. Of course, that isn't necessarily an issue. We can do engineered beams to redistribute the load, assuming the rest of the structure is sound. But the more structural work we create for ourselves, the greater the cost."

Brandon nodded. "Right."

"Not to mention, the fun of doing a house like this is to try and retain the character and old charm, right? So you don't want to make the layout *too* modern. And you might want to keep at least one of these walls to increase the amount of storage. You can, of course, put a big island in the middle, but you can't just have cabinets hanging from air, at least not without making the room feel really tight, you know?"

"Right. But if we do uppers and lowers along this whole wall, that'll give us several feet of counter space." Brandon walked over to the wall along which he wanted to run the kitchen cabinets. "So I'm thinking sink here, under this window, dishwasher here, then we do the stove over here, double ovens stacked here, then the fridge over here. We can put in stainless steel appliances, white cabinets, probably shaker style, light quartz counters, and a neutral backsplash."

Travis did the thing with his shoulders again.

Brandon sighed. "What are you thinking?"

"Honestly? I think you're eradicating the integrity of the house. If you put in the same kitchen a buyer could find in any other house in the city, what's the incentive for them to buy a historic house? Modernize it, sure. I'm with you on the appliances, I think your idea for the layout is sound, but the colors are just so… bland."

"What would you do?"

Travis looked surprised, and he took a step back. "I'm not a designer."

"No, but… if this was your house, what would you like to see?"

Travis walked back to the center of the room. "Keep your layout. But I'd do craftsman-style cabinets instead of shaker. Something a little more in keeping with the age of the house. Definitely stone counters, maybe marble if the budget allows for it. Then something bold for the backsplash. A tile with some kind of pattern, maybe blue or something else that pops. But I'm not a designer."

Brandon nodded. The ideas weren't bad. On the other hand, anything too specific meant that they'd have to find a buyer with similar taste. Brandon had built his entire career as a house flipper on making things tasteful… but neutral. Bold colors and old-fashioned cabinets were such a divergence from Brandon's usual style. He didn't want to argue on camera. Instead he just said, "Anything too custom could alienate buyers."

"Right."

Travis sounded sarcastic, and that irritated Brandon. The crew was still filming, so he took a deep breath and said, "I can't just run wild with design. The goal is to sell the house for a good profit."

Travis held up a hand in a gesture that said he was backing off the argument. "You asked my opinion."

Brandon took another deep breath. Yeah, his back was up. He didn't know Travis well enough to predict where a fight with him would go or how it would end. And he didn't intend to find out when the cameras were still rolling.

This was so bad. Travis riled Brandon up without doing much but writing notes on his clipboard. He stood there in tight jeans and a black

T-shirt looking sexy as hell, his hair hanging rakishly over his forehead, his stubble creating a shadow on his jaw. Brandon was attracted to Travis, but he could also tell Travis would work against him if given the opportunity. Oh, Travis would hold his tongue because he understood his role as a project manager—do what he was told, keep the project on schedule—but he would silently judge Brandon, and Brandon would know it. And Brandon didn't know what he wanted more—to pick a fight with Travis… or make out with him.

God, all of this was a mistake. Saying yes to this show, buying this house, working with Travis.

Had he really just been wishing for someone to play off of? At least Kayla would question his decisions with a joke and a smile. Travis would merely shrug and glare at Brandon, leaving Brandon to ruminate on what he'd done wrong.

"Cut," said Erik, one of the show's directors. He'd been lingering behind the cameraman through this whole discussion. The cameraman, who was basically wearing the camera as he followed Brandon and Travis around the house, let out a breath and slumped a little, the weight of all his equipment probably weighing him down.

"I have an idea," Erik said, walking between Brandon and Travis. "What if, for contrast, we let Travis make up a plan for the kitchen and we make a computer rendering of it to show how the two are different? Then, when we get to the point where we're choosing material, we can revisit these plans and discuss, possibly even pulling in some other opinions. Maybe we find a few potential buyers and have them vote."

"It's an idea," Brandon said, a little uncomfortable with it. He was the expert here, wasn't he?

"I'm not a designer," Travis said again.

"Yes, but it sounds like you have a different vision for the space. I'm not saying the whole house, just the kitchen. We show Brandon's rendering, which is very sleek and modern, and then we can show yours, with some more, er, vintage touches. There are lots of possibilities. Hell, maybe we could even throw the renderings on our social media accounts and ask fans to weigh in on which design they like better. Get some audience buy-in before the show premieres." Erik nodded to himself. "I like this a lot. I'll talk to Virginia about it."

Brandon glanced at Travis, who was frowning. "I mean, I guess I could do something. But it's still Brandon's show, isn't it?" Travis said. "He gets the final say. I've never had to sell a house. I just fix them."

Erik nodded. "That's fine. Let's do the rendering, at least to accompany the footage of you explaining what you would do. Then we can decide what else to do with it later."

"All right."

Brandon cleared his throat. "Great. Shall we look around upstairs?"

THE HOUSE was a structural nightmare. Once the cameras were gone, Travis and one of the reno team members checked the footings and structural supports under the house and the beams in the ceiling and attic. The foundation was cracked, a few of the walls Brandon wanted to remove were definitely load-bearing, and there were worrisome water stains in the attic.

In other words, just fixing the house and getting it up to code would be *expensive*, and that was before Brandon came in and did anything aesthetically.

Brandon's renovation plan bothered Travis, though. Travis might not have a real estate license, but he doubted anyone looking to buy in this neighborhood was really interested in a generic white kitchen. Victorian Flatbush *wasn't* modern. That was kind of the point.

Travis sat on the floor of the living room and finished writing up his recommendations. There wasn't really much more they could do today, so when Ismael, the head of the day shift crew, came to ask for his next set of instructions, Travis sent everyone home. He locked up the house with a sigh.

Brandon must have finished… whatever it was he'd been doing, and he stopped by Travis's spot in the living room to announce he was leaving for the day.

From Travis's vantage point on the floor, Brandon was impossibly tall. Travis had learned from watching *Dream Home* that Brandon's clothing aesthetic was basically patterned button-down shirts over jeans, and today he wore a long-sleeved navy number with little white birds on it. It was fitted precisely to his chest, showing off what was likely a gym-sculpted body. Brandon often seemed less everyday working-class guy and more like the star of a middlebrow nighttime soap playing the role of a construction worker.

And yet he was stupid handsome. Even though he had a hair and makeup crew that touched him up before he went on camera, he didn't really need them. He had straight white teeth and a square jaw and strong arms and jeans that clung nicely to his tight, round butt. It was shallow for Travis to judge Brandon by his outward appearance, but so far that was all Brandon had offered him.

But then Brandon said, "Erik wants to reshoot you talking about the kitchen design tomorrow."

"All right."

"I'm not saying you're right, because every wild decision we make narrows the buyer pool. Kayla and I put blue cabinets into a house once because they were trendy that season, and we had to lower our initial asking price before we got any offers."

"I'm not saying you have to take my ideas."

Brandon nodded. "I don't mean to be a dick about it, but I do have some experience with this sort of thing."

"I know."

"Restoration gave me a list of their approved shops in the region, so I'm going to go home and make some calls. Maybe we can see about getting some product samples."

"Cool. Are you allowed to go off-list?"

"Yeah, I think so. It's my money, after all."

Travis stood. "There's a flooring store in Red Hook that usually has some good deals. The company I used to work for dealt with them almost exclusively, so I know the staff there. I can put in a good word for you if you want."

"That would be great, thanks. I've never renovated a house in the city before. I have a couple of go-to places in the suburbs, but it would be better to source locally, if the price is right."

"Sure."

"What are you working on?"

"My report on the repairs we need to do. Do you want it now?"

"No, wait until tomorrow." Brandon jerked suddenly and then pulled his phone from his pocket. "My car's here. Gotta go. See you tomorrow."

Travis watched him go and shook his head, picturing the white kitchen in the otherwise vintage house again.

This was probably just rubbing him the wrong way because the house had a similar floor plan to the one Travis had bid on last year, but lost.

The house had been an old yellow brick row house off Flatbush Avenue in Fort Greene. Travis had known the house intimately because his grandparents had once lived in it. When Travis's grandfather had died about ten years ago, his parents had put the house on the market, and it had been bought by a family that had carved it up into apartments. After Travis had saved up a pile of money to buy a fixer-upper in the city, he'd seen the house up for sale again. He'd gone to an open house and could see dozens of childhood memories embedded in the walls, even though the interim owners had changed quite a bit and let the house fall into disrepair. Travis had made an offer on the spot, but he'd ended up losing the house in a bidding war. That was, of course, the problem with New York City real estate; you could scrimp and save to build the small fortune necessary to buy a house in the city, but there would still always be someone with more money. And that person would remove all the character from the house and cover the inside with gray paint and subway tile and put it back on the market eight months later for three million dollars.

Travis decided to walk home to shake off the day. He'd have to deliver a truckload of bad news to Brandon the next day—most of what he'd seen in the house indicated that the budget was beyond blown. They'd banked on asbestos and engineered beams but not foundation issues or a new roof. And Travis *would* make sure these repairs got done before anything else. He rubbed his chest, where his tiger tattoo was inked. Safety was paramount, especially in these old houses. There was no sense in putting some unsuspecting family in a home with modern touches but a horror show inside the walls. But Travis knew full well some unscrupulous developers in New York wouldn't think twice about it.

Really, this was one of those houses that probably should have been condemned and bulldozed to make way for something new, but the Landmarks Preservation Commission wouldn't allow for that, and buyers wanted the hundred-plus-year-old home, not a new one. If New Yorkers wanted new construction, they could buy a condo in one of the new high-rises in downtown Brooklyn.

Travis's studio apartment in Prospect Lefferts Gardens was tiny and still full of wallpaper books and tile catalogs even though he'd given up on buying his dream home a good while ago. The city real estate market was too volatile, too much of a financial risk, and he was tired of getting outbid for houses by rich people and celebrities looking to renovate or complete a lucrative flip. Maybe socking away some of the money from this Restoration Channel gig would increase the size of a potential down payment and he'd be able to buy something else in a few months, but for now, the dream was just that—a dream.

He dropped his stuff near the door of his apartment and sat on the sofa. His entertainment unit on the opposite wall had a lot of shelving, mostly for books. Travis spotted the one on the history of architecture in the region. Well, maybe he could show Brandon some examples of how a house from 1917 should have looked, and they could work on preserving it instead of obliterating its character and charm. Obviously the house should be brought up to code and modernized, at least behind the walls. And sure, take out a wall or two; that would help make the space more functional. But the house should be restored, not renovated.

Travis dragged his laptop across the coffee table and opened it. For now he'd focus on his report for what the house really needed. In the end, it wasn't his house; he had no financial stake in it, and Brandon and the Restoration Channel producers would do what they wanted. Despite his reticence about being on television, this was a good gig, and Travis didn't want to rock the boat too much either. So he'd do his job. He'd make a list of necessary repairs and argue that they'd have to be done in order to make the house safe. And if Erik wanted him to make a rendering of the design he'd use for the kitchen, then sure, what the hell? But from now on he'd make it a point not to fight with the host.

Not too much, anyway.

Chapter Four

BRANDON COULD tell from the expression on Travis's face that he was about to offer up a report that would utterly destroy Brandon's budget.

The tricky thing with a show like this was that though the Restoration Channel was taking on some of the financial burden, a lot of Brandon's money was still at stake. He could afford to take some risks, but he still worried about being over the budget. A failure of this magnitude was not an option, and the more work they had to put into the house and the longer the project took, the smaller the profit would be. Not for the first time since starting this project, Brandon could hear his late father—a New York real estate magnate in his own right—in his head, telling him he'd screwed up big-time.

His stomach churned as Travis came into the living room. A couple of cameramen stood nearby, ready to capture the kind of moment viewers ate up with a spoon.

Travis had on an old T-shirt that had probably once been black but had faded into a splotchy dark gray. It clung to his chest, revealing defined pecs and a fit body, and his tight jeans didn't leave much to the imagination either. Travis was the sort of man Restoration Channel viewers would love—he exuded raw sex appeal—and Brandon could already see the social media posts from women wanting Travis to, er, use his tools at their house. Hell, Brandon wanted that too.

But he had a show to focus on. Brandon looked around the house again and tried to take it all in. He tried to imagine how this room would look with the fireplace reconstructed, with fresh paint on the walls, with some nice stylistic touches. He couldn't remember the last time he'd had such a clear vision for a house or was this excited to renovate, although he was sure Travis was about to tell him there was a pile of work to do just to bring the building up to code. But Brandon knew even with that, he could do something amazing with this space.

"Basically," Travis said, "here's the rundown." He glanced at the cameras, clearly not completely comfortable with their presence yet.

"Cut," said Erik, the director, who stood quietly in a corner supervising. "Okay, Travis, I'm going to need you to sound a little more forceful. You're about to give Brandon some bad news. That sucks, and you can be regretful about it, but go ahead and just say what it is. But first I think we should actually show the damage to the audience. Just describing it isn't all that interesting."

Something changed on Travis's face. Maybe he understood what he was supposed to do better now. Brandon did not want to get bad news, and he hated that Erik was forcing them to draw this out—he wanted to know what he was dealing with so he could make a plan to fix it—but he understood that these kinds of scenes were the bread and butter of any home renovation show. These were the stakes; fixing a house this old and broken was nearly impossible, so how would our hero get out of this jam?

Travis nodded. "Come with me to the basement."

Erik ordered the cameras to start filming again as everyone followed Travis downstairs. Then Travis held court.

"I checked with the city, and according to the records, there was a renovation done on this house in 1983. But whoever did it cut some corners. So, first, let me show you this." Travis bent down and grabbed the edge of an area rug that rested against the basement wall. Brandon tried not to see the strip of skin exposed between the bottom of Travis's shirt and the waistband of his jeans.

The basement was unfinished, but there were plumbing hookups for a washer, dryer, and sink, so that was presumably how the previous owners had used the space. Travis peeled back the rug and gestured. "There's a crack in the foundation here. We'll have to get an engineer in to really find out what the problem is. It could just be that the house has settled after being here for more than a hundred years, but…." He glanced at the camera. "There could be a bigger problem too. There's also an issue here." He pulled a metal tape measure from his tool belt and unfurled enough of it to use as a pointer. "At some point in the life of this house, there was a wall or a few posts here, and whoever removed it did not properly support the ceiling. See where it's starting to sag here? So just to start, you've got a bigger structural issue on your hands than we initially thought."

Brandon let out a breath. His heart pounded. "All right."

Travis nodded. "I think you'd better come with me back up to the kitchen," he said.

So everyone followed Travis back upstairs. Travis went straight to the wall near a window in the kitchen's eating area. A section of the wall had been peeled away to reveal that some of the framing had rotted.

"What is this?" Brandon asked.

"Ancient termite damage. The good news is that the termites are long gone. The bad news is that all this wood will have to be replaced. And there are mice and cockroaches in the walls. There are also asbestos wraps around every heating duct I've found so far, but I'd recommend putting in an all-new HVAC system anyway because the existing one is not up to code for a house this size. Still, there's no asbestos otherwise, so the expense will likely be less than what we budgeted for. But we have to get exterminators and abatement teams in here before we can do much work."

Every word Travis spoke sounded like the ring of a cash register; Brandon saw the expenses piling up, and all of these items were things they'd have to do to make the house safe and salable. They'd budgeted for abatement and exterminators but not to repair concrete slabs in the basement. "Anything else?"

Travis crossed the room and touched one of the walls. He looked completely at ease, despite dishing out all this bad news. "This wall is load-bearing. We can still take it down if we replace it with an engineered beam, but, you know, that's a few thousand dollars. And I'd want to test for lead paint."

"Lead paint. I hadn't thought of that." Brandon sighed. "Do you have a sense for the financial damage?"

"It's hard to say. Depends on how bad the structural issues are. But we're talking at least fifty thousand dollars to fix all of the issues I've just shown you."

Brandon nodded. That was a big budget hit. "Does this affect any of our cosmetic plans?"

"I mean… we'll probably have to strip the walls anyway. In a house this old, it's lath and plaster, possibly even some wire mesh, and that will be a pain to remove. Labor costs are something to think about."

"That's accounted for in the budget, unless we go beyond our scheduled dates." Brandon pressed his lips together and looked around. "How much will all this extra work set us back, schedule-wise?"

"Could be as much as a week or two, depending on how much structural work is needed."

"All right. I can tweak the design budget to offset some of these costs. And this doesn't even get into plumbing and electrical, does it?"

"I'm not sure about plumbing yet, but we definitely have to upgrade the electrical. It's all knob and tube. None of it is to code. We need to do a complete rewire."

"All right. Well. Let's get the engineer and a plumber in here as soon as we can so we know for sure how big of a hit to the budget this is."

Travis nodded. At Erik's urging, he walked over to stand closer to Brandon so that they'd both be in the tighter camera shot. He opened his mouth as though he wanted to say something, then closed it again. Finally he cleared his throat and said, "Did you not have this place inspected before you bought it?"

"We bought it as-is."

"Mm-hmm."

Brandon could hear the sarcasm. He crossed his arms and leaned closer to Travis. "I'd much rather discover the issues and have our team fix them instead of having the previous owners trying to half-ass fix something in a hurry to sell the house. At least this way I know things will be fixed right and I'll be able to vouch for the house."

Travis met Brandon's gaze directly and held it as he spoke. "All right. I agree. But since we've barely started demo, I'm guessing there are still some surprises hiding in the house. Once we get everything stripped down, we'll have a better picture of what we're dealing with."

Brandon nodded. He was paying a crew to start demo today, but they couldn't do much if asbestos was on the pipes. "Is there anything we can start today?"

"You could take everything out of the kitchen and bathrooms. And I drew up a design plan for the kitchen, so we can talk about that too."

"All right, let's do it."

THE CAMERAS spent the next few hours filming the crew as they destroyed kitchen cabinets and hauled toilets and sinks to the dumpster out front. Erik told everyone to act very excited about "Demo Day!"

Travis didn't do much of the demolition himself. He spent about twenty minutes filming a segment where he described his own design plan for the kitchen; the style he was going for was antique but with modern conveniences. Brandon stood on the sidelines with his lips pressed together, as if he didn't approve.

Travis was constantly aware of Brandon's presence, and it unnerved him. Travis had been pretty determined to treat this like a job, just one on TV, and part of his code of ethics was to never get involved with a client. Brandon riled him up, there was no doubt about it. Part of that was that Brandon was wrong about the design, but a larger part of it was that the more time Travis spent near Brandon, the more he was attracted to him.

Today Brandon had on a short-sleeved gingham shirt with the top couple of buttons undone, and it pulled across his broad chest in a way Travis found really appealing. It was an unseasonably warm day, and Brandon was sweating a little, and as Travis described the color palette he had in mind, a bead of sweat escaped Brandon's hairline and dripped down the side of his face. It was all Travis could do not to lean over and lick it off.

Once that segment was, thankfully, out of the way, Travis picked up a sledgehammer and prepared to get demo started. Brandon grabbed one too, and went to town on the kitchen cabinets. Travis couldn't help but watch as Brandon's muscles rippled.

But then he spent the rest of his time being called in to monitor problems. There was water damage from a leaking pipe in one bathroom, ductwork in a weird place in the kitchen, and they uncovered all kinds of shoddy wiring and outdated plumbing. Anytime they found something, Travis had to track down Brandon and a cameraman to explain the issue. Travis could see that Brandon was growing more panicked with each new discovery.

Toward the end of the day, Travis tracked Brandon down one last time to close out for the day. "I hate to be the bearer of more bad news."

"Then just don't tell me." Brandon ran a hand through his already disheveled hair. "I can't take much more."

Brandon was joking, but Travis was not amused. "The termite damage in the kitchen is pretty extensive. We may have to do some work on the exterior wall."

"Geez. This house doesn't even have good bones, does it?"

Travis stopped himself from laughing. Because yeah, someone should have torn this whole structure down. "Not really. But everything is fixable… for a price."

Brandon blew out a breath and put his hands on his hips. "All right. We'll figure it out."

"I think that's a good place to leave it for the day," said Erik.

While the TV production crew started packing up, Travis walked over to Brandon. "I hope you don't think I'm deliberately causing problems."

Brandon shot him a sidelong look, then let out a long breath. "I knew going in that this would be a huge financial undertaking."

"I realize your budget has some limitations, so maybe we can compromise on the design. If we don't take down *every* wall on the first floor—"

"Modern buyers don't want a boxy old house."

Travis knew that wasn't true; he'd had a client the previous year who had asked him to *add* walls to his brownstone. But he wasn't about to argue. "That's not what I'm saying."

Brandon rubbed his forehead. "I know you aren't trying to undermine me or the production when you point out issues with the house. But I know what I'm doing with design."

"Have you ever flipped a house in this neighborhood?"

"No."

Travis paused for a moment, trying to decide if he really wanted to go in on this or not.

"Just say what you want to say," said Brandon, a little impatient.

Travis let out a breath. "I want the show to succeed. I want this project to succeed. I hope it's enormously profitable. So please know that this is coming from that place. And ultimately, this is your project, so if you want to make everything in this house look sleek and modern, that's your call. My point is just that, given the history of the neighborhood, it makes more sense to take a preservationist outlook rather than a house-flipper approach. We don't want the house to be generic. Buyers in this neighborhood want something unique."

"It won't be generic. But buyers who say they want charm almost never do. People don't like anything too 'out there.' They want open concept, they want neutral colors, and they want functional living space. The current layout is not functional. Hell, there isn't even a true master bedroom upstairs. No one wants to buy a house this size that doesn't have a master suite."

The heat in the room went up a few degrees. Travis disagreed. There was a time and a place for neutral, and some neighborhoods and building types called for that. Travis had worked on many an apartment that had been transformed from a dingy prewar space to something out of a contemporary design catalog. That wasn't what this house was, though. Travis could practically hear the old rotted beams begging him to leave some of the house's character. "Obviously. I'm not saying not to do what you have to do to modernize the house. I'm just saying, if possible, you should try to preserve some of what makes the house unique. We're probably going to have to lose the crown moldings when we do asbestos abatement, but we should photograph and recreate them after we put up new drywall. That sort of thing."

Brandon blew out a breath and put his hands on his hips. "Crown moldings, fine. But I still think we should do a modern kitchen. If not shaker, then flat-panel cabinets. Sleek, simple, nothing ornate."

"Flat panel? That's completely wrong for the time period the house was built."

"Nobody wants old-fashioned. They want 'charm,' by which they mean they want what they see on the Restoration Channel or in interior design magazines. Farmhouse sinks are hot right now in urban kitchens. That's what counts for charm. Trust me, I've been doing this a long time."

Travis had no interest in getting into a dick-measuring contest with Brandon, but he said, "I've been working on renovation projects in Brooklyn for fifteen years. It's a competitive market, and it's a lucrative one, but you still have to make your house stand out. If you want top dollar, it has to be unique. And no one who is buying a 1917 house is looking for something super contemporary. The adjacent neighborhoods are lousy with new construction for people who want that."

Brandon shook his head. "They'll say that, but trust me, I've done a couple of these old houses before, and the buyers who think they want antique never really do. People today have certain expectations, especially of a flip, *and* we have to make it look good on TV."

"And you think beige carpet and gray walls will accomplish that?"

"No, but—"

"I just hate to see all the charm of the house obliterated."

"I'm not planning to obliterate the charm." Brandon let out a huff.

The most ridiculous part of this whole conversation was that Travis couldn't escape the fact that he was super attracted to Brandon. The man was gorgeous when he was worked up, his skin flushed, his hair disheveled. Travis wanted to reach over and smooth those ruffled feathers—but he wanted to make this argument more. Because the odds of him ever getting any part of his heterosexual coworker were minuscule, but maybe he could persuade Brandon to take some of his design ideas.

Travis continued, "I don't want to tell you what to do, but please consider revising your design."

"I know what I'm doing." Brandon was prickly now, offended. Damn, Travis had pushed too hard.

Yet still, he said, "I know you do. But so do I. You keep asking for my opinion, so I'm giving it to you."

"Well, maybe stick to giving me reports about asbestos and termites, not design, all right."

Travis held up his hands. "Fine."

"I gotta get out of here. I'll see you tomorrow." Brandon's tone was placid enough, but he stormed out of the house, leaving Travis alone with the crew. That was okay. Travis still had a to-do list to finish that day, so he got back to work.

CHAPTER FIVE

"YOU DON'T think the dynamic would be better with a cohost?" Brandon asked.

Virginia and Garrett Harwood glanced at each other. They were all seated together in the conference room at the Restoration Channel's Manhattan office because Harwood had called Brandon in to get a status update on how shooting was going. Brandon was starting to wonder if he could really support a show on his own—nearly everything on the Restoration Channel was hosted by a couple or siblings or a pair of people of some sort who could bounce ideas off each other.

Brandon worried now that he looked foolish on film. Travis kept undermining his design ideas, but Brandon was supposed to be the renovation expert. He'd flipped hundreds of houses on *Dream Home*; he and Kayla had filmed close to two hundred episodes before those terrible photos of Kayla had hit the tabloids.

And now Virginia and Harwood were clearly having some kind of psychic conversation, because they kept looking at each other as if they knew something Brandon didn't.

"What?"

"Well," Virginia said, "we've been thinking about giving Travis a bigger role on the show. Not a costar as such, but we like the dynamic between you."

"Dynamic? But all we ever do is argue."

Harwood raised his eyebrows, and Virginia said, "Exactly."

"What?"

"You guys make great television. There's built-in conflict. The way you spar with each other… it's great."

"It's tense," said Harwood.

"It's compelling," said Virginia. "It's like how you and Kayla used to argue over her more eccentric design ideas. Remember that episode when she wanted to put a chandelier in the master bathroom?"

"Of course," said Brandon. It was one of the few genuine fights they'd ever had on camera. A chandelier in a bathroom, he still maintained, was a ridiculous extravagance. The six hundred dollars Kayla had spent on the thing would have been better spent on so many better things. Six hundred dollars was a few hundred square feet of flooring, was a bathroom's worth of floor tiles, was a new window.

"That stuff is gold," said Virginia as Harwood nodded. "It creates suspense. Can Brandon and Travis resolve this conflict? Will they meet each other in the middle?"

"Then they want to see your problem-solving skills at work," said Harwood. "They want you to compromise and then create a beautiful final product. That's what keeps the show interesting."

Of course. Brandon let out a breath. "Well, fine, so I'll host, I'll argue with Travis, but I need some design help, because maybe Travis is right—maybe my original design *is* wrong for the house and the neighborhood." In truth, Brandon was nearly persuaded already, but something about Travis made him dig in his heels. And since Travis kept reminding him he was not a designer, Brandon would need some professional help. "I was thinking of bringing in Kayla. Would that be okay?" Because Kayla was a great designer and knew more about things like craftsman cabinets and wallpaper patterns than he did.

Virginia tilted her head. "That might get some ratings—seeing the two of you struggle to work together."

"Struggle? Kayla and I still get along great. Just because our marriage didn't work out, that doesn't mean there's any enmity between us." And there wasn't, although they hardly talked to each other lately. Brandon missed that, missed being able to hash out design problems with her or just talk about anything over beers at the end of a long day.

"Really? You're telling me it was an amicable breakup, because I read that—"

"I'm not getting back together with her. But we're still friends, and she's got a good eye." And the more he fought with Travis, the more Brandon saw that he needed help.

Harwood frowned. "Well, we've already let Kayla out of her contract."

Brandon sat back in his chair and sighed. This was all wrong. Again, Brandon wished he and Kayla were still working together. He felt out of his depth with this show and could have used an ally. And as much as he'd liked Travis at first, Travis was turning into more of an antagonist than a cohost. He was always the bearer of bad news, even though everything Travis wanted to fix needed to be fixed. Of course, everything that needed to be fixed was also making the project budget climb.

And yet…. "I'll figure out how to pay Kayla out of the design budget if you won't. I could use her help, even if she's not on camera. She was always better at design than I was."

"That's true," said Virginia. "I think a lot of viewers tuned in more to see Brandon hit things with a sledgehammer than to do the interior design on the house." She tilted her head back and forth, clearly thinking it through. "Tell you what. Let's bring her in for a segment on design. We can pay her a per diem."

"Thanks. I think it will be good to have her on board, even if it's just for a day or two."

"You seem awfully eager to work with the woman who cheated on you," said Harwood.

"She didn't—that's not exactly what happened."

"Right. It's none of my business. But viewers think *she's* the bad guy, so maybe don't be too nice to her on camera."

Brandon sighed. "I know this is reality television, but it's not really *reality* television. People watch the Restoration Channel to be soothed or to think about paint colors or real estate in vacation destinations. Don't they? This isn't a Housewives show. We don't need drama."

Virginia crossed her arms. "You know I used to work on one of the Housewives shows."

"I know. I'm not mocking them. I'm just saying that's not the kind of show I'm making."

"The tension between you and Travis is compelling, though. Hell, if Travis were a woman, I'd guess it was sexual tension between you."

Brandon burst into laughter. The comment surprised him. There was, of course, the problem that he *was* attracted to Travis. Ridiculously so. But he'd pushed that aside because their relationship had grown so adversarial. Besides, there was no way they could get involved with each other—not if Brandon hoped to keep conveying this happy heterosexual image of himself.

"There's a real opportunity here," said Virginia. "I mean, the Chase name is practically synonymous with New York City real estate."

That nearly set Brandon off. His father, John Chase, had been a real estate mogul in New York in the seventies, eighties, and nineties, investing in huge construction projects and adding tall buildings to the skyline. His claim to fame was the glamorous St. Joseph Hotel on the Upper West Side. John Chase wasn't a name people knew outside of New York City, but anyone who paid attention to local real estate definitely knew who he was. Brandon's older brother Robert ran the family business now, which was fine by Brandon. He'd wanted to succeed in his own right.

He couldn't deny that he'd gotten some help from his family over the years, though. His inheritance from his father was a large portion of the financing for this current project, after all. The fact that he was using his father's money was probably the reason Brandon had been hearing his father's voice in his head more than usual. What his father would have thought about this job had been weighing on him the whole project.

John Chase had been a demanding man. His take-no-prisoners business style had made him a lot of enemies, but he'd also been smart and successful, and he'd demanded the same of his sons. Robert was the protégé, middle brother Luke was the apprentice, and Brandon, the baby, was the one with the independent streak. And yet how independent could he be when he was still using Daddy's money to buy houses? His father's words were never far from his mind: *Don't fail me, son. Never fail me. Failure is not an option.*

Brandon rubbed his forehead and tried not to let his distress show. "I'd really rather leave my family out of it."

"Fine," said Virginia, holding her hands up.

Brandon wondered if all of this wasn't spinning out of control. He'd worked so hard to create a safe, TV-friendly public persona, something he could parlay into the kind of real estate success that could have made John Chase proud if he were still here. He knew being on TV got him jobs and deals he wouldn't have been offered otherwise, and creating this name for himself made him feel like he wasn't always in his family's shadow. And okay, the part of him that had been a theater kid in high school did like the limelight—just not when the press about him wasn't great.

It was funny, though; that moment when Kayla had come to their home and explained to him what had happened at the restaurant and they'd decided their marriage was probably over, he'd been able to see a different life for himself—one out of the spotlight. He could almost taste the freedom he'd never had. But on the other hand, he'd worked so hard to build up his public persona that he didn't know who he was underneath it all anymore.

And now he'd been swept into this.

"We also called you here today," Harwood said, "because we've got a lead on another house. It'll take enough time to close on it that we might as well get moving on it now."

"This show will bankrupt me," Brandon said. He wanted to deal with this first house and its ballooning budget before taking on a second, although he understood that projects would have to overlap if they had any hope of finishing this show on time. He spared a thought for the house on Argyle Road, knowing Travis was there right now overseeing the crew as they got back to work now that the asbestos abatement was done.

Brandon loved that damned house. That was what had finally persuaded him to see the house as Travis did, as an old house to be restored, not plowed over or renovated. Travis was right, the house had charm, and it was that charm that had sucked Brandon into the project. It would be a shame to remove it.

And now here he was, trying to keep his shirt and make the best decisions for this new show and this house, not to mention his potential future projects.... He was completely out of his depth, and he knew it.

"We were thinking, just to keep it interesting," said Harwood, "that we could do a few shows in which you and your team renovate houses for buyers in the neighborhood. That would ease the financial burden somewhat. In this case, the buyer is Jessica Benton."

Brandon sucked in a breath. Jessica Benton was one of those anticelebrity celebrities who "just wanted to act." The New York paparazzi was pretty good about mostly leaving celebrities alone, but Jessica Benton still got her photo taken leaving her gym and getting coffee at a popular Park Slope café. Her husband was also an actor, albeit a lesser-known one, who had a major role on an HBO prestige drama series. Buying a house in Brooklyn would be a natural thing for her to do. "Is she buying it to move into or to flip?"

"It's not clear yet, but if she wants to flip it, that could be a fun episode," said Virginia. "Viewers would like the celebrity angle, and it's keeping within the theme of the show. Plus, she would foot most of the bill."

"I'm game," Brandon said, although working with a celebrity made him nervous. Of course, if the tabloid coverage of his divorce was anything to go by, he was also pretty famous. Still, the prospect of going in on a project with someone else fronting the money was enticing.

"Good to know," said Harwood. "I'll keep you posted. It's not a done deal, but I think we're close."

"The ratings, man," said Virginia. "Brandon is already a household name. If we do episodes with celebrities like Jessica Benton, people will make the time to tune in to the show. I can already see the preview ads in my head."

Brandon thought they were all being overly optimistic and couldn't quite figure out how this would ever work, but he was in too deep to back out now. So he smiled and said, "I'm excited," even though inside, he was terrified.

AFTER THE crew was gone for the day, Travis lingered to make some notes and set up a priority list for the next day's projects. Renovations were proceeding now that the asbestos abatement team and exterminators had moved through the whole house. They'd finished the demolition work, and the next major thing would be to fix the structural issues under the house.

Brandon walked into the living room, where Travis currently sat. Travis had a folding chair pulled up to a sawhorse, which he was using as a desk. He was surrounded by temporary support walls now that most of the lath and plaster had been removed, and could therefore see Brandon coming from across the house. And yet it still surprised Travis. Today Brandon had on a purple-and-black plaid shirt that hugged his torso and a pair of well-fitted jeans that, while not especially tight, showed off how fit he was.

Travis shook his head. He didn't want to find Brandon attractive.

"I want to run something by you," said Brandon, walking over to him.

"Okay."

"I'm trying to take your arguments about the design to heart, and I want to bring in an outside designer. I just got network approval."

"That's fine." Travis rubbed his head. "Who is the designer?"

"Kayla Chase."

Well, that was a surprise. "As in your ex-wife, Kayla?"

"Yes."

Travis couldn't fathom that. Then again, his last few boyfriends had not been the best men humankind had to offer, so he wasn't that broken up about never seeing them again. "You can work with your ex-wife?"

"As well as I can work with you. Better, actually, because she doesn't question me constantly."

"I don't question you constantly."

"You're doing it right now!"

Travis let out a huff of breath. "I'm not, like, deliberately trying to goad you. This is a good job and I want to keep it." Although the truth was, it was fun to goad Brandon. Brandon was dead sexy when he was ruffled up, and an entertaining sparring partner. It was damned inconvenient to be this attracted to someone he had to work with, especially when he wasn't out to anyone in the cast or crew.

Sometimes when they were in the heat of an argument about cabinet styles or load-bearing walls, Travis thought Brandon might be attracted to him too. But that was very likely just his imagination.

"The really stupid thing," Brandon said as he leaned against the exterior wall, "is that the network is eating it up. I had a meeting with Virginia and Garrett Harwood yesterday, and they say the fact that we don't get along most of the time makes for good TV."

"Are you serious?" The suggestion was laughable, but then, it was television. He supposed if this was a straightforward house renovation show where everyone got along and there were never any issues with the houses, the show would be pretty boring.

Brandon shrugged.

"So, wait, is bringing your ex-wife on board your way of adding even *more* drama to the show?"

"No." Brandon sighed. "You've convinced me that you're right about the design. The truth is that the network has more faith in my design skills than I do. I was running with what I've always done in the past—only I hadn't taken the neighborhood and the age of the house into account. Kayla's a far better designer than I am and will have a better sense for what buyers in this part of the city would like." He closed his eyes and leaned his head against the wall. "There never really was much drama between us."

"Uh, didn't she cheat on you?" Travis had taken to periodically googling Brandon because the tabloid stories about him were so bonkers.

Travis assumed only a fraction of them had even a hint of truth to them, but that she'd stepped out on him seemed to be the incontrovertible fact. Kayla had been photographed kissing another man in a restaurant in Manhattan. Brandon and Kayla's marriage had ended soon after.

"God, I'm tired," said Brandon, rubbing his eyes.

"I'm just saying," Travis said, "I've been cheated on a time or two. I don't exactly have kind feelings toward those exes."

"The story they're telling in the media is not exactly what happened."

"I assumed."

Travis waited, expecting Brandon to explain, but he didn't. Instead he pushed off the wall. "I should get home."

"Did I offend you?"

"No. I… ugh, I just hate the shit with the tabloids." Brandon ran a hand through his hair.

"You came out looking like the good guy, though."

Brandon rolled his eyes. "Is that supposed to be some kind of goddamned silver lining? Because I didn't want any of this to happen. I just wanted everything to stay like it was. And because Kayla did a really dumb thing, everything changed. And somehow the worst part for me is that I feel guilty because she lost her job over it."

"She did?"

"She's the villain and I'm the victim, if you read *People*. No one wants to watch a show hosted by a villain. But the network is banking on people feeling sorry for me and tuning in to, I don't know, make sure I'm okay?" Brandon walked a few paces into the middle of the room and kicked a reciprocating saw that lay in the middle of the floor. He threw his hands up in the air. "Well, I'm not okay! I lost my best friend, I had to move out of my house, and now I'm bleeding money on this fucking flip that I let the network talk me into because I loved this house." He walked over to one of the temporary walls and wrapped his hand around the frame. "And I do love this house. But this is so fucking hard, and I don't know how to do it. So I wanted to bring Kayla in because I need some kind of normalcy and another perspective and someone who understands me to help with all this, and she's the only one I could think of. But of course everyone will assume I'm stirring up drama."

Travis put his pen down and stood up. He wanted to help Brandon calm down, but he wasn't entirely sure how. "I'm sorry. I didn't mean to imply anything."

Brandon turned and looked at him. Their eyes met, and Travis could see just how close to the edge Brandon was, how difficult it was for him to hold it together. Travis's instinct was to pull Brandon into his arms and try to soothe him, but that would be wholly inappropriate.

"I didn't mean to unload on you. I just…. I used to love this work. But I feel like this project is trying to kill me," Brandon said.

Travis nodded as he thought that over. "All right. Well, let's find the love, then. Because I can't fix any of the rest of your problems, but I do know a thing or two about how to fix houses."

Brandon crossed his arms. "What do you mean?"

Travis walked over to the fireplace, still waiting to be demolished, and laid a hand on the mantel. "What did you love about this house the first time you saw it?"

Brandon looked around. "Its charm. And the fact that I could see the potential. This house has broken bones, but the layout is pretty good, and… well."

"What?"

Brandon sighed. "This is stupid, but with every subsequent walk-through, I started to picture a family here. A married couple, a few kids, a dog or three. It made me happy to think about that. Because that's why I do this, you know? I want people to have a good place to live, a home that brings them joy. And then… well, then I started picturing *my* family here."

"With Kayla?"

Brandon balked. "No. Some potential spouse with no name. And I don't even want kids, but sometimes when I start a new project, I try to put myself in the shoes of the potential buyer. For this house, I think it's a young married couple with a couple of kids, and this is their forever home. And I like that image, you know?" He shook his head. "It's absurd, I know."

"It's not absurd at all. I tried to buy a house like this last year for similar reasons."

Brandon looked at Travis's hands. "I don't see a ring. Are you married?"

"No. I'm not seeing anyone right now either. I broke up with someone a few months ago, and then I got this job, and as you know, I basically live here now."

Brandon nodded slowly. "Were you going to buy a house for just yourself?"

"Well, yeah. I'd move my hypothetical future spouse into it eventually. But I wanted a project." Travis shook his head. Man, avoiding pronouns sounded clunky. Did people usually use the word *spouse* this much in regular speech?

The specific house he'd wanted had been a happy place, a family home. When Travis had been a kid, the house had been full of children and laughter and rogue candy dishes. But he didn't want to dwell on his disappointment about losing part of his history. Some developer had bought the house and turned it into the kind of cookie-cutter nightmare Brandon wanted to make this place. Travis grunted. He knew his emotions were playing out over his face, and he tried to look as placid as possible.

Brandon didn't seem to notice. "It's a nice thought," he said. "I totally get it. I've worked on houses that I loved so much, I thought of keeping them. But I also just enjoy the process of making an old home new again, you know?"

"I do know. It's why I do this work too."

Brandon stared at the floor thoughtfully for a moment. He looked up and said, "I apologize if I've been dismissive of your ideas. You actually do have good instincts. I can see now that my initial approach was wrong and I was just being stubborn. You were right. When I pictured this place initially, I did want some modern touches, but I like the weird mantel over the fireplace and the wall sconces and the wainscoting too. The bannister on the stairs is beautiful, and I'm glad we were able to save it. I just… I need this to be successful."

Travis was touched that Brandon had apologized, and he realized suddenly that Brandon really was stressed about the project. Travis hadn't recognized the extent to which Brandon's life had been upended by his divorce and how much pressure he was under to make the project and the show successful. Travis's role in this was pretty minor—he had a salary and would get paid for his hours worked whether the show did well or not—but Brandon was financially and professionally tied up in it, with a greater personal cost if the project tanked. He had new sympathy for Brandon. "I accept your apology. And I'm sorry if I was more…

aggressive than I should have been. I just… I mean, this house should have been condemned, but you can easily picture how it once was. I hated to see all that wiped out, you know?"

"Yeah, I know." Brandon offered Travis a little smile.

"Brooklyn is a weird real estate market."

Brandon let out a sigh. He walked over to the door and picked up his backpack. "Well, we've had a moment, I guess."

Travis laughed. The bubble of tension around them popped so suddenly, Travis was surprised he hadn't noticed it was there. "We have."

"Thanks for listening. I have to get home. See you tomorrow."

Chapter Six

WHEN BRANDON walked into the house, he found Travis at work demolishing the fireplace. He had a drill with a chisel attachment that he was using to break up the mortar, and he removed the bricks in chunks. The sound of demolition throughout the house was so loud Brandon couldn't hear his own footsteps. In fact, Travis was focused on taking the fireplace apart and didn't hear Brandon approach.

That gave Brandon a moment to enjoy the view. Travis's plain black T-shirt clung to his chest and arms, and those corded muscles flexed as he removed each chunk of brick. His skinny jeans had seen better days—the holes in the knees looked like they were caused by wear and tear, and not like they were artfully put there by the store that produced them. But Lord, those jeans just caressed Travis's ass and thighs. Travis had a tool belt slung low on his hips, and he periodically put the drill on a nearby sawhorse and pulled a chisel from the belt to hack at the mortar. He was sweating so much that Brandon could see a bead of moisture at the end of the lock of hair that hung over Travis's forehead. And Travis sported a few days' worth of beard growth.

He was ridiculously sexy, masculine without being over-the-top, and looking at him made Brandon's whole body wake up and take notice.

This was so bad.

He cleared his throat and said, "Hey, Travis."

Travis turned his head. "Oh, hey. Didn't see you there. Making good progress on the fireplace."

"I see. Did the camera crew get any footage of you working on it?"

"They did. They filmed me for almost an hour. It reminded me of my boss at my first construction job. That guy used to hover and pick everyone's work apart. If he'd actually done some work himself instead of just supervising, we would have gotten our projects done a hell of a lot faster."

"Sure. But viewers love demo. I don't know why." Except that he totally did, because he could have watched Travis work like this all day.

Travis shrugged. "It's fun. I mean, this is a lot more tedious than bashing kitchen cabinets with a sledgehammer, but I'm actually finding it kind of therapeutic."

Brandon smiled at that. "Sure."

"Anyway, the cameras are downstairs filming the repairs to the foundation. I put Ismael in charge of overseeing that."

"That's fine. I trust Ismael."

"Good. His whole crew wore their company shirts today. I think Ismael is hoping the phone number on the shirt gets picked up on camera."

Brandon chuckled. It was the policy of the Restoration Channel to hire local when possible and therefore provide jobs for workers in the community where the show was filmed. Brandon and Kayla had used a half-dozen different companies for *Dream Home*, though they'd had a group of five project managers who alternated so that no single person got stuck doing too many projects at once. In their heyday, the now-defunct B & K Homes could work on five houses at a time.

"Okay," Brandon told Travis. "Kayla's coming tomorrow, by the way. Do you think we've demolished enough that we can start talking about design?"

"Mostly." Travis tucked his chisel back into his belt and stood. "I mean, all the demo is done except for the fireplace. You guys can get started on the design while we finish the last of the repairs. And some of the work we do will depend on what kind of flooring you want."

"You don't want to sand down and keep the old floors?"

Travis grimaced. "I'm of two minds. There are spots where the floors need to be repaired. You could have patches custom made, but that kind of work could end up costing more than just replacing the floors. Plus, given how creaky the floors are, we should probably pull everything out, replace the subfloors and make sure they're level, and then lay down new wood floors that mimic the look of the old floors. That's what I would do. But it's your project."

"Right." Brandon had noticed that the hallway near the front door was particularly creaky, moaning whenever anyone walked on it.

"We could patch the subfloors to fix the creaks. There are some cheaper workarounds. But I think, given how much I'm guessing you'd want to sell this house for, it would probably be better to just redo the floors. Sorry." Travis narrowed his eyes at Brandon. "You're tuning me out, aren't you?"

"No. Just thinking about what I'd like to do." Replacing the subfloors and floors on the entire first floor was going to be expensive. But so would the patches; Travis was right that custom patchwork was pricey.

"I'm really trying to keep your costs down," said Travis. "At this point, I think a good compromise would be to redo the floors entirely across the first floor, but then maybe not take down so many walls, because the steel beam we would need if we took down this wall over here?" Travis crossed the room and put his hand on the wall that separated the living room from the kitchen. "It's a few thousand dollars. Why not keep the wall and put the money toward the floors?"

"Buyers today want open concept."

"Some do, yeah. But not all. And didn't you just tell me you thought I might have been right about the neighborhood?"

"Yes, but not about the walls. That's a hell of a compromise. I can already see the open house. 'Oh, I wish this wall weren't here.'"

"You don't need the wall gone for the kitchen design. You can add more storage on the other side, in fact."

"I don't know. I have to think about it."

"I'm just saying. We're well over budget. Do you have a hard spending limit?"

"I do, yeah. We're not there yet. So I can spend a little more." Which was true. He did have a ceiling figure in mind—the top dollar amount he was willing to spend. Still, while he could go over budget, he'd feel better about the project if they didn't test that limit.

"We can also make some other compromises."

"I know."

"Houses like this weren't built to be open concept. These walls are keeping the whole house up. We can do engineered beams, but again, there are cheap and expensive options. You can have beams that hang across the ceiling, or you can cut holes and make them flush with the ceiling, or you can lower the ceiling height, or you can just… not take down every wall. I agree, lose the one between the hall and the living room so the front entrance doesn't feel so narrow, and get rid of the one between the kitchen and dining room to make one large entertaining space. But this wall? Let's keep it."

"I have to think about it."

"Or you can make compromises with materials. Granite countertops instead of quartz or marble. Prefab cabinets instead of custom. Keep the existing footprints in the bathrooms instead of moving plumbing around."

"None of these things feel like options."

"They all cost money."

Brandon grunted. "God, I know. I don't know what to do. This is why I called in Kayla." The walls of the house felt like they were closing in on him, even though they were mostly just framing right now and not actual walls. "But we can't put cheap finishes in a multimillion-dollar home," he said, though his voice came out shaky and thin.

Travis must have sensed his panic, because he reached over and put a hand on Brandon's shoulder. Which was just too fucking much, because Brandon could *not* have a man this sexy touching him and still somehow hold himself together. He jumped, his nerves getting the better of him, and stepped away from Travis's touch.

"Jeez," Travis said. "Sensitive much."

"Sorry." Brandon rubbed his forehead. "I know you're trying to help. But I just can't right now."

"Depending on what happens downstairs with the foundation, we may need to make some more decisions today."

"I know, I—"

"You do have experience with all this, right? I know this is your first solo show, but did you have other consultants on *Dream Home*? You seem uncomfortable here."

He *was* uncomfortable. For so many reasons. "Did I not cut open my chest and bleed all over here yesterday?"

Travis held up his hands. "That's a little dramatic, don't you think?"

"It's all very well for you to sit there in judgment of me. It's not your money or your reputation on the line."

Travis rolled his eyes. "No, I'm just the sidekick."

"Did I say that?" Lord, but Travis got Brandon's goat. "We can have these arguments on-camera or off, but it doesn't change a few fundamental things."

Travis crossed his arms. "I'll bite. What are those things?"

Everything kind of hit Brandon at once. Here he was, staring down the best-looking man he'd set eyes on in years, trying to figure out how to keep this house standing so he could sell it, a project that cost more with every problem they uncovered. That looming failure weighed on him heavily. He held up his thumb. "First, it's my money on the line. The Restoration Channel is taking on some of the financial burden, but if this first house is a big flop, that's it. I fail, the show gets canceled, and my reputation is a joke."

"Right."

"Second." Brandon held up his index finger and took a step closer to Travis. "Every decision I make impacts the value of the house, so yeah, I'm worried about how much I spend."

"I'm not questioning you. I'm just telling you the issues as I see them and trying to find solutions that won't bankrupt you."

"I know. I know that's what you're doing. And it makes me crazy every time you open your mouth, because of the third fundamental thing."

"What's that?"

They stood about a foot apart now. Travis dropped his arms, and Brandon could see the V of sweat at the top of his shirt. He even smelled good, like musky sweat and man, and it was so appealing that Brandon took a small step closer.

"The third thing," Brandon said under his breath, "is that I am so attracted to you, I can't see straight."

He hadn't meant to say that, but some combination of stress and being on a roll with his little rant had forced it out of his mouth. He braced himself for Travis's reaction. Construction guys like Travis were not the most open-minded folks, in Brandon's experience, and there was no way to know if he'd be okay with hearing another man confess his attraction.

But Travis just stared at him, unblinking. "You… what?"

"I didn't mean to confess that, but I haven't been able to stop thinking about it since I walked into the house today."

"You…. Jesus. Well, why didn't you say something sooner?"

"What?"

Suddenly Travis's lips were against Brandon's. Brandon hadn't expected this. A slap, a punch, but not a kiss. But Travis tasted delicious, and his lips were hot and wet, and Brandon finally got his hands in all that honey-colored hair on Travis's head as he sank into the kiss.

Then there was a noise downstairs. Travis pulled away suddenly.

"Good Lord," said Brandon.

"Hi, I'm gay, by the way."

Brandon couldn't believe the last thirty seconds had happened, but apparently they had, because Travis's face was flushed and his lips looked swollen. Not to mention, Brandon could feel a bit of the burn from Travis's beard on his own face. "Well, there you go."

"Making out on set is probably not the smartest thing we do today."

And before Brandon's brain could get anywhere near formulating a response, Ismael called out, "Hey, Travis!"

Then Travis was gone, cutting through the kitchen, probably headed for the basement door.

Brandon just stood in the middle of the room, dazed.

WELL, FUCK. Brandon Chase was bisexual. Who knew?

Travis zipped out of the room and toward the sound of Ismael's voice. "What's up, Iz?"

"Need your input on something."

Conscious of the fact that the cameras were downstairs, Travis took a deep breath and ran a hand over his face, hoping he didn't look too much like he'd just made out with the boss. Not that Brandon was his boss; technically, Travis was employed by the Restoration Channel. But still. Travis couldn't get his head around this. Brandon was attracted to Travis, and Travis had kissed him, which was reckless and unprofessional.

He took another deep breath and descended the staircase.

It turned out Ismael just wanted to confirm the plan before any concrete was poured, so once Travis was a free agent again, he went back upstairs to finish the fireplace. Brandon was nowhere in sight—Travis wasn't even sure he was even still in the house—so he picked up his chisel and got back to work.

The problem with a monotonous project like dismantling an old brick fireplace was that his mind wandered as he worked. Travis's imagination was suddenly alive with possibilities. Most of those mental images involved more kissing, some nudity, and preferably a bed, although Travis also considered the logistics of finding a place in the house where they could make out without getting stabbed by a stray nail or being caught on camera. They hadn't really done anything on the second floor yet, but he wasn't sure he wanted his skin to touch that ancient carpeting. Maybe if they put down a drop cloth or something….

He shook his head. This was a silly line of thinking. They had a job to do. If they hooked up and something went wrong, they'd still have to work together. With cameras around, no less. Or else Travis would get fired. Travis really liked this job and wanted to keep it.

But the next time he saw Brandon, they'd have to have an awkward conversation, and he wasn't really excited about that.

The crew finished up in the basement for the day around the time Travis was finally through hauling the broken bricks out to the dumpster. Since nothing more could be done until the next day, the night crew hadn't been scheduled. Travis said goodbye to Ismael and was about to leave, when Brandon came back, laden with shopping bags.

He dropped the bags near the front door. "Hi, sorry. Kayla wanted me to pick up a bunch of design samples. Is it okay if I just leave all this here? These bags are flipping heavy."

"Yeah, the crew is gone for the day. I'm the last one here. Leave stuff anywhere you like, as long as it's not somewhere Ismael will trip over it when he comes in tomorrow morning."

Brandon shoved everything toward the foot of the stairs. "How'd the rest of the day go? I see you finished the fireplace."

"Yeah. Everything was fine. The foundation repair is done. We have to give the concrete a little more time to dry before we do anything downstairs, but it's all poured and leveled. The next steps all depend on what we decide to do for design—which walls are staying and what we're doing to the floors, I mean."

"Good. Okay. Well, hopefully Kayla and I can iron out the design tomorrow, and then we'll be able to move forward."

"We're over budget but not behind schedule yet."

Brandon nodded.

Travis sensed Brandon would avoid the subject of their kiss unless Travis mentioned it. The easy thing would be to avoid it as well, but Travis wouldn't be able to get it out of his mind until they hashed it out. They had to set some boundaries. Or something.

"We should really talk about what happened today," he said.

"Are you hungry? Did you eat dinner?"

"I haven't eaten. I'd planned to grab some takeout on the way home."

"There's a good Chinese place on Church. It's a little on the fancy side, but the food is excellent."

Travis gestured at himself. The worn jeans and dust-covered T-shirt were not exactly dress-code appropriate. "My clothes are more storefront pizza than they are fancy sit-down restaurant."

"Oh. Yeah. Well, we could get something delivered here. Maybe sit on the floor and talk over dinner?"

"I… all right."

Travis didn't know what to do with himself while Brandon called the local pizza place. He pulled a roll of brown paper out of the closet and put some down on the floor so they wouldn't get any grease or tomato sauce on the floor. When he finished, Brandon said, "They're sending paper plates, and I asked for a couple of cans of soda."

"Worst case, we can pilfer from the craft services setup in the backyard."

"Really?"

"Well, plates and stuff. Maybe some sodas. They take most of the food away when they leave each day, but they set up a tent back there with a little refrigerator and snacks for the night crew."

"This isn't like a normal project, is it?"

"In a lot of ways, it is. But there's better food, and cameras follow me around."

Brandon chuckled.

Travis decided to be bold. "And apparently I sometimes make out with the hot host of the show."

"About that…."

Travis held up his hand. "I don't really want to sit on the floor. Let's do this." He moved the sawhorse he'd been using to the middle of the room, over the paper he'd just put down. Then he went into the kitchen and grabbed a couple of folding chairs.

"You improvise like this a lot, don't you?" Brandon asked.

"I worked on a brownstone in Park Slope last year, and we got so behind schedule that I literally slept in the house so I could get there early enough every morning to get it done."

"That must have been unpleasant."

Travis shrugged. "I've slept in worse places."

"Well, I appreciate your commitment to the job." Brandon opened one of the chairs and sat in it. "By the way, the network signed off on hiring the kitchen and bathroom guys you recommended. I figured we could have them focusing on those rooms while the other teams deal with the rest of the house. With that many people working, we'll have the rest of this project done in a flash."

"Oh, great. That's awesome. You'll like these guys. I used to work for Mike and Sandy before I broke out on my own. They're both good-looking Army vets who are great at what they do. So, you know, good TV."

"Well, that will work for our mostly female audience. But I hired them because of the 'they're good at what they do' thing. I mean, I did meet with Mike on Monday, and he is super hot, but that's not why I hired him."

"He's super married anyway."

Brandon laughed. "I should probably limit the number of people I kiss who are working on this house."

"Right. I think we should—"

The doorbell rang.

"I'll get it," said Brandon, bounding out of his chair.

A few minutes later Travis was sitting in the other chair, holding a slice of pizza on a paper plate.

"For what it's worth," Brandon said, "I don't generally make a habit of kissing people I work with."

"Except for your wife."

Brandon stared at his plate.

"All right," said Travis. "One thing at a time. You should know, I am very attracted to you too, but I realize that acting on that attraction is very bad for our working relationship. And also, I was all set to just push that attraction aside because I thought you were straight, but now, here we are."

Brandon nodded. "And I'm trying to stay in the closet for the sake of my job, so us getting caught together would be bad."

For some reason that idea hadn't entered Travis's mind, but of course Brandon was in the closet. Travis hadn't had an inkling Brandon was anything but a married heterosexual man, despite all the googling. But also…. "Get caught? That implies something might happen between us."

"Under different circumstances, don't you think it might have? I mean, I'm very attracted to you. It was driving me to distraction. I shouldn't have said anything about it to you, but it just… popped out of my mouth, as if I couldn't hold it in anymore."

"Oh."

They ate in silence for a few moments while Travis turned that over in his mind. He put his plate down. "Stupid idea."

"What?"

"I don't go around kissing men I work with either. But I can admit that part of why I pick fights with you is that I enjoy seeing you all riled up, and I had no outlet for this attraction. But if the attraction is mutual, it kind of seems a shame not to do something with it."

Brandon laughed softly. "I'm sure part of the reason I fought with you, too, is that I didn't know what to do with my attraction to you either. At least the powers that be think we hate each other, even though we were just pushing each other around on the playground this whole time."

"But I also really like this job."

"Right. And it's my name on the marquis, so you think that if something goes wrong between us, you'll get fired."

"Precisely."

"Quite a pickle."

Travis rolled his eyes and picked his plate back up. What was he doing even entertaining this idea? He shouldn't have an affair with Brandon. Sure, they were hot for each other, but that wasn't enough for him to risk a job this lucrative on. Hell, a few more months working for the Restoration Channel, and Travis would be able to buy any house he wanted.

Travis watched Brandon eat a few bites of pizza. "Ah, well. In another place and time. But I do think I was right about the design of the house, and you probably will have to compromise on some things if you want to stay anywhere near the top end of your budget."

They'd managed to polish off a whole pizza—Travis had been ravenous, truth be told—so he started to clean up. He took Brandon's plate and his own and threw them inside the box. "We can just toss all this in the dumpster. We don't really have a place to put other kinds of garbage. Craft services just takes the trash with them when they leave each afternoon."

"Yeah, all right." But Brandon seemed distracted now, staring at something on one of the wall frames.

"You okay?"

Brandon stood up. "No, I… God. I spent eight years of my life married to Kayla, and working with her, and I was so fucking careful not to let on to anyone that I'm attracted to men. And now that I'm divorced,

I should be free to pursue whoever I want to, but I can't… I can't get out of my own head. All afternoon, I kept thinking, *What would the network say if they found out?* The viewership loves these wholesome married couples. Hell, the best-rated show is hosted by a super religious couple with five kids."

"Really?"

"Do you even watch the Restoration Channel?"

"No, not really. I've seen *Dream Home*, but that was for research."

"Right. Well, a few years ago, the Restoration Channel aired this show called *Country Creatives*. It was these two guys who were friends and business partners who did splashy, over-the-top renovations on old houses in rural areas. It was a modest hit for the network. And then it got leaked to the media that the hosts were actually a couple and not just friends, and everyone lost their minds. The Restoration Channel wants to appeal to the widest audience possible, and a gay couple making over houses in red America was never going to fly, so their show got canceled and they got fired."

"Shit."

"Working in Brooklyn is a different can of worms, I know. But I just… I don't want to take any risks here. It's bad enough that a huge chunk of my money is tied up in this house. I can't risk losing the show too."

"Right. And getting involved with me is a bad idea anyway."

"Are you trying to convince me or yourself?"

"Both." Travis's mind swirled. Brandon was so sexy, he made Travis dizzy. His first instinct was to grab Brandon and shove him against the nearest available wall, but he shoved his hands in his pockets instead.

"We *will* get caught. There's no way to avoid that with this many cameras around."

"I know." Travis put the pizza box back down on the sawhorse. He hadn't known about the gay couple who had gotten fired. That did throw a wrench in the works. Travis didn't much care about who knew about his sexuality, and he'd inadvertently come out to Ismael by using the wrong pronoun when they'd been chatting the other day. Ismael hadn't even blinked, for which Travis was thankful. So when he'd come on to Brandon again tonight, the idea that the *show* could be at stake hadn't even occurred to him. But if there was a precedent for the network firing gay hosts….

Shit.

"Why did I agree to this?" Travis asked aloud.

Brandon let out a bitter, surprised laugh. "I ask myself that very question about thirty times a day."

"We'll have to exhibit a tremendous amount of self-control when the cameras are around either way."

"I do know. I was unsuccessful at that today. I'll try harder." Brandon laughed again. "You're not that great at holding yourself back either, you know."

"What makes you say that? Because I kissed you?"

Brandon flushed crimson, likely remembering it. "I just meant, you're not shy about expressing yourself."

"Ah." Travis smiled to himself. "I'm right, by the way."

"You're always right."

Travis rolled his eyes at the sarcasm in Brandon's voice. "Not *always*."

"Not for nothing, but I should be angry at you because you keep undermining me. I'm the host—I'm supposed to be the expert."

"I'm not trying to undermine you."

"Maybe not, but you're not afraid to speak your mind either."

"I love these old houses and I want them to be preserved. That's all."

"Preserved, not modernized."

"Are we having this argument again?" Travis was tired. Since there'd be no more making out with Brandon tonight, he just wanted to go home. "Do whatever the fuck you want, okay? The final word is yours."

"What I want?" Now there was an edge to Brandon's voice. "I never get what I want. If I could have what I want, Kayla would be here beside me doing this renovation. We'd work together to come up with a design that fit the house and the neighborhood, and I wouldn't feel like such a fucking idiot all the time. Because you're right—I'm out of my depth here, and I'm pretty sure you and everyone else working on this project knows that." He closed his eyes and pressed a hand to his forehead. "And I'd kiss you whenever I damn well felt like it. Because we're attracted to each other and we should be able to act on it."

"You want to kiss me?"

Brandon huffed and rolled his eyes. His body language said, *Duh*. "I've wanted to since the moment we first met. I think about it all the fucking time."

"This is pretty inconvenient, huh?"

"You make me *feel*. Inconvenient doesn't even begin to describe it."

"I know the circumstances aren't ideal, but—"

Suddenly Travis was pressed up against the wall right next to the fireplace he'd spent all day dismantling, and Brandon was kissing him as though he were trying to suck out his soul. Travis had been about to say that though the circumstances were not ideal, they could find a way to work together and push this whole attraction thing aside. But, well… this was good, too.

Brandon smelled great, and his body was warm and a little sweaty, and he tasted like pizza and promise. And—oh—Brandon shoved his hands up the inside of Travis's shirt and splayed his fingers across Travis's skin, and Travis could feel Brandon's arousal against his hip, and…. Holy shit, they were going to do this right here, weren't they?

So, fine, Travis was game. He unbuttoned Brandon's shirt and tore it off his arms. Brandon whipped his own undershirt over his head, and… wow! Brandon's body was tight and muscular, and the hair that spread across his chest had a red tint to it. Or at least, it did in the dim temporary lighting in the living room.

Brandon pulled off Travis's T-shirt, then got his hands on Travis's jeans. Oh, they were just… diving right in. Travis meant to protest more vehemently, but this felt amazing. Before he even really knew what he was doing, his hands were undoing the fly of Brandon's jeans, and he could feel Brandon's erection straining against his cotton briefs.

"You're going to kill me," Travis managed to groan.

"I know. We'll just have to combust together."

"No, I mean, this whole room is kind of a hazard. There are broken bits of brick on the floor and stray nails, and the walls aren't really secure and…."

Brandon jerked away. "Right."

"I'm not saying we shouldn't make out, because we definitely should, but maybe we could do it in a less hazardous place. Like my apartment. It's only like ten minutes from here by cab."

Brandon laughed and rested his forehead against Travis's. Travis took advantage of the proximity to run his hands over Brandon's delicious chest.

"You want to put this on hold and go to your apartment?" Brandon asked.

"That seems wise. For safety reasons. You know."

Brandon took a step back, then bent over to pick up his shirt. "We should probably… no. Fuck it. Let's go."

CHAPTER SEVEN

TRAVIS'S APARTMENT was tiny but neat. A shelving unit divided the studio roughly in half, and Brandon could see the end of a bed sticking out from behind the unit. "This is nice."

Travis rolled his eyes as he put his bag down near a row of hooks next to the door. "Whatever. It's small, I know. Let's just get down to business, all right?"

Brandon laughed. Travis was direct; Brandon appreciated that.

But Brandon was nervous. He hadn't gotten naked with anyone in quite a while. He wanted to have sex with Travis, no question, but he needed a moment. "Can I have a glass of water?"

"Sure."

The kitchen was tucked into the corner. There wasn't much to it—a fridge, a sink, an oven with a microwave over it, and about two square feet of counter space, with two upper cabinets above. Nothing like a chef's kitchen. But the cabinets looked new, and there was a mosaic tile backsplash—the exact thing that had been all the rage a couple of years before.

"Do you rent this place?" Brandon asked when Travis handed him the glass.

"Yes. I hate this tiny kitchen, but I didn't design it. This was supposed to be a temporary space while I was house hunting. But then I didn't end up buying a house, so I stayed."

"There's a whole show about that on the Restoration Channel."

Travis laughed and shook his head.

"So, okay, tell me this." Brandon looked around and spotted a little café table with two chairs at it. A laptop rested on top of the table, so this was presumably also what Travis used as a desk. "If you could do anything you wanted in the kitchen at the Argyle Road house, what would you do?"

"Are we not having sex? Because I wouldn't have been so eager to show off my tiny apartment if we weren't."

"We'll get there. Just humor me for a few minutes." Brandon sipped his water as Travis sat in the other chair and gave Brandon a wary look. "You don't think talk of home design is sexy?" he asked, smiling.

"I think *you're* sexy. But I think you'd be sexier if you didn't have any clothes on."

Brandon chuckled. Okay, this was helping him calm down. "I'll talk to you about home design with my shirt off, if you'd like."

Travis nodded solemnly. "I think that would help."

So Brandon indulged Travis and took his plaid shirt off before hanging it over the back of the chair and peeling off his undershirt.

"Better," said Travis. "You were saying?"

"Hypothetically, if you had an unlimited budget and the power to do whatever you wanted in the kitchen, what would it look like?"

"Is this foreplay?"

"Sort of. Just tell me."

Travis shrugged. "I'm not really a designer."

"So? You clearly have an opinion."

"Fine. I'll bite." Travis closed his eyes for a moment. "Craftsman-style cabinets, probably in a dark wood. We can get away with it in that kitchen, especially if you take the wall down between the kitchen and dining room, because there's so much natural light that comes in through the windows. Probably light quartz counters. Light gray or white, even, to break up the dark cabinets. Then—and here's where it gets a little zany—I saw these tiles a few weeks ago at a flooring store. I'm not sure if they'd work as a backsplash, but they're teal blue with… I don't know what it's called. A brown outline of a flower on each one. Actually, hang on, I'll show you." He got up and went to one of the bookcases in his apartment. He pulled a photo album off the shelf and flipped through the pages. He handed it to Brandon, open to a spread of a couple of children and an older man sitting on the floor of a kitchen.

"It's called a quatrefoil. Is this little boy you?"

Travis grunted. "Yeah. That's me and my cousin Jen with my grandpa at his house. And I saw tiles at the flooring store that looked a lot like those, but the teal was more vibrant. They looked appropriately Victorian, so I thought those would be good in the kitchen. But as the backsplash, not the floor."

"Teal is a bold choice."

"You asked my opinion."

Brandon tilted the photo album to get a better look at the tiles. They were pretty and might work as a backsplash, but they were awfully specific—not at all something Brandon would put in a home he intended to sell. He handed the album back to Travis and watched as Travis put it away, wondering about what his grandpa had meant to him. Probably a lot; Travis had looked at the photo with fondness.

Brandon cleared his throat. This was about foreplay, not getting deep into each other's personal histories. "So, you would take that wall down?"

"Yeah, I would. It would make the space function better. For the flooring, I might do a ceramic tile. I like those twenty-four-by-twelve ones that are popular right now. I'd coordinate the color to the cabinets, maybe light gray. But, like, a warm light gray. That color probably has a name, but I don't know it. Then stainless-steel appliances, obviously. Maybe black stainless steel, just to be different. And I've seen some great vintage-looking ovens in stores. Absurdly expensive, but one would look perfect in that space. Just saying—not that you should follow my ideas, necessarily. Then if there's space for an island—and I think there is—maybe we do the cabinets in a contrasting color, same countertop, though. Sink in the middle. A little bit of an overhang so you can pull up stools."

"So what I hear you saying is that this"—Brandon gestured at the corner kitchen—"is not your dream kitchen."

Travis smirked. "No, it isn't. I don't even cook much, but it's nice to have options. This toy kitchen is really only good for heating up takeout."

Brandon finished his glass of water. "You must feel left out, seeing as how you're the only person in this room with a shirt on."

Travis smirked. "Are you saying I should join the club?"

"It might expedite things."

Travis whipped his shirt off, then stood up. "Hell, why not take it further." He undid his fly and shoved his jeans down his legs. He stepped out of them on the way toward the bed, displaying his ass for Brandon as he walked by.

Travis's body was sinewy and strong. He was tall and lean, with body hair that looked a bit like sand clinging to his skin after a day at the beach. There was a tattoo on his right pectoral muscle and another on his arm and probably more on other parts of him that Brandon couldn't see because the object of his desire moved too fast. Travis disappeared behind the shelving unit, so Brandon followed, because he had to.

Brandon stood at the foot of the bed and looked at Travis, who lay there, still in his briefs, with his legs splayed. "What are you doing?"

Travis ran a hand down his own chest. "Expediting things."

"Yeah?"

Travis shoved a hand into his briefs and grabbed what must have been a pretty substantial cock. "I'm having sex tonight. Whether it's with you or not is up to you."

Brandon's heart pounded. Well, with an invitation like that….

Brandon pushed off his jeans and climbed onto the bed.

TRAVIS HAPPILY accepted the weight of Brandon's body on top of his and ran his hands down Brandon's back, feeling his soft, smooth skin. He opened his legs to let Brandon settle in the cradle of his hips, and he shifted his pelvis up so their dicks rubbed together. The zing of arousal that whipped through his body was warm and exciting.

Travis wanted to do this hard and fast. He didn't want to waste time on romance or sweetness. He didn't know Brandon well enough to judge how much foreplay or flowery language he needed, or if this could just be sexy fun.

So Travis decided to just go for it. He wrapped his legs around Brandon's thighs and shifted his weight so that he was pinning Brandon onto the bed. Brandon laughed, which was a good sign that sexy fun was on the menu tonight. Travis kissed him hard, biting his lip, and Brandon groaned into Travis's mouth, making his lips vibrate.

"So what's your deal?" Travis asked.

"What do you mean?"

Travis ran a hand down Brandon's chest. They both still had their underwear on, but Travis could feel that Brandon was hard as a rock. His eyes sparkled with a bit of daring. He was into this. Travis grinned. "You have things you like in bed? Top? Bottom? Whatever strikes you in the moment?"

Brandon kissed Travis, probably stalling for the best way to answer the question. Travis hadn't intended for this to become an interview, but he wanted to know if there were boundaries he should respect. Brandon had been married to a woman until recently; maybe he hadn't been with a man in a while. Or ever. Not wanting to dwell on that possibility, Travis deepened the kiss and shifted his hips against Brandon.

When Brandon dropped his head back onto the pillow without speaking, Travis said, "I'm game for pretty much anything. I can tell you what I'd like to do, which is to flip you over and worship that tight ass of yours, then fuck you into next Tuesday."

Brandon groaned. "Yes." The ecstasy in his voice told Travis that Brandon was definitely into that idea.

"Good." Travis knelt and scooted back from Brandon a little. "Roll over."

Brandon complied, smiling at Travis before he rolled onto his stomach with a bounce on the mattress.

Brandon's body was something else. He was so flipping tall, with long limbs like a swimmer, and his broad shoulders and long back were unmarred by scars or tattoos. Brandon's thighs were powerful, masculine, his arms well-muscled, his hips narrow, his ass nicely rounded. Everything about Brandon was TV ready. Travis was no slouch, but so much of his strength was due to throwing around sledgehammers and carrying around stone countertops; he wasn't molded in a gym, and he had scars and tattoos, nothing like Brandon's near perfect facade.

He pushed that thought aside and hooked his fingers into the waistband of Brandon's briefs, then pulled them down. Brandon's ass was similarly perfect, all firm, smooth skin.

"Do you have any physical flaws?" Travis asked, a bit in awe.

"If I do, I'm sure you'll find them."

Travis chuckled. Brandon did have his number. But he was done talking.

He pushed at Brandon's ass and got him to raise it a bit. Then Travis ran his hands over Brandon's skin, firm but soft to the touch, and slid his thumbs into the crack of Brandon's ass. When he bent down to lick the seam, Brandon groaned and jerked.

"Okay?" Travis asked.

"Good Lord, do that again."

Travis dove in.

Brandon smelled delightfully sweaty and musky. Travis had long been drawn to bodies like Brandon's, strong, possibly gym-sculpted, men who smelled like sweat and hard work. Brandon had a bit of made-for-TV polish, but in the hidden parts of his body, he was raw, sexy, imperfect. Travis pressed his face in, licked the entrance to Brandon's body, playing with his tongue and fingers to elicit all manner of grunts and groans. When Travis reached between Brandon's legs, he found Brandon's eager erection. Travis himself was hard and tingling everywhere, already beginning to lose himself in the sort of overwhelming arousal that made one forget his own name. And more than anything, he wanted to be inside Brandon.

He reached for his nightstand while Brandon, clearly lost in the same place Travis was headed, whined incomprehensible protest noises. Travis pulled a bottle of lube and a condom from the drawer, then resumed his place, this time lubing up his fingers and sliding them inside Brandon while he kissed and nibbled at Brandon's lower back.

"Oh, that's good," Brandon said, shoving his body back onto Travis's fingers.

Travis's cock was practically crying out to be inside Brandon. Brandon was whimpering, his skin flushed now, his body begging Travis. So Travis pushed off his own briefs and rolled on a condom. But he wanted to see Brandon's face.

He nudged Brandon onto his back. Brandon looked up with a question in his eyes. Brandon was pink from his face, across his chest, down toward his cock. Travis was hardly a size queen, but wow! He wrapped his hand around that cock and stroked it, sending Brandon's hips hopping off the mattress. Then, because he had to, Travis swallowed that cock, savored the salty taste of it and gave it a long lick.

"I'm dying," Brandon said. "This is what dying feels like."

Travis laughed and rose on his knees. "But what a way to go, eh?"

Brandon grabbed the lube and poured some on his fingers. He wrapped them around Travis's dick and slicked up the condom. "I need this inside me more than I need to breathe."

"Jesus."

It was Brandon who spread his legs and shifted his hips up, and Brandon who grabbed Travis's cock and steered it toward him. Travis bowed down and kissed Brandon as he started to slide inside.

After that, instinct took over. Travis had done this hundreds of times, only it had never been quite like this. Brandon's body was warm and tight, but Travis slid into it like he was meant to be there. Brandon put his arm around Travis as they continued to kiss and Travis started to buck his hips. There was nothing secretive about this, even though they wouldn't be telling anyone about it in the morning. No, they had all night, and all the lights in Travis's apartment were blaring, and they could see each other clearly. Travis lifted up, shifted his hips to get a deeper angle, and looked into Brandon's eyes.

Brandon was falling apart, his lips parted. He closed his eyes tightly as if he were fighting to hold on. He threw his head and shoulders back, bowing off the bed, and his cock was red and hard and pointed toward his chin. Travis wrapped his hand around it as he got the best angle, and the rest of the world became a little fuzzy. He focused only on Brandon, on the size and hardness of his cock, on the way his body squeezed Travis's, on the redness that spread across his chest.

Travis stroked Brandon harder. His singular goal was to get Brandon to come on his cock, to see Brandon fall apart beneath him before he himself succumbed to the pleasure their bodies were creating. Brandon's facial expression was anguished, but in a way that Travis knew meant he was just barely holding it together.

Brandon grabbed fistfuls of the sheets near his head and pushed his hips against Travis. Then his whole body seemed to surrender to Travis; his eyes rolled back, his shoulders fell to the mattress, and he let out the moan of the deeply satisfied. Then he came against Travis's hands, his body clamping down on Travis's cock, and it was all too much. Travis surrendered himself as well, giving himself to this moment, and came inside Brandon.

When he was aware of his surroundings again, his forehead was pressed against Brandon's sweaty chest. Travis slid out of Brandon and collapsed on top of him, his limbs limp.

Brandon laughed softly and put his arms around Travis. "That was awesome," he said, sighing.

Travis rolled onto his back and dumped the condom in the trash can near the side of the bed. He remained on his back and looked over at Brandon, who looked happily out of it. "It *was* awesome," Travis said.

Suddenly Travis felt a little overwhelmed. He'd just fucked a TV star. He'd fucked a guy he worked with, which he *never* did. He'd just fucked a guy he'd been arguing with in front of a camera. Had he really just done that?

He had, yeah. And he had no regrets. He rolled over to loop an arm around Brandon's chest and pull him close. Brandon rested his head near Travis's on the pillow. They gazed at each other for a moment. The way Brandon smiled indicated that hopefully, he had no regrets about this either.

CHAPTER EIGHT

TRAVIS COULD feel the gods of sleep luring him into unconsciousness, but Brandon flicked his earlobe and said, "I didn't notice you had pierced ears before."

Travis sighed and closed his eyes. "Something I did in my twenties. I still wear earrings when I go out, but I'm always worried about getting them caught on something at work sites, so I don't wear them on the job. Which means I don't wear them, because I pretty much only go to my job these days."

Brandon laughed softly. "Okay. Tattoos. Piercings. A job you have to do with your hands. You're a bit of a badass."

Travis guffawed. "Hardly. Can we go to sleep now?" He settled into the pillows.

"I should tell you something."

"Now?"

Brandon took a deep breath. "Well, given that we just had sex and we'll be spending tomorrow with my ex-wife, yeah. I think you need to know this."

Travis sighed and propped himself up on one elbow so he could look at Brandon. "Shoot."

"I'm telling you this because I trust you, by the way. This doesn't leave this room."

Travis was touched that Brandon trusted him, so he said, "Okay. Lips are sealed."

"Long before we were married, Kayla and I were best friends and business partners. We met at our real estate licensing class, actually. So basically, we founded B & K Homes, and we mostly handled real estate transactions at first, but then we started flipping houses in Dutchess County upstate."

"Sure."

"See, I'd always been interested in real estate because my father…. Do you know who my father is?"

"No. Should I?"

"John Chase."

Travis sat up. "*The* John Chase? Chase Tower? The St. Joseph Hotel?"

"Yes. I grew up in a suite at the St. Joseph."

"You… well, that's amazing. Was it amazing?"

Brandon shrugged, as if he didn't think so, but not in an arrogant way. He seemed nonplussed, in fact. "I don't know if amazing is the right word. I mean, don't get me wrong, the suite is gorgeous. The family doesn't live there anymore, although my brother Robert uses it as an office sometimes. But… my father was a hard man to live with. You have to have a certain amount of ruthlessness to get ahead in the New York real estate market, and he used that same ruthlessness on his family. Failure was not tolerated."

Travis was almost afraid to ask, but he did anyway. "What does that mean?"

"Well, like, my GPA dipped below 3.0 one semester in high school, and I wasn't allowed to hang out with my friends until I pulled my grades up. My brother Luke got a DUI once when he was nineteen, and when the story showed up in the *Post*, my father was so furious, he refused to pay Luke's rent that month. He never laid a hand on us, but he was stern and quick to dole out punishments. And if he disapproved of something we'd done, he'd freeze us out. He and Robert didn't talk for almost a month once because Robert bought a building in Queens that Dad thought was a bad investment."

Travis suspected Brandon was sugarcoating this story a little. He sounded almost apologetic about his father, which seemed like a sure sign of a lifetime of gaslighting and abuse. Travis also knew that John Chase had passed away about five years ago. Of course, most people were never quite free of a history like that.

"Anyway," Brandon said. "I'm telling you this to explain the situation I was in. Robert took over the family business when Dad started having health problems. Luke helped out sometimes too, although Luke has… well, he's got his own stuff to deal with. And I decided that I was interested in real estate, but I was the rebel, and I wanted to get by on my own. Kayla and I moved to Poughkeepsie and set up shop there just when there was a boom of people from the city moving upstate. We made enough money that I didn't need Dad's financing. I didn't want it, frankly. Dad probably would have invested in my business if I'd asked, but his help would have come with strings, and he would have wanted more control than I was willing to give up. So Kayla and I made the business a success without his help."

"That's admirable," said Travis, lying back down.

"I was proud of the work we were doing. And then we were watching some Restoration Channel show one evening when Kayla said, 'We should do *that*.'"

Travis traced a line through Brandon's chest hair with his finger. "Be on TV?"

"Yeah. Kayla had a friend who was an entertainment agent here in the city, and she managed to discover that the Restoration Channel was putting out feelers for a house-flipping show hosted by a married couple. Restoration's whole thing at the time was that its viewers were getting really invested in each couple. Fans wanted to get to know the couple more than they wanted to see the end results of the home renovation. So Kayla decided we should get married."

"Well, if you rushed into marriage to get your fifteen seconds of television fame, I suppose that could be a reason for divorce."

"It worked, because we got the job."

"And then lost it when your marriage fell apart."

Brandon looked at the ceiling. "Here's the thing I need you to understand. It was a marriage of convenience. In case you haven't figured it out, I'm gay."

Wait, what? Travis assumed Brandon and Kayla had been in love with each other—Brandon always talked about her fondly—and that Brandon was bisexual, especially since Brandon kept going on about how much he missed Kayla and wished she were with him on the site, but… no. He was gay.

"My father was conservative," Brandon said. "He threatened to disown me when I came out, and my mother encouraged me to stay in the closet to keep him happy. So I did. Imagine how different my life would have been if I'd…. Well, it's too late for that now. But at the time Kayla suggested we get married, it solved two problems. It made my family happy and it gave us the opportunity to do *Dream Home*. Dad was very excited about having a son carrying on the family tradition of real estate supremacy on television."

"So, wait. You and Kayla had a fake marriage."

"We had a legal marriage. There was a ceremony at City Hall and everything. We just never consummated it."

This was blowing Travis's mind. He didn't know anyone in modern times who still did things like this. "So, wait. The tabloids all say she cheated on you."

"We had an arrangement. We shared a house near Poughkeepsie to keep up the ruse, but we agreed that forcing each other into a sexless marriage was an awful thing to do, so we agreed we could see other people as long as we were discreet. And then about a year and a half ago, Kayla started dating this guy named Dave. They fell in love… and she got careless. They were out for dinner one night in Manhattan, and someone snapped a cell phone photo of them kissing. That person posted the photo on social media. Then the tabloids went *crazy* and ran with the story."

Travis let that hang in the air while he tried to puzzle through what Brandon was telling him. "In other words, you and Kayla had a legal but fake marriage, and everything was going fine until the tabloids saw Kayla kiss another dude and assumed she was cheating. And that was enough to get your show canceled?"

"The Restoration Channel had another house-flipping show that was hosted by a married couple who got divorced in the sixth season, and the whole show fell apart. Viewership dropped off, the episodes weren't as good because the couple was constantly fighting with each other, and the show itself became about their divorce drama instead of house flipping. Restoration wasn't willing to make that mistake twice. And since the narrative was that we were getting divorced because Kayla was cheating on me—and not because Kayla wanted to marry the boyfriend she had my blessing to be with—Restoration pulled the plug. Plus, you know, we were hired because we were this cute, happy newlywed couple. It's hard to sell that image when out here in the real world, everyone is talking about how our marriage fell apart."

Travis remembered something Brandon had said earlier. "And you feel guilty because Kayla kind of got shafted here, but you look like the injured party."

"Yes. I hate that this is how it played out. Kayla insists she's okay and she and Dave are happily flipping houses out of the spotlight in California now, but… it's all ruined."

"To be fair, she's the one who kissed a guy in public."

Brandon rubbed his face. It was clear that the whole situation still brought him a great deal of anguish. "We decided to get divorced because it was the healthier thing for both of us. My father died five years ago and my mother and I rarely talk, so there's no reason to hide who I am from my family. I don't work for the family business, so they don't get a say anyway. Kayla wanted to pursue a relationship with Dave, and she thought I should burst out of the closet once I was free of the show, but instead I took this job."

"But you and Kayla are still friends, which is why you wanted to have her on the show."

"That, and I could really use her expertise. I thought I could handle a solo show, but it turns out I work better as part of a pair. Without getting feedback from someone else, I don't know how to make decisions." Brandon rubbed his face. "Sorry. Just… nothing this year has turned out the way I thought it would, and it's really thrown me for a loop."

Travis shifted closer to Brandon. He wished he had known Brandon was this much of a mess *before* they'd fucked. Because this was a lot: an abusive father, the weight of family expectations, a marriage of convenience, and now pressure from both the network and Brandon himself to make the show a success. This information made a lot of things click into place for Travis, though—Brandon trusted Kayla, so it made sense for him to want her opinion, and he didn't have any enmity toward her because she didn't really cheat on him. He was driven to succeed, too, both because of and in spite of his family, and Travis was sympathetic to that.

Travis's own family had been less ambitious. He'd come from a long line of New York construction workers—his grandfather had worked on the Empire State Building—and he liked working with his hands, so why not keep up that tradition? Then again, his parents lived in a little bungalow in Queens with vinyl siding, not the St. Joseph Hotel. Expectations for their children were different, and Travis had always felt that his parents had just wanted him to be happy. Because who would have thought a working-class kid with a fairly thick Queens accent could have even gotten this close to being a TV star?

Travis suspected he'd only really scratched the surface of what made Brandon the man he was now, and knew he'd find some messy challenges once he dug deeper. On the other hand, he still liked Brandon a lot. He put a hand on Brandon's chest and tried to be comforting, even though he'd never been very good at that. Travis had a few relationships under his belt, but he was generally a love 'em and leave 'em type. It had been only on rare occasions that he'd met a man who was worth more than a few tumbles in bed.

Brandon might be worth more, though.

It was hard to know. Brandon had spent so much time putting up a careful facade, Travis wondered if Brandon even knew who he was beneath it all. And no wonder Brandon had wanted to turn the Argyle Road house into a neutral wonder; he'd spent years of his life trying to make one thing into something else—an old house into a new house, a quirky house into a generic one, a gay man into a straight one.

But Travis saw what was really there, at least with the house. And he wanted to see who Brandon really was too.

"I suppose I didn't help matters by questioning everything you did at the house," Travis said.

"Actually, that did help, because I had someone to discuss my ideas with. I need that. I need a partner. Not even romantically, just on the show. I tossed the idea of getting a cohost to Virginia and Garrett Harwood, but they wouldn't bite."

"So you want me to fight with you? Because I will."

Brandon laughed, which had been Travis's intention. They smiled goofily at each other for a moment.

"I just.... I wanted you to know all this because I didn't want there to be any misunderstandings between us. But we still have to keep up appearances when the cameras are around."

"Of course." Well, Travis resented having to hide his feelings on camera, but if the circumstances had been different, it wasn't like it would have been PDA City with Brandon anyway. Travis had never been especially touchy-feely in public. He could keep his hands to himself. "I look forward to arguing with both you and Kayla about design tomorrow, then."

Brandon sighed. He put an arm around Travis and pulled him close, so Travis tried to touch Brandon in a comforting way. He felt inadequate.

Not that Travis's life had been devoid of emotional turmoil, but he'd learned how to cope with it. But he didn't know how to anticipate what other people needed. He wasn't very good at being nurturing. That Brandon had shared as much of himself as he had in such a short amount of time was… well, it was nice to be trusted that way, but Travis was a little uncomfortable.

Still, he put his arm around Brandon and laid his head on his shoulder.

"Thank you, Travis. For listening, if nothing else."

"No problem. Anytime." He snuggled a little closer. "Are you staying the night?"

"Do you not want me to?"

"I want you to. It was just a question."

"I don't want to go home right now."

"Then stay."

"I'll have to get a change of clothes. Your little jeans will never fit me."

"Where do you live?"

"Brooklyn Heights."

"Well." Brooklyn Heights was a neighborhood well beyond Travis's means. He supposed a long-running successful television show and some family money earned one some luxuries. "It's just a few stops on the subway. Twenty minutes on the 2 train."

"All right."

Travis picked his head up and gave Brandon a long, lingering kiss. He knew how to do that, at least. When Brandon wove his fingers through Travis's hair, Travis felt like he'd done something right.

Travis lay back down. "Let's get some sleep. We've got an early day tomorrow."

BRANDON HAD set a phone alarm for six in the morning so that he'd wake up in time to go home, shower, change clothes, and be back at the house in time to welcome Kayla. But he needn't have set an alarm, because he spent a good portion of the night lying awake. Part of that was the unfamiliarity of a strange apartment, but a bigger part was that he still couldn't quite believe he'd said so much to Travis. He kept replaying the conversation in his head, wondering if he should have been so honest, if he'd shown too much vulnerability, if Travis thought he was a fool for marrying Kayla to begin with.

Travis, of course, slept soundly. He didn't have much of a snore, but his soft, even breathing and the occasional puffy exhale told Brandon Travis was out cold while Brandon fretted.

He didn't… do this. Brandon didn't have long-term relationships because there was no way to explain his relationship with Kayla that didn't make it sound like he was a closeted man in the 1950s. And the biggest reason he'd agreed to the divorce was that what had once seemed like a good idea for the sake of his career had started to feel increasingly silly the longer it went on. Over the years he'd had a few discreet affairs, but nothing that could be considered a real relationship. And he had the potential for something significant here, except for the part where they still worked together. He could understand why Travis had been reluctant to start anything.

Brandon told himself he could compartmentalize everything, but he wasn't sure that was true. And he felt self-conscious now, having shared so much with Travis that he'd never shared with anyone. And he blamed himself for everything that happened with Kayla.

But he'd felt that Travis needed to know that Brandon had never had romantic designs on Kayla, especially if they were all going to work together.

He needed Travis to know that the carefully constructed persona Brandon had built for TV was a facade. The problem was that Brandon had no idea who the real Brandon was anymore. And this was what kept him awake most of the night.

When the phone alarm went off at six, it was almost a relief. Brandon grabbed his phone and turned off the alarm. Travis grunted and rolled over and then was quickly back to sleep, so Brandon checked one of his social media accounts. The latest news was that it had somehow leaked out that Kayla would be doing a guest segment on Brandon's new show, and what did this all mean? Was Kayla in New York to beg for Brandon to come back to her?

Brandon closed out of that app quickly and got out of bed.

A few minutes later he walked back into the bedroom to find his clothes. Travis was sitting up in bed, rubbing his eyes.

"Are you abandoning me?" Travis asked.

"I need to change clothes. The film crew will surely recognize that I'm wearing the same clothes I had on in yesterday's dailies."

Travis nodded and rubbed his eyes. Then he slid out of bed, still naked as the day he was born, and sauntered over to Brandon, who was now half-dressed. Travis took Brandon's face in both of his hands and gave him a long, soft kiss. "Think of me fondly during our separation."

Brandon laughed. "What, you mean the whole hour and a half we'll be apart?"

Travis leaned over and whispered in Brandon's ear, "I hope you relive last night the whole time. I hope when you're in the shower, you think about what it was like for me to fuck you. I hope you picture me naked when you grab your cock, and I hope you jerk off in the shower thinking of me. And then I hope that when I see you again back at the house, you're all worked up, but there'll be nothing you can do except wait for the end of the day when I can take you back here."

Travis was naked and hard and pressed against Brandon. It felt amazing. And maybe that was all this was—just a physical thing. A roll in the hay. A release of tension. Maybe everything he'd told Travis didn't matter.

Sex. Brandon could do that. The emotional stuff was what he was less sure about.

But he was willing to run with this now. He moaned and grabbed Travis's bare ass, pulling him close and kissing him hard, sucking Travis's lower lip into his mouth and sinking his teeth into it. Travis groaned and pulled Brandon back toward the bed.

"I have to go, Travis."

"This'll take, like, eight minutes, tops."

Brandon laughed and sank back into the bed with Travis.

Chapter Nine

Brandon had put on a clean plaid shirt and jeans for work, and was somewhat surprised when Kayla walked into the Argyle Road house dressed to the nines. She wore a plum-colored blouse and black pencil skirt with low wedge shoes that were impractical for the state of the house. She looked fantastic—just inappropriate for the building she'd be walking around in.

"Design day is very exciting," she told one of the cameras in the living room.

Brandon was excited to do this walk-through, but a lot of thoughts swirled through his head. Travis stood near the front door, a wry look on his face, likely taking in this whole scene.

Virginia walked over. "Okay. Here's how I think we should do this. Travis, come over here."

Travis glanced at Brandon as he walked over. Brandon was embarrassed to say he couldn't take his eyes off Travis. Today Travis wore a T-shirt advertising the kitchen and bath company they'd hired tucked into dark-wash jeans. His work boots were scuffed, announcing that he worked hard and didn't dress for style. The shirt clung to Travis's torso, though, belying a bit of vanity on Travis's part.

Brandon wondered what Travis did with his off-hours.

But he didn't have time to think about such things right now. He turned to Virginia.

"What are the major design decisions?" asked Virginia.

"We're stalled until there's a design plan," said Travis. "The obvious things are kitchen layout and design, bathroom layout and design, flooring throughout the house, and whatever we're doing with this fireplace. The materials we order could take a week or two, so we should figure everything out now. Paint and stuff that's purely cosmetic can wait a bit. But mostly I need to know which walls are staying and how much plumbing I'm rerouting."

"That… sounds right," said Brandon, feeling overwhelmed.

"Okay. So, let's do a walk-through today. Brandon and Kayla can make final decisions about walls and plumbing with consultation from Travis. Then tomorrow, Brandon and Kayla can go shopping for materials while Travis starts implementing the plans. Yeah?"

"Sounds good," said Kayla. "You boys ready to begin?"

"As I'll ever be," said Brandon.

"Great. Then let's start right here. Are the cameras ready to go?"

Brandon had forgotten how good Kayla was at this sort of thing. She felt completely comfortable in front of the cameras in a way Brandon never did. He mostly got through the shoot by pretending the cameras weren't there, and eventually his brain just stopped acknowledging that they were always in his peripheral vision.

Travis seemed unfazed too. When Erik yelled, "Action!", he walked over to Kayla and said, "Hi, I'm Travis, the project manager."

"Nice to meet you, Travis. You keeping this one in line?" Kayla poked Brandon's arm.

"I'm trying. I am glad you're here, though. Brandon and I had a bit of a tiff over the design early on. He wanted to generic the hell out of this place."

Kayla's grin was positively evil. "Well, buddy, you're about to learn that Brandon is great at figuring out practical things like room layouts, and he has good taste if you give him some options, but he's afraid of color and pattern."

"I'm really looking forward to this," said Travis, smiling at Kayla.

"You're about to have a lot of fun at my expense, aren't you?" said Brandon.

"It's the best kind of fun. Come along, my ex-husband. We're going to design the heck out of this house."

They started in the living room. Travis whipped out his clipboard, on which he had a sheaf of paper. Brandon looked over Travis's shoulder as Travis flipped through the pages clipped to the board. Each page was a rough blueprint drawn on graph paper, one room per sheet. Travis found the one for the living room, which had the old walls drawn on and the fireplace marked.

"We're taking out the wall between this room and the hallway, right?" Kayla said. "It's unnecessary. We'll get a few more feet of space for this room if it goes all the way to the staircase."

Travis crossed out the wall on his blueprint. "Yes," he said. "It's one of the few things we've agreed on."

Travis was mostly quiet while Kayla and Brandon discussed the relative merits of different fireplace treatments before they settled on a stone surround for a gas fireplace and the reclaimed mantel.

"I'll have to run gas lines in here," Travis said. "And dismantle the chimney."

"You said chimney, but I heard a cash register ring," said Brandon.

Travis just raised an eyebrow.

Kayla said, "A gas fireplace is easier for the homeowner. It's not like there's an abundance of wood to chop around here."

"Yes, but dismantling a chimney is expensive. Why bother if we can easily clear out any blockage?" said Travis.

"Can we?" asked Brandon.

"Yeah, I think so. It's still cheaper than taking down the whole thing. And you can buy firewood at the grocery store on Church."

"I guess some buyers might think a wood-burning fireplace is quaint and charming," said Kayla.

"Fine. Let's keep it." Brandon took a deep breath, willing himself not to get too fired up. Travis was right in this case; converting the fireplace was an unnecessary expense that wouldn't add any value to the house.

They moved on to the kitchen next. Travis already had the wall between the kitchen and dining room crossed out, so at least they agreed there. As Brandon decided where each appliance would go and how far the cabinets would extend, Travis drew out the plan on his blueprint page. It came in handy that Travis had drawn it to scale, because he could tell them exactly how big a kitchen island they could build.

Brandon had already lined up the various samples along the wall between the kitchen and living room.

"What are we doing with this wall?" Kayla asked.

"Keeping it," said Brandon. "Travis made the excellent point that we can put more storage here. Maybe a big pantry or something."

Kayla nodded. "Sound plan." She looked at the samples. "So, shaker cabinets are all wrong for this space, but I like these." She ran her hand along the top of the craftsman-style cabinet door that lay against the wall. "Not this color, though. This gray is awful. We should do something warmer. Maybe a natural wood color. But dark wood. That cherry color is so 1990s."

Travis snorted.

Brandon glanced at him. "I take that noise to mean 'I told you so.'"

"Did I not tell you dark wood, craftsman style?" Travis tapped his head.

"What were you thinking for flooring?" Kayla asked.

Brandon sighed, sensing he was about to lose all of his arguments. "Originally I thought hardwood through the whole house, but if you're thinking dark wood for the cabinets, how will that work with the floors?"

"Depends on what color you're staining the floors."

"I like this one," Brandon said, pointing his foot at a floor tile.

And so it went for the next half hour, as they debated the pros and cons of the various samples. Eventually Kayla concluded, "We have to do some shopping. I don't like any of these backsplash options."

"All right," said Brandon, thinking about the tiles Travis had shown him. Travis's face betrayed nothing now, but all of the samples Brandon had grabbed from the store were solid colored.

"But I think we should do the same cabinets and counters in the bathrooms. This light gray quartz is just the thing, I think." Kayla bent down and picked up the sample. "I like the sparkle in it."

"And the sparkle is real authentic to the time period," Travis said.

Ah, there he was. "I don't think we're going for authentic so much as practical here," said Brandon. "Quartz is low-maintenance. Good for families. It's not porous, so it doesn't stain." Which Travis of course knew, but Brandon still said it for the sake of the cameras.

"Right," said Travis.

"I think Kayla will agree with me that most buyers want something that feels evocative of the era, but they also want modern kitchens and bathrooms," Brandon added.

Kayla nodded. "Let's do stainless everything. Appliances, sink. We can do an antique-looking vent hood over the oven. I saw these hammered copper ones a few weeks ago that would look great here."

By the time they had finished with the last bathroom, Brandon couldn't pay attention anymore. It was mostly Kayla and Travis conferring. Kayla wanted to move all kinds of plumbing around, but Travis was mindful of the budget and talked her out of it except in one bathroom, where it really did make sense to move the shower.

And finally they were in the family room. Travis and Kayla had a spirited argument about whether to get rid of the wall between the dining room and the family room and ultimately decided to just make the doorway bigger.

"Tomorrow we'll go to this place I know in Dyker Heights," said Kayla. "It's like a tile clearinghouse. We should be able to get some good deals on quality product. That okay with you, Bran?"

"Yeah, that works." He turned to Travis. "What do you think, Travis? Is Kayla's design more in keeping with what you envisioned for the house?"

"You guys have the final say."

Virginia made a "keep talking" motion from behind the camera.

"Tell me your opinion," Brandon said.

"I like most of Kayla's ideas. It all comes down to which materials you choose. I think you want to go for timeless over trendy here. But you can add a little color or something unique here or there."

"Can you imagine something that really pops here?" Brandon asked, gesturing to the blank wall. "A wallpaper feature here. A Victorian pattern, something that could have been put in the house when it was built."

"I salvaged some of the original wallpaper," said Travis, "so maybe you can find something close to it."

"That's an amazing idea," said Kayla. "Brandon, you and I will scare up some samples tomorrow too."

"Sounds like we have a design," said Brandon, grinning for the camera, even though his stomach was sinking.

TRAVIS WAS surprised by how much he liked Kayla. Oh, she was loud and pushy sometimes, but he liked her ideas, and she was upbeat without being insufferable.

They wrapped up filming for the day, leaving Travis with an interesting quandary. He'd been wanting to get Brandon back to his apartment since the morning, but Brandon seemed eager to spend time with Kayla. That was fine; Travis had no claim on Brandon's time. Truth be told, he was still processing everything Brandon had told him the night before. It was plain that Brandon and Kayla were good friends; they had the easy rapport of people who had known and been fond of each other for a long time. Travis could see how that chemistry could be mistaken for romance; Travis himself had felt jealous a few times as the day had gone on. He told himself he was being ridiculous. Sleeping with a man one time did not mean they had any claim to each other.

He sighed and shook his head. It didn't matter. They worked together. It was probably just as well that Brandon looked like he'd be hanging out with Kayla tonight. Travis should go home and talk himself out of ever being with Brandon again.

But then Brandon walked over to him. "We're going to dinner. Kayla wants to check out some new restaurant on Cortelyou Road. You want to come with us?"

Dammit. Travis's instinct was to say no. But that seemed rude. Plus, he did kind of want to spend more time with Brandon.

"I'm not asking you to solve a complicated math problem," Brandon said. "It's just dinner."

"I know, I'm sorry. I'm not the best at navigating complex social situations. But sure, I'll go to dinner."

"It's only, like, a fifteen-minute walk or a couple of stops on the subway, but Kayla's getting a cab. Come on, pack up, let's go."

And that was how Travis found himself squashed into the back of a cab with Brandon and Kayla. It was thankfully a short ride, and then they were parked in front of what looked like a brand-new pub. The decor outside had the sort of artificial distressing that Travis kind of hated; blowtorches and hammers could make a piece of metal look old, but they also left telltale signs.

The restaurant turned out to be kind of a hipster joint, which Travis could have guessed from the outside. There were a lot of beards and flannel shirts among the clientele. A waitress with purple hair escorted them to a table in the corner, where she handed them menus that were pieces of paper stapled to slabs of wood.

"This is rustic," said Kayla.

Travis laughed because he could hear the sarcasm in her voice.

She smiled at him in return. "So, the gimmick with this place is that they have a cheesemonger and a beer expert on staff. I don't know what a beer expert is called. Like, you know how wine has sommeliers? What is a beer expert?"

Brandon got out his phone. "Google says a beer expert is called a cicerone."

Kayla tilted her head as if she were considering that. "Interesting. Well, this place has a cheesemonger and a cicerone on staff. You can get a cheese plate as an appetizer with a flight of beer and they'll explain which cheese to try with which beer. And then nearly everything on the menu integrates some unusual cheese and tells you which beer to drink with the dish. They have, like, a hundred and fifty beers on tap. Look behind the bar."

Travis looked. The number of taps reminded him of a self-serve frozen yogurt café with dozens of handles. There were so many options, he didn't know how he would even begin to choose. He liked beer—generally lighter, crisper beers over bitter IPAs—but he was game to try anything. He looked at the menu. Hipster prices too, a little high for this part of Brooklyn, but hell, he was making good money arguing with Brandon on camera, so he could eat an elaborate meal now and then.

Kayla ordered the cheese plate with the flight of beer; then they each chose entrees. Travis decided to order the beer recommended to pair with his chicken dish.

Brandon asked the waitress why beer instead of wine. She replied, "Cole, our beer expert, could tell you better than I could, but he thinks beer and cheese taste better together because of the similar ways they ferment, or something like that. I can send him over, if you like."

"No, that's okay. I was just curious."

"This place is trying really hard," said Travis when she left.

"I lived in this neighborhood years ago, before I met Brandon," Kayla said. "It was almost entirely Afro-Caribbean. Now look at it!" She shook her head. "Hipsters everywhere."

"Yeah, it gentrified pretty quickly," Travis said. "The company I used to work for did a ton of projects in this neighborhood. Before I got hired for the show, I got steady work gutting and renovating kitchens and bathrooms in neighborhoods like this all over Brooklyn."

"Sounds like a lot of work."

"Well, some of these kitchens and bathrooms aren't very big. But landlords have cottoned on to the fact that a certain type of renter is willing to pay a little more for a bathroom that doesn't look like the standard black-and-white-tile one every New York apartment has. I mean, I rented a whole series of apartments that had identical layouts and finishes, as if the same architect had built every building."

"I take it from your accent that you're from New York originally."

"Yeah, Queens."

"What brought you to Brooklyn?"

Travis glanced at Brandon, who shrugged. Travis hadn't expected to be interrogated, and he supposed it was an innocuous enough question, but he didn't love talking about himself. He cleared his throat. "Uh, well, I grew up in Forest Hills, but my dad is from Brooklyn and my grandparents lived in Fort Greene. When I was in my midtwenties, a buddy of mine needed a roommate, so I moved over here." He shrugged.

"Sorry, I didn't mean to be nosy." Kayla smiled. "I'm just really fascinated by why people move."

"Speaking of that," said Brandon, "how is Orange County treating you?"

"I love it! Dave and I are looking to buy a house near the beach now. I don't love LA, but once you get a fair distance from the city, it's sunny and warm and beautiful all the time. Well, the fact that it never rains is a problem, but we've been playing around with drought-tolerant landscaping at some of the houses we've flipped, and I like it."

Brandon chuckled. "Always a positive spin."

"We actually just bought a bungalow in Santa Ana that a few major film stars of the fifties once owned, but it has since fallen into disrepair. We got it for a song because it was in such sad shape when we bought it. But Dave's letting me run with the design. I want to do a super retro midcentury modern design, but with a lot of pops of color, so it will be like living inside a Shag painting."

"Shag?" asked Travis.

"He's a SoCal painter who does these really cool, colorful retro paintings. Very mod era, early 1960s. I love them." She looked at Brandon. "Brandon's breaking out in hives. Whenever I wanted to do something like paint a wall purple, he used to freak out."

"I suggested teal tiles for the backsplash in the kitchen," Travis said, "and he nearly passed out."

Kayla nodded. "That seems right."

"Come on, guys. I need to sell this house for a lot of money if I have any hope of recouping my investment. If it's too specific, I'll never be able to find a buyer."

"Look, if you do it right, it will look chic and custom." Kayla picked up her phone. "The first house we flipped in Orange County was in this cute little up-and-coming neighborhood. Nobody there wanted the standard package. Let me show you what I did in the kitchen."

Travis sipped his beer while he waited for his turn to look at the photos, and he felt a little smug. When Brandon handed him Kayla's phone, he was treated to several photos of a *very* specific kitchen. Bright electric blue flat-panel cabinets, a backsplash with white and light gray subway tiles arranged in chevrons, dark wood floors. "Wow, I like this blue. Staging it with the pops of yellow was a good choice."

"Right? And we sold the house like that." Kayla snapped her fingers. "I mean, we got two offers right after the first open house. The house was only officially on the market for about eight hours."

Brandon grimaced. "It's just so bold."

"All right, Mr. Expert," Travis said, knowing that calling Brandon that would get his goat. "You asked me yesterday what I would do to the house if I could do anything. So let me turn that on you. If this was your house, not a flip but a place you'd actually live, what would your design choices be? Assume an unlimited budget."

Brandon's eyebrows knit together. "All right, fine. What I'd do?"

"Oh, here we go," said Kayla, crossing her arms.

"Tile floors instead of wood," Brandon said. "And none of this wood glaze bullshit. Ceramic tiles that look like ceramic tiles. But just in the kitchen and dining room, since they're still separated from the living areas because we decided not to take the walls down. So, my thought is, warm gray floors, a warm wood for the cabinets, maybe walnut. Then polished concrete counters, chrome finishes."

Kayla shook her head. "Your taste is so industrial and masculine. You had me until the concrete counters. I hate that look."

"I know. You never let me put them in, but we're not partners now and this is imaginary, so I can do what I want. I'd do white quartz in the bathrooms, though. The one with the sparkle like we picked out today. In the kitchen, I'd do a pop of color backsplash. Not electric blue, but a softer blue would work. You need some color to balance out the gray." He sighed. "I'd paint the bedrooms different colors, or at least do a feature wall in each."

"What would you do in the master?" asked Kayla.

"Feature wall with a wallpaper that has a geometric pattern behind the bed."

"Not geometric," said Travis, laughing. It seemed like such an odd thing for Mr. Neutral to choose.

Kayla put a hand over Travis's. "He picked out this wallpaper for our house upstate that had a bit of gold metallic in it."

"Metallic, eh? Is that not a bold choice?" Travis raised an eyebrow at Brandon.

"It was for my own house." Brandon looked frazzled now. "I wasn't trying to sell my old house when I designed it."

"As I recall, we left the wallpaper when we sold it."

"We could do some of those things in this kitchen," Travis said. "I'm not opposed to polished concrete counters."

"Really? I'm surprised you didn't just tell me that something like that was all wrong for a house in this neighborhood."

"I mean, it is. But I don't hate your idea for the kitchen design."

Brandon smiled, looking pleased. "Well, I don't think that's the right design for *this* kitchen. And actually, if it was my house, I wouldn't do concrete counters. Concrete is really porous and you have to reseal it regularly, plus it still stains easily. It's a bitch to maintain. It's just a look I want to try at a flip now that I have free rein. Maybe in the next house."

They talked shop as they ate, and Travis genuinely liked Kayla even more the longer they discussed house design. He could see why she and Brandon were friends.

Eventually they split the check and wandered outside. Kayla called another cab to take her back to her hotel. As it pulled up, she said, "Tile shopping tomorrow, big guy. You ready?"

Brandon smiled. "As I'll ever be."

She blew him a kiss and got in the car. As it pulled away, Travis said, "She seems fun."

"I miss seeing her every day. We were great roommates. But such is life."

Travis worried this would get maudlin, so he said, "So are you coming back to my place or…."

"Sure." He patted his shoulder bag. "I brought a change of clothes this time."

"Good thinking."

Chapter Ten

As Brandon lay in bed, Travis took a phone call from Ismael. They discussed the work plan for the next day while Brandon felt like a fraud.

These guys were doing the actual work on the house. Sure, Brandon had thrown a sledgehammer a couple of times, and there'd be plenty of footage on the show of him laying tile or painting a wall, but he wasn't the one actually working on the house. He wasn't even responsible for most of the design now that he'd brought in Kayla. What the hell was he doing?

Travis got off the phone and glanced at Brandon. "You all right?"

"I should have said no to this show. It's giving me an existential crisis."

Travis laughed. "But *darling*," he said, his voice teasing and sarcastic, "then you would have never met me."

Travis's tone made a shiver go up Brandon's spine. "Don't call me *darling* like that ever again."

Travis laughed, crawled back into bed with Brandon, and lay beside him. He grinned. "Big project for tomorrow is to start putting up drywall. Are we doing anything with the basement?"

"Let's put up insulation and drywall but otherwise just leave it as an open space. What's the floor like down there?"

"Just concrete. But it looks decent because it's new. Maybe we should stage it with some rugs and good lighting so it doesn't look too barren. You can claim it's a great room or something. Plus, the laundry is still in the basement, so you don't want it to look too scary."

"Okay."

"The house I grew up in had a dark, terrifying basement. It scared the crap out of me as a kid. My mom used to put stuff she didn't want me touching in the basement because she knew I was too afraid to go down there."

Brandon liked the mental image of Travis as a little boy afraid of monsters in the basement. He put an arm around Travis and stroked his back. Then he let out a sigh. "Are we making a mistake?"

Travis was silent for a long time. Finally he said, "What do you mean?"

"I guess it's my turn to have the freakout about us potentially getting caught together."

Travis frowned. "Are you freaking out? About what we just did or…."

"No, not about you. About the show. About how we act on the show. Or… about everything."

"So it's like an overarching crisis you're having."

Brandon took a deep breath and stared at the ceiling. "Here's where I'm at right now. I'm a man who has been putting up this front of heterosexuality for years, and everyone who watches or produces the show thinks I was part of this nice, happy marriage until it fell apart, and now I'm this wounded bird who just needs the right woman to come along to fix me. I actually read that in a tabloid article, by the way."

"Gross."

"I know. But I've cultivated this image that is intended to help attract the sorts of viewers who watch the Restoration Channel. I felt like I needed to act a certain way in order to be successful."

"Like a house you make generic to appeal to as many buyers as possible."

It bothered Brandon how astute that was. "I feel like I've painted myself into a corner. And I'm enjoying spending time with you. Dinner tonight was fun, the sex after was even better, and I even enjoy arguing with you when the cameras are around. But I'm worried now that we'll get caught and then… then it'll be all over. That my reputation will be blown to bits."

Travis pulled away and sat up. "Okay, first of all, there's nothing bad about being gay."

"I didn't say that."

"You implied it. That's what you're worried about, isn't it? That everyone will find out you're gay and this perfect piece of fiction you've created will fall to pieces? As if being gay was a character flaw?"

"Some might view it that way." Brandon put a hand over his eyes, hating how well Travis had him pegged.

Travis's eyes went wide. "Do you?" His tone was angry.

Shit. "No, of course not." Although Brandon had always been quiet about that part of himself. Even prior to working on *Dream Home*, he'd kept under the radar. Sure, he'd gone to a few gay bars, but he'd never been to a Pride parade, never engaged much with gay culture. And maybe that was something he had to work out with himself, but he didn't feel like now, with this new show on the line, was the time to do much self-exploration.

And there was his father in his head again. *Do you really think anyone wants to do business with a fairy? No one will take you seriously.*

Brandon knew that was wrong, that it was hateful and homophobic and out of touch with how most people thought these days, but he still struggled to shake free of it. John Chase had been overjoyed the day his son married Kayla, even though he'd wanted a big wedding instead of a city hall ceremony. Pleasing his father had become a habit with Brandon, one that was very hard to let go of.

Except he really wanted to be with Travis.

Brandon never would have known Travis was gay if they hadn't kissed that first time. He almost said as much, but he already knew Travis would be offended. And looking around at Travis's space, it was clear Travis wasn't shy about much. There was a little rainbow flag sticking out of a pencil holder on top of his dresser, photos of him with various men—friends? lovers?—in frames all over the apartment, and there were books on LGBT history in the shelving unit.

Brandon had loved doing *Dream Home*. He and Kayla were good enough actors that they could be persuasively affectionate on screen. He was successful, he was popular, and the show had been John Chase approved.

Had he really thought a fake marriage with Kayla was sustainable? That a time wouldn't come when one or the other of them wanted to have a real relationship… with someone else? Had he really thought the charade could just go on indefinitely?

What a goddamned mess he'd gotten himself in.

"You've spent a lot of time in the closet," Travis said. "I understand why you felt you had to, but let's be clear—it was a personal choice. No one held a gun to your head and made you be on television."

Brandon recognized that he'd stepped in it. He did sometimes feel like being gay was a character flaw; he had to hide it in order to keep his job. "No, but just as you want to keep this job, I want to keep mine." He blew out a breath. "All I meant was that the Restoration Channel has built itself on a platform of showcasing charismatic heterosexual couples who make over houses. I am not heterosexual, and I'm worried that if you and I get caught together, that could cause trouble for me with the network."

"Ah." Travis scratched his chin. Brandon could sense he was still angry. "Well, we'll just have to keep our hands to ourselves when cameras are around."

"I've pissed you off." Brandon could sense from Travis's tone that Brandon had said something wrong.

"No. Well, yeah, you kind of did. It's… I've never dated a closeted guy before. It's a lot to think about. I wouldn't have been all over you in public anyway because that's not my style, but I take your point. We each have something to lose here, I guess."

"I'm sorry."

"Apology accepted. But know that I'm not shy about who I am. If anyone asks, I'll tell them. If someone on set gets a whiff of the fact that I'm a gay man, well, that's fine with me. What can they even do? It's not like my sexuality affects how I do my job."

"That's fair."

"But if you're going to be paranoid about us being caught together, maybe it's better to end things now."

Brandon shook his head. That wasn't what he wanted at all. He'd just wanted to let Travis know to use some discretion, but now he'd opened this whole can of worms. And though he'd love to be able to say that if they got caught, he could live with the consequences, he kept picturing Harwood's and Virginia's faces when they got the news. "I want to keep seeing you," he said. "We just won't make out on camera."

"I think I can hold myself back."

TRAVIS FLOPPED back on the bed. He didn't mind pretending they were just coworkers for the sake of the cameras, but now that he was seeing the depths of Brandon's insecurity, he was starting to feel less confident that this could work out.

Then again, Brandon was in his bed, albeit with a sheet covering the good bits of him. Could this be a fling the length of the job? A way to add a little extra fun to a job that he liked but that involved a lot of long hours and difficult work?

"You're mad."

Travis rubbed his face. "I'm not mad. I'm just trying to figure out what this is."

"Do we have to define it right now?"

"No. We don't. I can play dodge-the-cameras with you for a while." After that, who knew? They'd only hooked up twice—it was probably too soon to put much thought into that, anyway.

"All right. By the way, Restoration told me about another house in Victorian Flatbush. This one's on Rugby Road, just a couple of blocks from where we are now. It's just as decrepit as the Argyle Road house. But here's a stroke of luck. Jessica Benton is buying the house. We're just loaning her our expertise and doing the work to flip it."

Who was Jessica Benton? Travis tried to connect the name to a face in his mind. "The actress?"

"Yeah. So at least this one would not put the financial burden on me. I thought it could be a good project to overlap with the Argyle Road house."

"So you're really fronting the majority of the money for this renovation?" Travis knew that intellectually, but he'd assumed that the Restoration Channel was absorbing a lot of the risk too. No wonder Brandon was so on edge.

"Yep. Well, my father's money. I've been sitting on an inheritance in search of a project. Basically, Restoration and I each put in half the money for the house, and they gave me a renovation budget up to a certain amount, so that when we sell the house, we'll split the profits fifty-fifty. But anything above the renovation budget is mine to cover, and we're about a hundred thousand dollars past Restoration's limit."

"Hence your concern about budget. Although I gotta be honest, the kinds of figures you're throwing around… it's like, what even is money?"

"I know. Like, woe is me, I'm rich, what problems could I even have?"

Although Travis did judge Brandon a bit for his rich-people problems, it wasn't hard to see how much this was stressing Brandon out. But what was really going on here? The revelation that Brandon had invested money he'd inherited from his father was enlightening, although Travis didn't completely understand what it told him. Brandon had a domineering father who didn't allow for failure. That likely weighed on Brandon as he invested it in this particular project. Brandon had constructed an image of himself that he thought would create the most success. Brandon was willing to sacrifice a lot for that success, if his marriage to Kayla was anything to go by; he needed to maintain a certain image, and he was willing to forego his own happiness—his own identity—to get what he wanted. This was ambition Travis had never encountered before, and it intimidated him.

So, all this was kind of fucked-up, but underneath it all, Brandon was a damaged man who had likely lost track of exactly who he was. No one in his life had ever loved him for who he was, just for what he could achieve. No wonder Brandon was so worried.

So, the question was… why did Travis think he was the man right for this task? Why did he think he could offer Brandon the love he needed? Travis usually ran from these kinds of emotional entanglements.

But Brandon was a good man despite everything. He was smart, he worked hard, and he'd built a real estate brand all his own without relying on his famous father. Given his childhood, Brandon could have grown up to be a monster, but Brandon's moral compass pointed in the right direction. Brandon might be confused about who he was, but he wanted to do the right thing. He wanted the people in his life to be happy—Kayla was Exhibit A—and he wanted to take old, run-down houses and make them safe, comfortable places for families to live. He had a good soul and he deserved love.

Travis smoothed his hand over Brandon's chest, and they snuggled together on the bed.

"I didn't mean to vent all over you," Brandon said. "I kind of dug my own grave here. I wasn't ready to sign on to do a show by myself, and I didn't think it through. All I knew when I signed the contract was that I loved the house and wanted to fix it."

"So focus on that for a while. Think of the house first before all the other bullshit. If you love the house, fix it, because you know how to do that, and then trust that everything else will work itself out."

Brandon closed his eyes. "Good advice, but…."

"Feel free to vent to me." Travis was surprised to realize he meant it. Getting involved with Brandon seemed like asking for trouble, but he… liked Brandon. A lot. And life wasn't always rational. Maybe Travis wasn't the right person to love Brandon the way he deserved to be loved… but maybe he was.

"Thank you," said Brandon. He kissed the top of Travis's head. "I'll pull it together soon."

"Once we get this first house, everything should go smoother." Travis said that with more confidence than he felt.

"Here's hoping." Brandon took a deep breath. "God, it's like I've opened a vein and bled all over you. You must think I'm really fucked-up."

Travis let out a little burble of laughter. "I mean, yeah, I kind of do, but I think I understand why."

"I don't suppose you have some deep, dark secret you want to tell me, just to even things out."

Travis didn't have many secrets, but he took Brandon's point. Brandon had shared a whole lot of himself, probably because he was so stressed out, he couldn't hold it in anymore. Travis hadn't shared as much. Maybe Brandon was asking because he didn't feel like he knew Travis very well.

"Uh, well…." Travis tried to come up with something. "Maybe just ask me something. I'm a pretty open book."

"Okay. Hmm." Brandon appeared to think for a moment. "Okay. I somehow doubt renovating homes was your lifelong ambition. What did you want to be when you were a kid?"

"An architect." That was an easy thing to answer, at least. "Or an artist, maybe. But I liked building practical things more than I liked painting landscapes, if you know what I mean. I built a dollhouse for my sister out of Legos."

"Wow."

"Yeah. But then I got to college and figured out pretty quickly that it wasn't for me. I became a licensed, bonded carpenter instead, then sort of stumbled into renovation work. Mike and Sandy's company was looking for someone to build some shelving on one of their projects, so I applied for the job, and while I was there, I helped out with all kinds of other things. Ultimately I got my contractor license."

"A carpenter."

"I like woodworking. It's one of those things that started as a hobby and became my whole job for a bit. I made this headboard, actually."

Travis pointed at it. The whole bed frame had been an early project, something he'd done in his parents' garage before he'd moved out for good. It was simple, two posts connected by a panel into which he'd carved some swirly designs, but he'd always really liked it.

"You made this?" Brandon asked.

"I made the chairs over there too."

Brandon looked at where Travis was pointing. "Wow. I wouldn't have guessed. That's some really strong work. So if I decided I wanted some built-ins in the family room instead of a wallpaper accent wall…."

"Basic shelving? I could do that in a day."

"Good to know. I'm filing that away for later." Brandon gazed at Travis's body. "Tell me about this tattoo." He tapped the art deco design that wrapped around the top of Travis's arm, near his shoulder.

Travis nearly laughed; Brandon had randomly chosen the tattoo that would be easiest to explain. "It was something I drew when I was, I dunno, nineteen? Kind of an homage to my grandpa, who was a riveter on the Empire State Building. But it was also kind of a nod to architecture styles I like."

"It's cool. I like it."

"That's not much, as far as secrets go, I guess. But I don't have anything big lurking behind the curtains or anything. I had a pretty normal childhood. My parents are supportive. I've never been married or really found anyone I've wanted to marry yet. I dated the Power paper towel guy from the commercials, but he dumped me for a younger model, and I don't think that really counts as a secret anyway."

"Wait, the deep-voiced beardy guy? 'Powerful enough for your toughest messes'? That guy?"

"Yeah. We were together for, like, three months a few years ago… before all that fame went to his head."

Brandon laughed. "I hope I'm not flattering myself when I say you definitely have a type."

Travis shrugged. Maybe he did. Brandon had some similar lumberjack qualities to Travis's ex, but in a more polished way. "I mean, come on. You can't throw a rock in New York without hitting an aspiring actor. And you're on TV. So dating the paper towel guy isn't that remarkable."

"So what you're saying is, you're boring and well-adjusted."

"Pretty much."

"Do boring, well-adjusted guys get piercings and tattoos?"

"If they are doing it in a weak attempt to rebel against their parents, yes. Mom wasn't even mad I got my ears pierced. She thought it was cute."

Brandon laughed. Then his face turned serious again. "I don't know what my father would have done if I'd gotten a piercing or tattoo. The thought never entered my mind."

"Middle child syndrome, I guess," said Travis. "My older brother was the first, and my little sister was the baby, so, you know. Look at me!"

"Does your mother know you have a tattoo on your hip?" Brandon ran a finger over the star that was the result of a dare when Travis was twenty-three.

"Nope. And we will not be telling her."

"So you *do* have a secret."

Travis laughed. "Sure."

Brandon lay with his hands behind his head and stared up at the ceiling. After a long moment he said, "You know, after season two of *Dream Home*, a Restoration Channel executive floated the idea of how great it would be if Kayla and I had a baby. When the idea grew legs among the showrunners, Kayla lied and said we'd tried but were having fertility issues, and it was too hurtful to talk about, so she wanted people to stop."

"Wow. They told you to have a kid for ratings?"

"Basically, yeah. Not Garrett Harwood, though. His predecessor was the one who made that suggestion."

"I hope Harwood doesn't get any ideas in his head like that for our show."

"That doesn't seem to be his style, thankfully."

"I like you and all, but I'm not having your baby, no matter how much it brings up our ratings."

Brandon laughed and hit Travis with a pillow.

Chapter Eleven

BRANDON WAITED as Kayla climbed into the SUV the network had provided. She looked around. "No camera?"

"Nope. I asked them not to ride in the car. They don't need to see us drive around. We're meeting them at the store."

"How long is the drive?"

"Depends how bad traffic is on the BQE. The GPS says fifteen minutes."

It took twenty, but by the time they got to the tile and flooring store, the crew already had cameras set up. The store was opening a couple of hours early just for them so that they could browse without being interrupted much.

"Go, go, tiles!" Kayla said.

The selection inside the store was overwhelming. Brandon had never been here before, but Kayla seemed to know her way around.

"I scoped this place out the last time I was in New York. It's supposed to have a great selection and reasonable prices. They've got the standard things, but also a lot of really unique items. Do you have a particular goal here?"

"To not make my house look ridiculous?"

Kayla rolled her eyes. "We're agreed that we're not doing anything basic like white subway tile, right? We need flooring, we need a kitchen backsplash, and we need tile for the bathrooms."

Brandon pulled a piece of paper from his pocket. "Travis made a list."

"He seems very organized. Is he a good project manager?"

It took every acting skill Brandon had not to react to that question. "Yeah, he's very good. He's kept us on schedule so far, which was a nearly impossible task."

"Let's deal with flooring first, because that's an easy choice. How do you feel about tile in the kitchen?"

Kayla and Brandon walked through the store, picking out flooring for the kitchen and dining room—Brandon was still leaning toward carpet for the second floor, mostly for budget reasons, and wood for the rest of the main floor, which they'd have to buy at a different store—and tile for all three bathrooms. Kayla had talked Brandon into making a lavender-and-white powder room with an accent wall done in a gingham print wallpaper she'd seen in a magazine, and Brandon wasn't totally sold—he worried it was too feminine—but he was willing to go along with her choice for the gray floor tiles.

What remained, finally, was the kitchen. Brandon had already talked to his supplier about ordering the craftsman-style cabinets everyone had agreed on, and the next stop on this odyssey with Kayla was to pick out the quartz slab for the countertops. So now it was just the backsplash. Kayla pointed to a blue mosaic tile that Brandon thought was hideous.

"Absolutely not," he said. "Those random metallic tiles are all wrong for this design."

"Yeah… but it's pretty, don't you think?"

"No."

Kayla laughed. "All right. You agree we're not doing plain subway tiles, though, right?"

"Not white subway. I think blue would look good with the cabinets we ordered. We could do larger glass tiles or gray subway tiles. Or, actually…."

A display of four-inch-square ceramic tiles caught his eye. Most of them were solid colored, but one display had a variety of ones with different patterns. And there in the middle was a teal tile with a brown overlay painted on. It wasn't exactly the style of tile Travis had shown him, but it was close and quite eye-catching.

Suddenly Brandon could picture the whole kitchen. He could see the floors going in, the way they complimented the dark cabinets, and then this pop of teal. It was the dream kitchen Travis had described, in this house, this crazy house they were fixing together. This money pit of a house that Brandon nonetheless thought was beautiful and charming and heartbreaking and, well, kind of perfect. And it should have the perfect kitchen.

"This is a little out-there," Brandon said, "but what do you think?"

"These are gorgeous. This brown is very close to the cabinets, so it will match well. But it's such a busy pattern that I wouldn't use it for more than the backsplash, maybe this high." She held her hands about eighteen inches apart. "These are pricey, though."

Brandon hadn't looked at the price. He just knew these were the tiles Travis had wanted in his dream design.

Fuck the price. "Worth it. I want these tiles."

Kayla nodded. "They are pretty. Sometimes design is like that. It just snags your eye."

Brandon looked at the measurements Travis had given him and worked out the price because he needed to for the cameras, but he knew these were the tiles he had to have. And it was such a dumb thing, to be feeling this way about kitchen tiles, but suddenly he could picture exactly what this kitchen would look like. And it would be perfect.

After an hour in the store, Brandon felt satisfied with the choices they made. It would take a few days for everything to be delivered, but Brandon was suddenly eager for Travis to see all the purchases he'd made.

Erik directed the cameras to shut down and told Brandon they had some good footage of the shopping expedition. Presumably the viewers liked this design stuff. Brandon wondered idly how many hours of footage they already had for a forty-two-minute episode.

"Are you filming the great countertop decision?" Kayla asked Erik.

"Yeah, meet you there?"

"Sure," said Brandon.

A few minutes later, he and Kayla climbed into the car and Brandon punched the address for the stone shop into his GPS.

"We're alone now, right?" Kayla asked.

"Yeah. The car's not bugged or anything. No cameras here. Is something up?"

"I happened to notice back there that you picked out teal tiles. Didn't Travis say something at dinner last night about teal tiles?"

Leave it to Kayla to notice that. Brandon put the car in gear and pulled out of the parking lot before answering. "I picked them because they matched the kind of tiles he told me he'd like to put in the kitchen. His design instincts have been pretty good so far, despite his continual reminders that he's not a designer, so I decided to defer to his opinion there. And they are beautiful tiles. Even you thought they'd work well in the kitchen."

"You like him, don't you? And not just as a contractor. You *like him*, like him."

"What are we, in ninth grade?"

"You have a crush on him. Buying the tiles he described is your way of showing it. You forget that I was your best friend for a long time, Brandon Chase. I know how you operate."

"In three hundred feet, turn left," said the GPS.

"Fine, I like him, but that's not why I spent four hundred extra dollars on tile. I believe in the design."

"Aha! Do you need me to play matchmaker? Pass a note to him in study hall?"

Brandon laughed. "No. We… we've figured out enough on our own."

"You're sleeping with him already, aren't you?"

The starkness of the statement hit Brandon so hard, he almost missed the turn. "Jesus, Kayla. I mean, yes, but no one knows. And don't tell him I told you, because he will freak out."

"Oh-ho! Is this a real thing?"

"No, it's…. We've hooked up a couple of times, that's it. It's not really anything yet. Which is why you won't say anything."

"Lips are sealed." She mimed zipping her lips. "And I do really like him. I hope this does become a thing, because I think he'd be good for you."

"In what way?"

"He's straightforward in a way you're not. And he's practical and organized and understands little details. You've always been more of a big-picture guy. You can dream things up, and he can make those dreams happen."

Brandon fought against rolling his eyes as they moved through an intersection. "Please. This is not as big as all that. It's… sex. I mean, I like hanging out with him, but if anyone at Restoration found out about us, it would be all over. And we work together, so if something went wrong, it could really complicate the show. Getting involved with him was a tremendously stupid idea."

"Or a brilliant one!"

"Your destination is ahead on the right," said the GPS.

"Tamp it down," Brandon said. "Don't let on that you know anything. It probably won't last past my selling this house, so don't go planning my wedding yet, all right?"

"You should so marry him."

Brandon pulled into the parking lot and found a spot near the entrance. Then he did roll his eyes. "We're back on camera now. We discuss only slabs of stone. Got it?"

"You can trust me, Brandon."

He wasn't so sure about that. Although he blamed himself for how things had gone down, there was still the fundamental truth that Kayla had kissed Dave in public and managed to get photographed doing it. She was either cocky about their privacy or lazy about adhering to their plan for behaving in public. Or both. And that *had* been her fault, even if Brandon took responsibility for the rest of it.

They both got out of the car and let a store manager escort them out back, to an empty lot full of rows of stone slabs. Kayla beelined for the stone in the color she wanted, and Brandon was content to let her pick out one she liked, provided it didn't have too much sparkle. He watched her like a hawk the whole time, worried now that she'd forget the cameras were around, but she kept her ongoing stream of dialogue limited to stone countertops. They found a slab they both agreed they liked that was, happily enough, on clearance. As they rang up the purchase, Erik called, "Cut!" and herded all the cameras out of the store.

"I saw you watching me," Kayla said as she got into the car. "I behaved."

"We good? Anything else you want to pick out?"

"Not today. Shall we go back to the house and check on your boyfriend?"

Brandon sighed and put the car into gear. "He's not my boyfriend."

"He should be."

"Let it go, Kay."

"You'll see."

TRAVIS TRIED to see the kitchen the way the kitchen and bath guys did. Travis's old boss, Mike McPhee, owned a renovation business that mostly made over the kitchens and bathrooms of the rich and famous in Manhattan, and he'd already explained that he didn't know the Brooklyn real estate market as well, but his business partner, Sandy Sullivan, had just made over his own house in Crown Heights and had lots of opinions.

"Here are the plans," Travis said, holding up his sketches. "It looks like a blank canvas now, but we made a lot of the design decisions yesterday."

The assistant director, Glen, was in charge of shooting while everyone else was out shopping, so Travis made a big show of displaying his plans on the table he'd made with a sawhorse, about where the new kitchen island would be.

"I haven't done a gut job like this in a while," said Mike. "Our last few kitchen gigs were mostly cosmetic. Painting cabinets, adding backsplashes, that kind of thing."

"Have you guys dealt with the plumbing yet?" Sandy asked.

"Some of it. We moved the pipes to that corner over there, but we still have to deal with gas lines and water lines here. We're keeping the footprints in all but one of the bathrooms, so we only need to move plumbing around in that one. The plumber's coming tomorrow to deal with the remainder of the pipes. My crew and I can do the rest."

Mike and Sandy glanced at each other, then Mike nodded. It wasn't the most glamorous of gigs, truth be told. Travis had talked Mike into it by saying he and Sandy could wear shirts advertising their business and would get a good plug from being on the show.

They talked about the plans for a few minutes before Glen cut and told everyone to take five.

"Some cushy job you've got here," said Mike when Glen was gone.

"It's not bad. I mean, this house was a complete disaster. You can't tell that now that we're starting to get drywall up, but every possible thing you can think of was wrong. Asbestos, bugs, structural problems, water damage, the whole shebang."

"It still looks pretty rough outside," Sandy said.

"The siding is actually in pretty good shape—it just needs a power wash and a new coat of paint. That's on the agenda for next week."

"So you're flying through this renovation."

Travis nodded. "We've got day and night crews, so we get through everything faster. The reno is costing Brandon a pretty penny, though."

Sandy leaned against the sawhorse. "This Brandon fellow. My husband likes his old show because I guess he has a thing for foxy contractors." He gestured at himself. "So I've seen a few episodes. Is Brandon as handsome in person as he is on TV?"

"Better."

The front door banged open then, and Brandon hollered out, "Travis?"

"Speak of the devil." Toward the front of the house, Travis shouted, "Kitchen."

Brandon and Kayla appeared a few seconds later. Brandon grinned at Travis, and something inside of him melted.

Mike cleared his throat.

"Oh, Brandon. Let me introduce you to Mike and Sandy." Travis gestured to each man as he said his name. "They're the kitchen and bath guys."

"Nice to meet you. I'm Brandon Chase."

Sandy grinned as he took Brandon's hand. "Very nice to meet you in person. And Kayla too!"

Brandon looked wary, but Kayla was all over the situation, grasping Sandy's hand in both of hers. "It's great to meet a fan."

"Well, we got everything ordered," said Brandon. "We should have almost all the materials by the end of the week. The kitchen backsplash tile might be running behind."

"That goes in last anyway," said Travis. "If we can start installing cabinets by early next week, we'll be on schedule."

"Good."

Mike stepped forward. "Travis showed us his plans, but why don't you talk a little about what you've got in mind. Layout, materials, the whole thing."

Brandon nodded and launched into his description.

Travis stood to the side and enjoyed watching Brandon talk. Erik walked in and signaled to the camera crew that they should be filming this, so Travis kept his mouth shut and tried to subtly manipulate Sandy so that his back of his shirt—with the name of the company and the office phone number, as well as a little rainbow flag near the bottom—was showing to the camera. Travis wondered if anyone would notice. He'd had a ton of fun working for Mike and Sandy when he was breaking into the business, in part because they were great bosses, but also it was nice to have some LGBT friends in the industry.

They looked at each bathroom in turn, with Mike and Sandy offering suggestions here or there, but most of the decisions were locked in now that materials had been ordered. Travis was a little curious about what

Brandon had picked, but he figured he'd see it soon enough. Hopefully Kayla hadn't let Brandon buy anything generic or beige.

As if Travis had said that aloud, Kayla elbowed him. "I think you'll like the materials we chose. This house will have character when all is said and done. All new, totally safe, modern amenities, but it will feel like an old house."

"Cool," said Travis, not sure how to react to that.

"I know you were worried. I'm trying to reassure you."

"I appreciate that. But at the end of the day, it's still Brandon's house. Putting in a cookie-cutter white kitchen would be a shame, but it's still his decision."

"No worries on that front. I've saved him from himself."

Chapter Twelve

THE NEXT night Travis followed Brandon home, and was somewhat intimidated by his apartment. Brandon was renting out the second floor of a brownstone on a charming block of Brooklyn Heights, in a house that was likely around 150 years old. It was a long, narrow apartment, not a great deal of square footage, but with french doors at the back that led out onto a little deck. The apartment itself was white and a little stark. When they came up the stairs, they were in Brandon's living room. A narrow hall took them to the bedroom and the kitchen in the rear. The kitchen was the stuff of Travis's nightmares: white cabinets, white marble counters, no color, no character.

"I didn't do this work," Brandon said. "It's a rental."

"Good. Because yikes."

"This is the dream kitchen of a good number of clients I've worked with, though. Lots of people like white kitchens."

"They can have them."

"Why does it mean so much to you?"

"It doesn't." Travis shrugged, but it nagged at him.

Brandon could likely tell he was lying. "Come on. It obviously means something to you."

"You really want to know?"

"Yeah."

Travis rolled his eyes. "I'm gonna need some booze or something first."

"I've got beer in the fridge. Have a seat at the island."

Because of course the model generic kitchen had a huge island. The stools beside it were the only pops of color in the room, dark wood with blue upholstery. Travis slid onto one as Brandon grabbed two beers from the fridge.

When they were seated beside each other, Brandon lifted his beer and said, "Cheers."

Travis clinked his bottle.

"So talk to me about why you are so passionately opposed to white kitchens. Have I finally unearthed one of your secrets?"

"It's not white kitchens that I abhor, exactly. It's this trend toward making everything so bland and homogenous." Travis sighed. "Fine. So, I know intellectually that owning property in New York City is in some ways a good investment, and in other ways it's just pissing money away. But my parents own their house in Forest Hills, and I guess I always assumed I'd own a house someday. I worked for Mike McPhee for a few years before striking out on my own, and I was making a good enough living that I was able to sock away some money. And a little over a year ago, I found this house. It was perfect." Travis knew he was going to get emotional, although he didn't want to. "Well, the house was my grandfather's."

"Really?"

"Yeah. My parents sold the house after my grandfather died, but it came back on the market, and I jumped at it. I could afford it because calling it a fixer-upper was kind of an insult to fixer-uppers, but I figured I could do a lot of the work myself over a few months before I moved in."

"Where was it?"

Travis sipped his beer while he collected his thoughts. It seemed like such a small thing in retrospect, but it still bothered him. "Fort Greene, on a residential block that was a real hodgepodge of architectural styles. And this house, man…. Two stories, ancient wood siding, tiny lot, but still a detached house. The people who bought it from my parents divided it into apartments, but it should really be a nice single-family home. Three bedrooms, compartmentalized main floor that could be opened up, and a finished basement, albeit one that was finished around 1972. I loved that house. A lot of my favorite childhood memories took place there. The interim owners did some weird things, but I could have restored it to be exactly what I wanted, a beautiful home for me and my hypothetical future husband and maybe a dog."

Brandon smiled. "So what happened?"

"I got outbid. I had enough money under my mattress to put down a solid down payment and could have secured a loan that would have allowed me to offer over list price. I had all my ducks in a row. And then a fucking house flipper outbid me and bought it." And that still stung. All that work, all those savings, all the plans he'd made, but it was New York

City, and there was always someone waiting in the wings with more money to spend.

"I'm so sorry," Brandon said. "How do you know it was a flipper?"

"The house went on the market again three months ago—at one point three million! Can you believe that? That's more than half a million more than the asking price the year before. I was curious, so I went to the open house. And you know what they did? They converted it to a single-family home, but the inside was just a sea of beige. All the character of the house had been completely stripped away." Seeing the house after renovation had broken Travis's heart. He knew a flipper going in and modernizing the house would be contrary to his vision for it, but for this guy to have modernized everything, to have torn down walls and tiles and stripped all the personality from the house, was like an insult.

"I'm sorry," said Brandon, looking somewhat chastened.

"I know I was kind of aggressive about it, but after losing that house, I couldn't stand the idea of someone going into an old Victorian house and making it just another cookie-cutter place. Those houses are historic and beautiful and interesting. The interior design should reflect that."

"It will. I'm excited to show you the materials we picked out."

Travis leaned an elbow on the counter—the marble was cool against his skin—and he rubbed his forehead. It still stung, losing that house, and he wasn't sure if he could explain how it had felt to have his dreams dashed the way they had been. How he'd almost left New York after the house sold because he was so fed up with the city, tired of renting, tired of putting white kitchens in other people's houses.

"You're still upset you lost the house," Brandon said softly.

"I… yeah. I am. I just think these old houses should be preserved, not stripped down and made to look like every other house in Brooklyn. One of the fun things about this borough is how eclectic its architecture is. Because you've got brownstones and big brick apartment buildings, but also houses with vinyl siding and old mansions and ranch houses that look like they should be in the suburbs. You've got beach houses near Coney Island and gorgeous old homes on the Prospect Park Gold Coast and, hell, the Grand Army Plaza arch and the Brooklyn Museum and Plymouth Church. There's so much character everywhere. You can't just come into this city, into *Brooklyn*, and make it look like a Restoration

Channel show, you know?" Travis paused and realized he was thirsty, so he took a sip of his beer. "I'm speechifying."

"Keep going."

"I just think…." Travis took a deep breath. These old houses were his passion. He found joy in fixing them, in breathing new life into them. When he'd struck out on his own, he'd started billing himself as an expert in *restoration*, not renovation. He'd spent hours and hours learning about architectural styles and vintage materials and Victorian design. "I just think that the whole point of your show should be to restore these old houses, make them look the way the original builders intended, within reason. Modernize, sure. But show the country what Brooklyn is, how it looks, how the people live. You know?"

Brandon nodded slowly. "I do know. And I love that house. Sure, I wish I hadn't rushed to say yes, but honestly, there was no other option for me. I really wanted to get my hands on the house."

Travis's emotions were too close to the surface. He'd already given too much of himself away. He sipped his beer and was surprised to see it was nearly gone. He sighed and wiped a bit of condensation off the bottle with his thumb.

"The thing about this neighborhood, about Argyle Road, is that it's like another planet," said Brandon. "You take that turn off Church Avenue and suddenly you're transported into an entirely different place. My first impression of it was that it was like walking back in time. I want to respect that."

"I appreciate that." Travis downed the rest of his beer and reached across the island to put the bottle in the sink.

Brandon ran a hand over his back. "I love that you care about this stuff so much. It shows me you were the right person for this job."

Travis's eyes stung—stupid emotions—so he blinked a few times and nodded.

"I didn't mean to upset you."

"You didn't," Travis said. "I'm still bitter about losing that house. But there will be others."

Brandon looked thoughtful for a moment. "There will be," he said, sounding a little dreamy.

Brandon reached over and cupped Travis's face. He smiled before moving in to kiss Travis. Travis opened his mouth, accepting the kiss, grateful that Brandon was so kind and so sweet and understood exactly what Travis was saying. Travis wasn't one for grand displays of emotion, but that didn't mean he didn't feel things. And a year ago, he'd felt his whole life plan slip out of his hands.

But maybe he was getting it back now. Sometimes being with Brandon made it feel that way.

Brandon pulled away slightly. "I know that feeling—wanting to plant roots. I never had that. I grew up in a hotel." He sighed. "The first piece of property I ever owned was the house I bought with Kayla, and even then it wasn't home. We had separate bedrooms. Part of me always knew it was temporary."

Travis put a hand on Brandon's shoulder and touched their foreheads together. "We're a mess."

Brandon laughed softly. "I know. I'm just trying to say, I get it."

Travis closed his eyes for a long moment. Brandon *did* get it. And Travis felt vulnerable, which he hated. It kicked up old anxiety. He would have answered any question Brandon had asked of him, but he didn't generally dig very deep below his own surface. He didn't like exposing that much of himself to another person. Explaining the reasoning behind his tattoos was one thing; expressing his emotions was another. He'd been with other men before, but he didn't love them, and he was slow to trust.

But he trusted Brandon.

Travis pulled away slightly but kept his hands on Brandon. How could it be that this man had so quickly worked his way under Travis's skin? How could it suddenly feel as if life had possibilities again just because he'd joined the cast of this ridiculous television show? And how could a man like Brandon—a sexy, passionate man, a sweet man, someone who clearly felt things deeply—how could *this man* be looking back at Travis with such affection in his eyes?

"Thanks for listening," Travis said.

"Of course. You okay?"

"I'm fine. I don't… do this a lot. Talk about my feelings."

"I got that impression. I won't hold it against you."

The smirk on Brandon's face defused some of the tension. Travis let out a breath and tried to relax.

"So. Wanna go to bed?" Brandon waggled his eyebrows.

Travis laughed, and it felt like relief. "I thought you'd never ask, baby. Forget this emotional crap. Let's have sex."

TRAVIS DRIFTED off to sleep, leaving Brandon with that itchy feeling in his legs, as if he could run a few laps around the block.

He didn't want to leave Travis, though, so he lay there, mulling over his thoughts.

What Travis had said about his grandfather's house, about wanting to build a home… Brandon felt that in his gut.

He and Kayla had made five seasons of *Dream Home* and would have made many more had Kayla not been discovered with Dave in that restaurant. It had been a popular show and a lucrative enterprise. Brandon and Kayla had fronted most of the money for their projects, but the Restoration Channel had thrown in money here or there to keep the show going. And so Brandon and Kayla had snapped up lots of shabby houses in the New York exurbs, a couple hours' drive from the city but in a far less densely populated part of the region. They'd made good money doing it, especially when they'd bought into up-and-coming neighborhoods. But the New York winters got to Kayla, so they'd been looking to move the show to Orange County, California, where there were plenty of old, shabby houses in otherwise nice neighborhoods, the perfect opportunity to flip houses for a profit.

And he'd been happy, to a point. He loved the work, and he loved working with Kayla. They'd owned a gorgeous house near Poughkeepsie: four bedrooms, a completely open first floor, a modern kitchen with all the bells and whistles that Brandon hadn't had much time to cook in. But those bedrooms allowed Brandon and Kayla to each have their own room and each have an office, and the arrangement worked for them. They really were like roommates. Neither minded when the other brought someone home, which was how Kayla's relationship with Dave had had the room to thrive. And Brandon had periodically brought men home, but he was so paranoid about the network finding out he was gay that no one had lasted longer than the third date. And truth be told, most of the men he'd gone out with had found his arrangement with Kayla too strange and complicated to want to navigate.

The end of the show could have been the doorway into the next phase of Brandon's life—one in which he could be open about who he was and search for a romantic partner. He was staring down forty now and was beginning to worry that his whole life would pass him by before he'd truly lived it, that he'd never fall in love or have a family or do any of the things he wanted. But now he was back where he'd been, albeit beside Travis, at least for now.

Travis wanted a home, one he had a hand in designing. Brandon wanted the same thing. This apartment was only intended to be temporary until he could decide where he wanted to live more permanently.

And that house on Argyle Road.... Despite everything, Brandon still loved it. He loved the charm of it, loved the layout, the size, the design, the neighborhood. He loved the finishes they'd picked out, especially those backsplash tiles that he knew Travis would love too. It was almost a shame, after all the work and thought he'd put into it, to sell that house.

So what if he didn't sell it?

Brandon was so surprised by the thought, he hopped out of bed, then walked to the kitchen and poured a glass of water.

But... what if he kept the house?

What if he moved into it? Well, the house wasn't just his. Sure, he had a significant financial stake in it, but he'd been thinking of the house as his and Travis's. Travis had done quite a bit of the work himself. His literal blood, sweat, and tears were in the house.

Brandon shook his head. It was a dumb idea. The only way to recoup his losses on the house was to sell it. That had always been the plan.

But he could buy out Restoration's part of it. It would set him back for a bit, but there would be other houses to flip. Hell, Virginia had been sending him almost daily emails about houses in the neighborhood that were on the market. His per-episode salary would keep him afloat while he figured out his next moves.

It was such an out-there idea. He needed to sell the house. He had no business thinking about buying it... or thinking about moving Travis into it with him. They'd just started seeing each other. There was no way the first good sex Brandon had had in a while would pan out to be the kind of commitment in which they shared a house. Life didn't work that way.

Unless it did.

He put his glass in the sink and tried to push the idea out of his mind. He and Travis were barely even dating. Thinking about living together was a ridiculous thing to even contemplate.

When he got back into bed, Travis stirred and said, "You okay?"

"I'm fine. Go back to sleep."

"Mmm."

Travis rolled onto his side, his back to Brandon, so Brandon took that as an invitation. He slid alongside Travis and put his arm around Travis's midsection, then pulled him close so that they spooned together. Travis sighed, and it sounded happy. Brandon kissed the top of his head and held him close. He wasn't sleepy and didn't imagine he'd be able to drift off now, but holding Travis, he felt content.

This was the way things were supposed to be. Brandon should have a man in his bed, someone he could see himself loving and sharing his life with. Maybe Travis wasn't that man, but this was still something Brandon hadn't even known he'd been missing. Or maybe Travis *was* that man, and they were working toward something. Brandon didn't know now, but as the sleepless night wore on, the idea of buying the house on Argyle Road and making it his own home started to seem less silly.

Chapter Thirteen

AS HE arrived at the Argyle Road house, Brandon was still riding the high of fantasizing about buying the house coupled with some spectacular early morning sex with Travis. Travis had snuck out to both go home and change and to not make it seem as if they were arriving at the site together. Travis was clearly irked by the subterfuge—and probably by having to get up early—but Brandon had insisted that showing up at the house together would look suspicious.

So maybe not everything was bliss. But Brandon still felt good. Travis had beat him to the house and was already at work mudding some of the drywall in the living room. He smiled at Brandon when Brandon walked into the room, and that made warmth spread in Brandon's chest.

So Brandon was sleep-deprived and a little giddy, but happy about things with Travis. On the other hand, he was consequently so tired, he couldn't remember what he was supposed to be filming today. He walked to the back of the house, hoping to find Erik to ask, but he found Kayla instead.

"Ah, there you are," she said.

"Hi. I thought you were flying back today."

"I am. But my flight doesn't leave for…." Kayla glanced at her watch. "Six more hours. I wanted to grab a word with you first."

"All right. On camera or…."

"No, privately. There's a cute little coffee shop on Church. Can we go there for a few minutes?"

"Sure. Let me just let Erik know."

Leaving the set ended up being a lot more complicated than he'd anticipated, even though Brandon had no particular agenda for the day. Erik had been hoping to film Brandon helping Travis out with the drywall, but after some persuading, Erik let Brandon go.

Viewers didn't really care about drywall. Thirty seconds of Travis mudding would get the job done.

Still, it was almost a half hour later before Brandon and Kayla were seated at a corner table in a coffee shop. Brandon sipped his latte. "What did you want to talk about?"

Kayla looked around. "No paparazzi here."

"They don't generally lurk around coffee shops in Brooklyn neighborhoods this far from Manhattan."

Kayla nodded, then reached into her purse and came back with a small jewelry box. "I wanted to give this back to you."

Brandon took the box and opened it. It was Kayla's engagement ring. The ring had once belonged to several generations of women in Brandon's family. Brandon had wanted to give the heirloom to Kayla as a gesture of good faith that despite the unusual nature of their marriage, he was committed to the life they were building for themselves. That was naïve, in retrospect. But Brandon's attachment to the ring was more symbolic than anything else, especially now that he and his mother were estranged. Brandon had frankly forgotten that he'd given the ring to Kayla at all.

"Uh, thanks," he said, placing the box on the table.

"It seemed like the right thing to do to return it. I know you and your mother barely talk these days, but still, I feel bad. It was all my fault this thing between us blew up."

"Kayla…."

"No, it was. I was careless. I forgot where we were and that there would be people who recognized me around. Who even watches the Restoration Channel? Well, a lot of people, it turns out. I just…. Dave and I were getting serious and I wanted to show him some affection, and I just wasn't thinking."

"You know what, though? I think… I think you did me a favor."

"What?"

Brandon took a deep breath and fingered the ring box. "You deserve to be with Dave, to really *be* with him instead of having a husband holding you back. *I* deserve to find someone I can love too. I know we had an arrangement, but I couldn't let myself really be with anyone else while I was still married to you. I know it sounds dumb, but besides the lack of sex, I took our commitment to each other seriously."

Kayla reached across the table and covered Brandon's hand with her own. "I know you did, sweetie. I did too, for what it's worth. But Mama needs some sugar sometimes."

Brandon laughed. “I know.” He sighed. “But I can’t help but think that you got the short end of the stick here, at least in the media. Everyone thinks you cheated on me. Restoration bought you out of your contract.”

Kayla shrugged. “You know what? I’m okay with how things turned out. Dave and I are going to settle in Orange County. I want to keep flipping houses, but I don’t need to do that in front of a camera. Don’t get me wrong, I loved doing the show, and I’m so happy to have had that experience, but after a few years in the spotlight, I’d rather lead a quiet life. I want to get married and have children. And I don’t want those future children to be on camera, but Restoration would expect that. Besides, Dave doesn’t want to be on TV even a little. It’s really better this way.”

“Are you sure?”

“Yes. I’m happy, Brandon. Don’t worry about me. Dave and I are great together, and I want to live with him in a nice house on the beach and have his babies.” She grinned.

Brandon shook his head. “This is not at all how I saw this going.”

“How long could we have really stayed married?”

That was the question, wasn’t it? Brandon had never been foolish enough to think marriage would cure him of his homosexuality—he’d never harbored any hope that he’d develop an attraction to Kayla, whom he loved like a sister—but part of him was determined to make the arrangement work. He’d wanted to build a successful brand, of which his marriage and business partnership were the cornerstone, and failure was not an option. The marriage clinched the deal with the Restoration Channel and made his father happy, and Brandon had never let himself think beyond that. But of course, Kayla was right. This careful image Brandon had invested years of his life into building up had always been destined to topple over.

Kayla looked at the table and said quietly, “I would have ended it eventually. I want to marry Dave and have a real marriage, not a fake TV one. Even if I hadn’t met him, you would have met someone eventually. That plan we made, it was good for the show, but it wasn’t a good life plan.”

“You’re right. You deserve to be happy. And now that we’re not married anymore, I feel like I have permission to find something real too." He sighed. "But I miss you. I miss having you around. I miss your friendship. I miss talking to you every day."

"You can still do that, you know. They have these newfangled things called telephones."

"I know. But it's not the same."

Kayla smiled. "I love you, you know. I miss our friendship too. Let's be better about talking regularly, okay? Even if it's just texts on the fly between you adding grout to tiles and banging Travis."

Brandon rolled his eyes. "I will." Then, feeling inspired, he slid the ring back across the table. "You can keep this, if you want. It doesn't…. I wanted you to have it. It has nothing to do with my family."

Kayla stared at the box. "It is a beautiful ring. I always liked it."

"It's yours. Call it a friendship ring."

"Oooh, like in elementary school when you and your BFF got those necklaces where one of them said 'Best' and the other said 'Friends'? Well, in my case, my best friend and I got necklaces that had the word 'Best' above 'Friends,' so when they were divided in half, hers said 'BE FRIE' and mine said 'ST NDS' so we called each other Be-fry and Stinds for a while. Good times."

Brandon laughed, because he couldn't not. God, he missed Kayla. "It's not exactly like that."

"I suppose not. But I will take this token of your affection and keep it close to my heart."

They chatted amiably as they finished their coffee; then Kayla walked him back to the house. "I'm gonna get a car and do a little shopping before I collect my luggage from the hotel and go to the airport. But this was great, Brandon, really. Don't be a stranger."

"I won't."

"And send me photos of the place when it's finished. I can't wait to see how it looks in the end."

"I definitely will."

Kayla hugged Brandon, and he put his arms around her and leaned his head on hers. She kissed his cheek as she pulled away. He waited with her for another minute until her car pulled up.

"I'll see you, big guy," she said as she opened the door. "Good luck with everything."

"Yeah. Thanks. You too. I want a wedding invitation."

"Of course, dearest." She blew him a kiss and got in the car.

He watched the cab drive down the street and felt a little sad, but also satisfied. It felt like a door to his past had closed.

He took a deep breath and walked back into the house.

MUDDING DRYWALL was a messy task, and also a boring one. Erik packed up his crew and left early for the day so that he could get some exterior shots from around the neighborhood before giving everyone the afternoon off.

Mudding was the process of adding drywall compound to the joints, nail holes, and divots in the drywall to make the walls as even as possible. It would help the paint go on easier and make the walls look like one smooth surface rather than individual panels of drywall. Travis had put on an apron to do the job, because he was good at getting the drywall compound all over himself, and sure enough, the apron was covered in white blobs now.

Brandon had been doing busywork tasks around the house, and Travis didn't see him at all until the sun started to set.

"Do me a favor?" Travis said when Brandon walked into the dining room where Travis was working.

"Sure."

"Send Ismael and the evening crew home. Once I finish this wall, we're done for the day. I'm gonna have the night crew start painting upstairs, but there's not much we can do down here until all this dries."

"Sure."

Brandon disappeared for a few minutes. Once Ismael and the crew stomped through the house and left for the day, Brandon returned. "I had a thought about upstairs."

"All right."

"I was going to do carpet for budget reasons, but at this point, why not go whole hog? Let's do hardwood up there."

Travis took a step up the ladder so he could smear compound over a divot close to the ceiling. "You sure?"

"Yeah. At this point the budget is so blown, we might as well go for it. I hate carpet. I'd rather see hardwood."

"You're saving some money by putting tile in in this room instead of wood, so that will mitigate some of the cost."

Brandon nodded. "I've decided I don't want to make any compromises on this place. We've still got a little room before we get to the spending limit, so let's just go for it."

Travis held his trowel away from the wall. "You're not going to make me tear down walls now, are you? Because we *just* got these done."

Brandon laughed. "No. Keep everything we've already done. But the thought of putting carpet upstairs was starting to bother me."

"Then yeah, sure. You're going to have to order more wood."

"No. I had this thought when Kayla and I were shopping. I ordered extra wood flooring in case I decided to do the second floor. I figured I could return whatever we didn't use. I haven't gotten around to ordering carpet, which tells me I'd really rather do hardwood."

"Okay."

Brandon shifted on his feet, a sign that he wanted to tell Travis something.

Travis cleared his throat and asked, "So, how was your coffee date with Kayla this morning? She make her flight okay?"

"Yeah, she texted me when she boarded the plane. She's in the air right now. She, uh, took me to coffee to return her engagement ring."

Travis had to stop what he was doing again because he was so surprised, but he supposed it made a certain amount of sense. People returned rings when engagements ended. Why not marriages? He took a deep breath and went back to mudding.

"We had a good talk," Brandon said.

"Good." Travis pulled a scraper from his tool belt and smoothed over the work he'd just done before climbing off the ladder. "You feel okay?"

Brandon nodded slowly. "I'm fine. It was… a little intense. But it was good."

Travis regarded Brandon carefully for a moment. They'd shared a lot with each other. After seeing them together, Travis understood that Brandon and Kayla were good friends, and their divorce really had wrecked something, even if they hadn't ever been romantically involved.

Travis wanted to ask if Brandon felt like he was moving forward, but he couldn't figure out how without sounding like a therapist.

"How's all this going?" Brandon asked.

"We're basically done with the drywall on this floor." Travis took the apron off and draped it over a folding chair so it would dry.

"Hopefully the floors show up tomorrow like they're supposed to so we can start putting those in."

"So it's coming along."

"Yeah. We're on schedule."

Brandon seemed a little distant, thoughtful.

"Are you sure you're okay?"

Brandon smiled. "I am. A little sad, maybe. I really feel like an era ended today. But I needed that, I think. Closure on that part of my life. I need to… turn to the next chapter."

Travis nodded. He stopped to listen for a minute. Once he felt confident that everyone had vacated the house, he leaned over and ran a hand down Brandon's arm. Brandon seemed to need a hug, so Travis pulled Brandon into his arms.

Travis closed his eyes and leaned into the embrace as Brandon squeezed him a little tighter. They definitely had something going here, and if they were at the stage where they were sharing secrets, maybe they had some real intimacy. Travis hadn't experienced this before, but the longer the show lasted, the more he could picture things working out with Brandon.

Assuming he didn't get himself fired.

With that cheery thought, he backed off.

"You want to have dinner with me?" Brandon asked.

"Sure. Especially now that I've gotten bits of drywall on your shirt. Sorry about that."

"We could just go to my place and get something delivered."

"Solid compromise."

Chapter Fourteen

A FEW days later, Ismael suggested they start painting while they waited for the floors to be delivered. Erik got a bunch of shots of Brandon and Travis with paint rollers. Brandon could already picture this as part of an "adding the finishes" montage. Sometimes he still marveled at the way this show was being put together. Two months of work distilled into forty-two minutes.

They were nearly done painting the first floor when the day shift ended. Ismael volunteered to stay behind to help finish, so Travis assigned him to the dining room while he and Brandon completed the living room.

Travis was efficient with a paint roller, probably from having painted hundreds of walls. He seemed to be lost in some kind of painting zone, totally focused.

Brandon had picked an off-white with a warm, yellowy undertone for this room, something neutral but still bright and happy. Travis hadn't commented on it, so Brandon assumed that meant he liked it, but it was hard to know. Brandon quite liked how it was coming together. They'd paint the crown moldings, baseboards, window frames, and other trim bright white, all matte paint so it looked soft. That sunny color, contrasted with the dark hardwood, would be perfect.

"How are you feeling about the paint colors?" Brandon said, perhaps tempting fate.

"They're fine."

"Thanks for your unbridled enthusiasm."

Travis stopped what he was doing and took a step back. He put the roller down in the tray, then crossed the room to get the ladder. "It's not gray."

Brandon rolled his eyes. "What would you prefer? Hot pink? Highlighter yellow? Electric blue?"

Travis set up the ladder, clearly aiming to start painting the crown moldings on the section of wall where the paint had already dried. He poured white paint into a tray, grabbed a wide brush, and climbed the ladder.

"You're not gonna put up tape or anything?"

"Nope. You're gonna do the patchwork when I'm done, though."

Brandon watched for a moment as Travis expertly painted the molding, clearly experienced with this kind of thing. He painted all the molding within reach without dripping paint anywhere and managed to cover about three feet. Then he came back down and moved the ladder.

"Are you going to just stand there gawking at me, or…?"

Brandon shook his head. The wall was done and just the trim remained, so he set up a tray with white paint and prepared to start the baseboards. "Can I help it if I enjoy watching you work? And you didn't answer my question."

"What question?"

"You hate the paint colors, don't you?"

Travis sighed but didn't miss a beat painting. "Honestly? I'd probably pick something similar. I'd punch up the colors in this room with the furniture."

"Really?"

"Sure."

"Because it means a lot if you approve."

Travis stopped what he was doing and stared at Brandon. "Why?"

Brandon couldn't exactly say *because I want for us to live here together*, so he said instead, "I value your opinion."

"It's a nice color. Totally inoffensive."

Brandon laughed. "You know what? I'll take it."

Travis went back to painting trim, grinning now. It warmed Brandon to know he could make Travis smile like that.

Brandon knelt to paint the baseboard and started moving toward the ladder. When he could go no further, he stood up and saw Travis looking at him.

"What?" asked Brandon.

"Nothing. Well, I need to move the ladder, but you're in the way."

That little smirk on Travis's face was too much. Brandon stood up, lifted himself on his toes, and leaned close to Travis. Travis leaned down and met him in the middle. They kissed, and Brandon never wanted it to end. He loved the way their lips fit together, the way Travis tasted, the way Travis smelled. Travis threaded his fingers through Brandon's hair and held him there by the back of his head.

It was growing increasingly difficult for Brandon to keep his hands to himself on set. Some after-hours kissing soothed him a bit. But Brandon found he didn't want to hide this relationship, or whatever this was, when they spent so much time together. The consequences of getting caught, though….

He sighed into the kiss. Best to worry about that later.

Then there was a bang, and Ismael shouted, "Hey, Trav! Can I—?" He walked in the room and stopped short. "Oh."

Travis jerked away from Brandon, making the ladder wobble, and stared at Ismael for a long moment.

Brandon tried to find something to say, but in his panic, he couldn't come up with anything.

Travis said, "We were just—"

"It's fine," Ismael said in his soft Puerto Rican accent. "I already knew about Travis. I just didn't know Brandon was…. But it doesn't matter. I just came to say I'm done in the dining room and I was gonna clock out for the day."

"Yeah, that's fine," Travis said, his voice shaky. "Brandon and I can finish the trim in here, and then we'll do the feature wall in the family room tomorrow." He glanced at Brandon, then turned to Ismael. "You won't… say anything, will you? This thing… it's not supposed to be public knowledge. I mean, not a word to anyone."

"Hey, boss, I can keep a secret. No big deal to me."

"All right. Thank you."

Brandon's heart pounded and his veins were icy. Ismael was acting awfully casual about this. Would he really keep quiet? Had Brandon just done the very thing he'd blamed Kayla for doing? It had been so incredibly foolish to kiss Travis in the house when people were still around. Why had he done it?

Travis came down off the ladder and rested a hand on Brandon's arm. "It's fine. It's just Ismael. I trust him not to tell anyone. We're fine."

"If anyone from the network found out…."

"I know." Travis stroked Brandon's arm.

"I swear I'll keep my mouth shut," said Ismael. "I understand what's happening. Don't worry."

"We're good," said Travis. "I'll see you tomorrow."

Ismael waved and left. Travis looked up at the unpainted molding, then glanced at Brandon. Travis took a deep breath. "You're clearly flipping out. Why don't you go on home? I'll finish the trim and meet you there. Okay?"

"If anyone finds out…."

"I know. I trust Ismael, though. He'll stay quiet. We're fine, Brandon."

Brandon took several long breaths, trying to get a handle on his emotions. Maybe it would be okay, but this just demonstrated how precarious this situation was. Brandon felt like he'd lost control of the situation and didn't know how to reconcile that.

"Please calm down," Travis said.

"I'm trying. I'm sorry I'm freaking out."

"It's fine. I understand. But freaking out is not getting this trim painted, and there's nothing more we can do tonight."

Brandon took another deep breath. He was starting to calm down. Travis was right, there wasn't much they could do that night. "All right. I'll, uh, get some takeout. Maybe pick up banh mi from that place on Montague near my apartment. That sound good? Then by the time you're done and get to my place, I'll have dinner set up."

"Yeah, that sounds great. Get me whatever you're having, but easy on the spices." He walked over and wrapped his arms around Brandon, rubbing his back. "Please be okay."

"I am. I just… I freaked."

"I know. It'll be okay, I promise."

Brandon sighed and rested his forehead on Travis's shoulder. "You can't promise that."

"Well, *this* at least will not be our undoing."

Brandon pulled away gently, then gave Travis a brief, soft kiss. "I'll take that promise."

"Now get out of here so I can finish."

TRAVIS WAS losing the battle to stay calm in the face of Brandon going off the deep end over Ismael catching them together.

He'd finished the trim after Brandon had left the house, and he'd spent the whole forty minutes or so that it took him to finish mulling over what had happened. Travis had known Ismael from his years working as a contractor, and while they weren't close friends or anything, Ismael had never given Travis a reason not to trust him. So Travis left the house feeling pretty confident Ismael a) didn't care at all about who was sleeping with whom, and b) wouldn't tell anyone what he'd seen.

It was, however, a good reminder that he and Brandon had to be more discreet.

And that was fine, he reflected in the cab to Brandon's place. It bugged him a little, but it was like a niggle in the back of his mind. For now, this was okay. If he and Brandon made any sort of commitment to each other down the line, that might change things.

Maybe it was too late, though, because rather than being turned off by Brandon's freak-out, he wanted to rush to Brandon's side to calm him down.

What the hell was wrong with him? This was not how Travis usually operated.

When he got to Brandon's place, they ate banh mi and Brandon seemed calmer. As they finished and Brandon cleaned up the takeout bags and wrappers, Brandon said, "If you really trust Ismael, then I will too. I'm sorry for freaking out."

"It's fine."

"You staying calm is…. You know, Kayla thought you and I might be good for each other."

"You told her?" That was a surprise. Travis had assumed Brandon wouldn't breathe a word to anyone.

"She kind of intuited that we were more than just coworkers, and pulled the confession out of me. But she thought we'd be good together because we kind of complement each other. And here's proof—you stayed calm while I freaked out. And that was comforting. I think if we'd both panicked, I'd be in a coronary unit right now."

Travis nodded but kept the fact that he was having second thoughts to himself. He couldn't see a reason Ismael, who was always so chill about everything, would feel compelled to tell anyone. In fact, Travis didn't think Ismael cared at all. And yet, if Ismael casually mentioned it to one of the guys on his crew, and then that man told someone on the TV crew because they'd been getting pretty chummy with each other… then word would get back to Virginia….

Travis just wanted to fix houses. He didn't need all this drama. He should be able to just walk away, but… he couldn't.

To change the subject, Travis said, "The night crew rolled in when I was leaving. They're painting upstairs."

"The matte eggshell, right?" said Brandon.

"Yep. And before you ask again, yes, it's the right choice. Paint colors matter more on the first floor and the exterior. People want to customize their own bedrooms. If the family who buys the house has a daughter who wants to paint the room fuchsia, well, paint is cheap."

Brandon smiled. "I've seen a few episodes of this competition show for interior designers hosted by the Restoration Channel. In one episode, the contestants each had to design a room in a model home. Now that's a case where you want to appeal to as broad a group of people as possible. You kind of want it to be a blank canvas—because people will want to customize—but you stage it well so that people can picture themselves living in it, right?"

"Sure."

"On the show, the designers went bonkers. Bright colors on the walls, clashing wallpaper in the office, quirky furniture all over the house. And the judges were like, 'Who would want to live in this house?' I always think about that when I pick interior paint colors."

"Fair. Paint is one of those things that can turn off a buyer, even though it's easy to fix."

"Once at an open house that Kayla and I were running, a woman came through who insisted on having a white kitchen. The kitchen in this house was massive, so we'd decided to go modern and had put in these dark gray flat-panel cabinets. It was one of the better kitchens we ever designed. And this woman walked in and was like, 'Nope.' Her husband pointed out that cabinets could be painted, but she just would not move into a house that did not have white cabinets."

"Hence your paranoia about quirky design and color."

"In that case, the woman was being unreasonable. I can admit that."

Travis chuckled.

"Oh, I should warn you, Virginia wants to bring a photographer by the set so we can do some promotional prints."

Ugh. Travis had known this was coming. Brandon was the host and would be in most of the ads, but Virginia had mentioned in passing that she wanted a few action shots of Travis doing stuff around the house to put on the website.

"I can tell by your facial expression that you're very excited," said Brandon.

"I've never been a big fan of getting my photo taken."

"Really?"

"Why does that surprise you?"

Brandon grinned. "Because you're so hot. If they take some full body shots of you working and put you on the billboards and subway ads, we're golden. Your thighs alone could get us top ratings."

Brandon walked over and ran a hand up Travis's thigh. Travis had never thought about his own thighs in this way; he certainly admired strong legs on other men but hadn't known they were something Brandon admired on him. "Um, thank you."

Brandon leaned close. "I mean, I'd put you on posters to try to sell this show. I think a lot of viewers are going to see you and start lusting after the sexy project manager. You're like the sleeper on this production. They'll tune in to watch me, but fall in love with you."

"You say nice things, but that's ridiculous."

"Well, I'd tune in to watch you."

"You can watch me anytime you want, babe."

"Oh, I have been. That's what's going to get me in trouble." Brandon sighed.

"Well, you can watch me right now, how's that? There's no one around. It's just you and me."

Brandon slid his arms around Travis's waist and started creeping up the back of his T-shirt. "Oh, yeah. I think we should be wearing less clothes."

Travis kissed Brandon, glad that they were moving forward with their real purpose here and not talking anymore. He could feel the edges of panic creeping in—about Ismael, about getting his photo taken for promotional purposes—but he didn't want Brandon to see that, so he surrendered himself to the feeling of Brandon's lips against his and Brandon's hands on his body.

"Take me to bed," said Travis.

"You didn't even have to ask."

Brandon took a step back, so Travis slid off the stool and followed Brandon into his bedroom. They peeled each other's clothes off and lay on the bed, and Travis tried to turn his brain off, to just let this be sex.

But he knew better. And as Brandon took him into his arms, as their skin slid against each other, as their cocks pressed together and tingles of arousal curled through Travis's body, he knew this was much more than sex. He'd allowed himself to be soft and vulnerable with Brandon. He cared about Brandon, wanted to soothe him, wanted him to be okay. He *cared* in a way he had never cared about a sex partner before. And as they kissed, Travis knew that something was different here, that his feelings were involved.

"I want you inside me," Brandon whispered.

Travis wanted that too. He'd spent the night at Brandon's apartment often enough now to know where things were, so he reached for the nightstand drawer.

When he slid inside Brandon, they faced each other, and Travis thought he could see some of his feelings reflected in Brandon's eyes. What felt good, what Travis wanted with his heart, started to subsume what was practical and what Travis thought he should do. Because this relationship could get him fired from a good job, and could, in fact, cause all manner of disasters.

And yet it was hard to remember that when he was inside Brandon, when they were kissing, when Brandon put his arms around him. They were wrapped up in each other, murmuring about how good it felt, and Travis knew there was something happening here that he'd never experienced before.

He was falling for Brandon.

Later, when they lay in bed tangled up in each other and basking in the aftermath, Travis said, "This is so going to blow up in our faces."

Brandon didn't even need to ask what he was talking about. Instead he just said, "Worth it."

Chapter Fifteen

After Travis's workday ended, Mike proposed they all get a drink. It had been a backbreaking kind of day, installing the antique tub in the master bathroom and laying most of the bathroom tile upstairs. Brandon had plans with his brothers anyway, so Travis had the night to himself.

They walked down to Cortelyou Road and found a bar that looked simple enough. The little rainbow flag near the awning was encouraging. Inside there was dim lighting, exposed brick, an old-timey brass railing around the bar, and a meat-forward pub-food menu that was just the thing Travis needed after a long day of work.

They settled at a booth in the corner and ordered beers while Travis tried to decide which decadent, toppings-laden burger he should order. His stomach grumbled in anticipation.

"So," said Sandy. "This is a pretty weird project."

"The cameras are unnerving, aren't they?" said Travis. "By the way, I'm really grateful to you guys for coming out to help."

"A big paycheck and a chance to advertise the business?" said Mike. "Easy decision."

Travis nodded. "I've never worked on a project with this kind of budget. It's like Brandon can just pull money out of thin air."

"So is he related to John Chase or what?" asked Mike.

Travis wasn't surprised that Mike knew who John Chase was. Travis had since done some research and discovered that John Chase had built a dozen buildings in Manhattan, and his family still owned several developments in the outer boroughs. The crown jewel was the St. Joseph Hotel, a Gilded Age relic the elder Chase had bought for a song in 1975—the year of the infamous *Ford to City: Drop Dead* headline—and restored to glorious heights. The St. Joseph was now one of the finest hotels in the city, famous for its sumptuous finishes and luxury service. But the Chase family also owned a massive apartment complex near Riverside Park, a few office towers in Lower Manhattan and Midtown, and another big apartment building near Lincoln Center. Newspapers in the eighties and nineties had called Brandon's father the King of the

Upper West Side. They'd also called him a grim taskmaster, a man who never laughed or smiled, and he seemed to win real estate bids mostly through intimidation and throwing money at lawyers. And he said at least once, in nearly every interview Travis had read about him, "Failure is not an option."

No wonder Brandon had such a complex.

"John Chase was Brandon's father," said Travis. "My understanding is that Brandon finances his real estate projects with his own money that he earned from the business he ran with Kayla, although he mentioned some inheritance money as well. But he's not directly involved in the Chase family real estate business, and I think that's by design. I get the impression he and his family do not get along."

"John Chase seemed like a piece of work," said Mike. "I renovated a condo in Chase Plaza maybe eight years ago, and the list of things we could and could not do in the building was like a homeowner's association on steroids. We could only use certain colors and materials, we could only work during certain hours, and the condo owners could only buy products from an approved list of vendors. That project almost made me quit."

"Oh God, I remember that," said Sandy.

"The good news is that Brandon is a lot more easygoing," said Travis.

"Is he now?" said Sandy, seeming intrigued.

Travis trusted his friends, but he wasn't super eager to talk about his relationship just yet, so instead he said, "So how are things with you guys? Your families okay?"

"Great," said Mike. "Well, Emma's leaving for college soon, and I'm not ready for it." Emma was Mike's daughter.

"Wasn't she ten years old five minutes ago?"

"She was a *baby* five minutes ago," said Mike. "She's all grown up now, and I'm in denial."

"She's not going far," said Sandy.

"That's true." Mike explained that his husband, Gio, had helped Emma get into Juilliard, where she'd be studying voice and opera in the fall.

"Alex is starting first grade in the fall," said Sandy. "I'm a mess over that, so I can only imagine what seeing Emma off to college will be like."

Both seemed happy, which was the main thing. Travis envied their settled home lives. Maybe it was a side effect of turning thirty-five a couple of months ago, but he was starting to feel tired of casual dates and random hookups. That was what wanting to buy a house had been about, hadn't it? He'd been saving money long before his grandfather's house had shown up on the market because he wanted a home to settle into, a place to build a family. He wasn't sure about kids; he couldn't see himself as a father the way Mike and Sandy were. But a nice house with a husband and a dog—that was something he could get behind.

"And what about *you*?" asked Sandy.

"Uh, well." Travis wasn't sure if he should mention Brandon. "I mean, I pretty much just live at the Argyle Road house now."

Sandy leaned toward Mike. "Do you see how that was not an answer?"

Travis sipped his beer and shrugged.

"You're banging Brandon, aren't you?" said Sandy. "He *is* pretty foxy. I mean, I've seen a zillion episodes of *Dream Home* because Everett is obsessed. He wants to redo the kitchen again, by the way."

"Your kitchen is fine," said Mike.

"I *know*. I built it. Anyway, I always thought Brandon and Kayla were a super cute couple, but then I met Brandon in person, and he makes my gaydar light up like a five-alarm fire. And the two of you have some chemistry, so I thought, you know…."

Travis crossed his arms, but he knew he was smiling. He couldn't help it. "What do you think you know?"

Sandy held up his hands. "He's a great-looking guy who is very publicly single. You work together all day long, sweating and lifting heavy objects. Things are bound to happen."

Travis hesitated to speak. He worried that the fact that he and Brandon were sleeping with each other might get out into the world. So he said, "He's a complicated guy."

"Uh-huh," said Mike.

"Look, he and I have talked some, and I get the impression his childhood was not a happy one. If I'm reading between the lines correctly, I think John Chase was verbally abusive to his kids. Brandon has built up this false front for himself, and he's very reluctant to take it down. He wants everyone to believe he's just this happy-go-lucky straight guy who had a bad break, but he's picking up the pieces now to create this new show. None of that is true, incidentally."

"The plot thickens," said Sandy, sitting forward.

"It's not my place to tell his secrets," Travis continued, "but it's just… this show, his career, his 'brand,' are the most important things to him. I can't help thinking that anyone who tried to get close to him would lose out to all that."

"So just fuck his brains out," said Sandy.

"No, I see what Travis is saying," said Mike. "That sounds like a lot to deal with."

"See, this is because you're a romantic," said Sandy.

Mike raised his eyebrows. "Do you know what you told me the first day you met Everett? That he was the hottest guy you'd ever laid eyes on."

"Right. And I did, in fact, fuck his brains out shortly after that."

"And then you married him. You've got at least one romantic bone in your body."

Sandy crossed his arms and huffed.

Travis laughed. "This is fun and all, but really, I don't see much happening with Brandon. Also, you know, we do work together. He's not my boss, technically, but it could still get awkward. And even though I'm not super stoked about having all my work filmed, I do really like this job. I'd like to keep it."

"I was putting up tile in the master bathroom today while this camera guy just lingered behind me, and I was suddenly terrified to make a mistake!" said Sandy. "The job took three times longer than it needed to because I was extra careful. Thankfully, after about half an hour, the camera guy figured out that putting up tile is extremely boring, and he took off."

"This is excellent publicity," said Mike. "I'm going to add 'as seen on the Restoration Channel' to our website."

"That was basically my thinking," said Travis. "I do this for a couple of years, I earn money and get some good publicity, and then I can build my own business and put 'as seen on TV' all over my website."

"I bet you're good TV too," said Sandy. "You've got that whole badass-with-a-heart-of-gold thing going. Women eat that shit with a spoon."

"It's not women I'm trying to attract here," said Travis.

Sandy sat back and considered Travis for a moment. "No, you're right. It's one handsome TV star."

THE PRESIDENTIAL suite at the St. Joseph Hotel was technically an apartment. It had four bedrooms, a spacious common room, a full kitchen, and two full bathrooms. The whole Chase family had lived here until John Chase had passed away and Robert took over the family business. Brandon's mother had moved to Massachusetts, having decided to spend her retirement years at the family vacation house in the Berkshires. Now Robert used the suite mostly as an office/meeting space; he and his family lived in a palatial apartment farther uptown. When Brandon arrived for dinner with his brothers, he quickly saw that half the suite was under renovation.

"This is different," Brandon commented.

"Yeah," Robert said, getting up from behind his desk, which was stationed roughly where the family sofa had once been. "No one is living here now, so I figured I'd change one of the bedrooms into a conference room and make some other changes while I was at it." He walked around the desk and shook Brandon's hand. "How are you, brother?"

"I'm all right."

Robert led Brandon over to a dining table and gestured for him to take a seat. "The hotel is catering dinner. Luke should be here any minute."

Brandon was already bothered by how stiff and formal this felt. He and Robert were brothers, for God's sake. They shared the same DNA, had grown up together in this very suite, and yet Robert was treating Brandon like a work acquaintance. They'd never been close—there was an eight-year age gap between them, after all. Brandon probably should have known by now not to expect much from his family, but it still grated on him that Robert was so cold sometimes.

"How's Hannah?" Brandon asked. Hannah was Robert's wife.

"She's good. She would have come, but she wanted to pick up Chloe from soccer practice. She doesn't trust the kids to get home on the subway by themselves yet."

Chloe, Robert's oldest, was only ten, so Brandon didn't blame her. "I haven't seen the kids since I moved back to the city. We should have lunch or something."

"Sure, I'll see when everyone's free."

Just then, Luke arrived. As with Brandon, Luke had a key to the suite and let himself in.

He looked rough. His hair was a little too long, and he hadn't shaved in a few days—and not in the deliberate way Travis maintained his stubble. Luke looked like he just hadn't bothered. And his clothes were more casual than Brandon expected—a simple T-shirt and jeans.

Luke was employed by the Chase Group. Last Brandon had heard, he was managing some of the properties the company owned in Brooklyn and Queens, so he and Robert were in much more frequent communication than Brandon was with either of them.

Brandon also knew that each of them dealt with the Chase legacy in different ways. Robert had become their father, essentially. Brandon had been so anxious to be the son John expected him to be that he'd created his own business and married a woman to create the perfect image he needed for success. And Luke, well. Luke drank. And it was starting to show.

He hugged Brandon, at least.

An attendant from room service arrived then with a cart full of food, which he dutifully laid out on the dining table. It was a sumptuous feast: a platter with three filets mignons, several bowls of vegetables and potatoes, two bottles of wine, and a platter of petits fours for dessert. Brandon recognized the china plates the attendant set out as belonging to the hotel's set, a unique design specific to the St. Joseph, variations on which they'd been using since Brandon had been a kid.

"So how is the television show?" asked Robert once they were seated and had served themselves.

"It's going well so far."

"I was sorry to hear about Kayla," said Luke. "I always liked her."

"She's not… that is, you know…." Brandon sighed. "Kayla and I are still friends."

"I couldn't be friends with an ex," said Luke, filling his wineglass nearly to the brim.

"That's not… I mean, it wasn't a real marriage. You know that, right?"

Luke shrugged.

"And I'm seeing someone now, anyway," Brandon said, not meaning to confess that much but irritated that Luke had forgotten the arrangement.

Robert raised an eyebrow. "Are you?"

"Is she hot?" asked Luke.

Brandon put his fork down, slamming it harder than he meant to. Both of his brothers stared at him. "No. I mean yes, *he's* hot, but I'm seeing a man, not a woman. In case you guys forgot, which you conveniently seem to do every time I leave town for longer than five minutes, I'm gay. I respected Dad's wishes not to come out publicly while he was still alive, but jeez, guys. It's not like that changes. I'm dating a man, okay? I'm keeping it quiet while I'm filming the show because I don't want any trouble from the network, but you guys are supposed to be my family."

Brandon knew full well that neither Robert nor Luke wanted Brandon's homosexuality to have any effect on the family business—and Brandon had no idea how that could happen, but he understood the way his brothers thought—so he knew they'd both be quiet. But he felt frustrated that they didn't seem to know him at all, didn't acknowledge what his life really was.

Robert looked chastened, at least. Then he ruined it by saying, "You'd better not bring him to lunch with my kids."

Brandon stood. "I'm leaving. I'm done."

Robert stood too. "No, sit. I'm sorry."

They stared each other down for a minute; then Brandon sat.

Something clicked for him then. All he'd wanted to do for most of his life was please his father. *Failure is not an option* was basically the Chase family motto, and Brandon had internalized it. Robert had always been the heir apparent, so Brandon had made a decision when he was a teenager that he'd go off on his own. Brandon and Kayla had started as Realtors and built up enough money in commission to fund their first house flip, so Brandon had never relied on family money. And Brandon had always reasoned that if he was earning money on his own, then he was not beholden to his family.

Except he always had been.

He'd never been able to get out from under his family's shadow. John Chase was not a household name outside of New York and people who studied real estate, so Brandon could be Brandon on TV, not John

Chase's son. But John Chase was always around him, in his ear, on his shoulders.

Just as John Chase loomed over both of his brothers.

Robert internalized the family motto and used it to keep the business going. Recently, he'd expanded to invest in residential properties in Brooklyn. He worked long hours and didn't see his kids much.

Luke worked for Robert sometimes. He periodically left to get other jobs, but then he'd get fired and come back. And he dealt with the family motto by drinking to forget it.

And Brandon had tried to get out, but he'd never been able to escape.

His brothers were his blood relations, but they weren't close. He still considered Kayla family, but they hadn't had a true marriage. And he'd grown up in this ridiculous hotel suite. He'd never had a family. He'd never had a *home*. And he'd spent his whole damn life finding and making homes for other people.

He ate a bite of potato and rubbed his forehead.

"Now that you're based in Brooklyn," said Robert, "I've got some vacancies in the new building on Schermerhorn. I'd give you a good family discount."

The last thing Brandon wanted was to be beholden to Robert. "No, I'm good. I like the place I've got now."

"You're *renting*," said Robert, as if that was something only the plebes did.

"For now. I'm not quite ready to buy a place yet. Let's see if the show is successful first."

"You don't think it will fail, do you?"

Brandon sighed. How had he never quite seen this before? His family exhausted him now. "No. It's going well so far. There are just a lot of things I can't predict. Ratings, whether the show gets a second season, whether something goes horribly on a house.... I think it'll be fine, but I don't want to count my chickens yet."

"Your name is on this project. The Chase name is on this project."

And now Brandon was really done. "Did you ask me to dinner just to make sure I wouldn't embarrass you?"

"No, of course not."

"Because it's actually *not* the Chase name. It's the Brandon Chase name. Do you think housewives in Iowa know who John Chase was? Do you really think your next deal hinges on whether or not *I* lose money renovating a mansion in a neighborhood in Brooklyn I'm guessing you've never set foot in? Do you think the fact that I'm dating a man right now will have any effect on your business? Dad didn't approve of my being gay, but I thought both of you were better than that."

"You were married," said Robert.

"I was. And I love Kayla. But being married to her didn't cure me. The secret's safe for now, but it's time for you to prepare yourselves for the possibility that one of these days, I'm going to quit TV and live my life." Brandon stood. "I have spent my entire life trying to live up to John Chase's expectations. And now here I am, thirty-five years old, lonely, and tired. I've never been in a real relationship because I've been too busy building a public image acceptable to those housewives in Iowa. And John Chase is dead. What have I been living this shell of a life for? I'm done."

Luke stood and followed Brandon around the table. "Brandon, come on. Finish dinner."

"I'm not hungry."

Robert remained at the table, staring at his plate.

Brandon let out a breath. "Maybe you never noticed. John Chase might have been a successful man, but he was not a good man, and all three of us are miserable as a result. Maybe you guys want to spend the rest of your lives trying to please a ghost, but I'm completely, totally, 100 percent done. Call me when you can have a conversation with me without talking to me as if I'm a leper."

Brandon stormed out of the suite without waiting for a response. As he rode the elevator, he reflected that this was not the most mature thing he'd ever done, but it felt good at the same time. Sure, it would probably be a while before either of his brothers contacted him, but he was okay with that.

He'd only ever lived for other people. It was time to live for himself. Past time. He wasn't entirely sure how he was going to do that, especially not with the show, but he had to find a way. A life and a home and a real love story—that was what he wanted. And he would not become like Robert or Luke, both shadows of men now, in different ways. No matter what their last name was.

Chapter Sixteen

TRAVIS HAD taken the B35 bus across town—taking cabs all over Brooklyn was an expense he didn't need—and so he was dismayed to see it raining before he even got to the house. He hopped off the bus near Argyle Road and dropped into a dollar store to grab a cheap umbrella.

So by the time he got to the house, he was damp, disgruntled, and late.

Ismael was standing in the foyer looking grim when Travis arrived.

"What is it?"

Ismael frowned. "We have an issue."

"Uh-huh."

Travis was irritated that Ismael was dragging this out, but then he realized Ismael was stalling to wait for the camera to get closer. Travis made himself look at Ismael and not the camera, and waited expectantly.

"So you know how it hasn't really rained at all since we started construction here?"

Travis nodded, sensing what Ismael was about to say. It really hadn't rained, at least not with any force. There'd been a few drizzly days, but no real storms. "There's water in the house."

"You better come with me."

Travis followed Ismael up to the master bedroom, where indeed there was so much rain that the new paint on the ceiling was bubbling. Travis almost dropped an F-bomb, but conscious of the camera, he said, "Oh crap."

"Do you want to see for yourself?"

"Yeah."

Travis followed Ismael over to the closet. The ladder that led to the attic had already been pulled down, and Ismael had left a couple of flashlights on, so Travis could see reasonably well. He didn't even need to go all the way into the attic to realize the issue. The roof had completely given way above the master bedroom, and water was starting to pool on the floor, where it was leaking right through the ceiling.

Travis climbed back down the ladder. "Is this the only room affected?"

"Yes, but you can see how much water damage there is to the attic ceiling. The documentation we had said the roof had been patched a couple of years ago, so we thought the water damage was old. Turns out…." Ismael gestured toward the attic.

Well, fuck. "*Was* the roof patched?"

Ismael rocked on his heels. "It was. Patches didn't hold."

"So we need a whole new roof."

"We need a whole new roof."

Well, that would certainly thrill Brandon.

"Cut," said Erik. "Brandon's downstairs. Let's tell him." There was nervous glee in his voice.

Travis rolled his eyes, but rather than making everyone traipse up and down the stairs again, he called out, "Brandon!"

"Two minutes!" Brandon hollered back.

"Can we get some tarps or drop cloths or something up here to stop *more* damage?" Travis asked.

"Not until Brandon sees it," said Erik.

"I've got a tarp downstairs," said Ismael, far more practical than the director. "I'll go grab it. I think there are some empty buckets down there too."

As if he had an internal timer, Brandon appeared in the master bedroom doorway exactly two minutes later, just as Ismael arrived back carrying a couple of empty buckets and a big blue tarp folded up and tucked under his arm.

Brandon waited for Erik to cue the camera again before he said, "What's up?"

"Fun story," said Travis. "The roof is leaking." He pointed to the bubbling paint on the ceiling.

Brandon went pale. He put a hand over his mouth and then moved it away slowly. "What does this mean?"

"The roof is old. When we did the initial inspection, we saw that the roof had been patched, so we thought the water damage in the attic was old. We were just going to repair it. But the patches aren't getting the job done anymore. We need a new roof."

"You can't just patch it again?"

"I mean, you *could*," said Ismael. "But this roof is so patchy that you're better off just replacing it. That's better for the buyer anyway, isn't it? You can warrantee a roof for ten years."

"What'll it cost?" Brandon asked.

Travis assumed Brandon had worked on enough houses to know exactly what roofs cost, but he played along and said, "House this size? Eight thousand, probably. Maybe eighty-five hundred."

Brandon frowned. "I mean, we have to do it." He looked up at the bubbling paint on the ceiling. "Can we put some buckets in the attic or something to keep this from getting worse?"

"On it!" said Ismael, moving toward the ladder.

Brandon stood in the middle of the room with his hands on his hips. "Can we not tell the difference between new and old water damage?"

Ismael was up in the attic, and there were a few other guys standing around looking a little terrified, so Travis supposed it was his role to take this one. "Not really. Water damage is water damage. Good thing it rained or we wouldn't have found this issue."

Brandon sighed. "But it seems like such a big issue. How did we not find this in our inspection? A roof leak that's this bad?" He pointed to the ceiling. "We should have seen that."

Travis did feel bad that they'd missed the leak. As Ismael's grunts came through the ceiling as he positioned the tarp and the buckets, Travis wondered how they could have failed to notice it. They'd hired an inspector to take a look at the house, and he'd missed the roof. Travis had taken a look when he was putting together the initial cost of renovation, and he'd missed it. Ismael had missed it too. The attic had been dry when they'd done the inspection—there had been evidence of past roof repairs, but everyone had assumed the water stains in the attic were old. It was common for homeowners to fix leaks and not repair the damage the leak had caused; Travis saw that kind of thing all the time, especially in cases like this, where the attic was unfinished. If no one went up there, what did a little water damage matter?

"I'm sorry," Travis said. "It's also possible that this damage is cumulative, or that the sheer amount of rain today made the leak worse than it had been. Hell, we've had plenty of light rain days since construction started and there was no indication that there was a leak, so it could have been that the patches were holding until met with a real test. Or this is a new leak. I haven't looked at it close enough to determine. But this house was abandoned for a while before you bought it, right? I'm guessing the roof is no longer under warrantee. Ismael's right, it's a good idea to replace it anyway."

"At great expense. When we're already way over budget."

Travis shrugged. "You can't *not* fix it."

Travis was starting to get to know Brandon well enough that he could see the anger contained under Brandon's stiff facade. That anger was justified. Even if Brandon had all the money in the world, the way this house was racking up expenses would be stressful for anyone.

"Everything's ordered," Brandon said. "We can't make any more cuts or compromises."

Meaning: Brandon had thought he was done spending money. There were no more compromises to design he could implement. Travis knew there was a line item in the budget for staging, that they'd hire a company to make the interior look good while they tried to sell it. But aside from a few things here or there, everything had been paid for. They'd saved some money where they could, but they were still quite a bit over budget.

Brandon was shaking his head while he stared at the ceiling. "I knew this was a risk."

"It'll pay off," Travis said. "You know as well as I do that houses in this neighborhood are selling for upwards of two to three million dollars."

Brandon sighed. "My profit margin keeps shrinking. But, fine. New roof."

Travis nodded.

"I can't believe this," Brandon said. "What else is going to happen?"

"No guarantees. But this has got to be the last thing on the interior."

Brandon turned to Travis sharply. "Does that mean things could still go wrong on the exterior?"

"No, I don't really think so." The day team had already power-washed the house, patched the siding, and demolished the busted-up front walkway. They still had to paint and put in a new walkway, but that had all been budgeted for. "I can't make any promises, of course, but the siding work is done. Everything else that has to happen to the exterior is cosmetic. We can paint the front door instead of replacing it, which will save you some money. And we can do a less expensive treatment on the walkway since we haven't bought the pavers we picked out yet."

"Is that what you think we should do?"

Travis didn't want the power of decision here. "It's your house."

"We had a minimal budget for landscaping because I figured we could spruce up those flower beds out front and put down some grass seed on the dry patches and call it a day. I didn't budget for sod, though. Can we… can we assess the outside? Make sure there's nothing else that could go wrong? Because we haven't put down grass seed yet, and we haven't painted the exterior, and this house is scheduled to go on the market in two weeks, but there's still so much to do…."

"We can go back to the carpeting plan for the second floor, which would save a lot of money over doing hardwood everywhere." Travis wanted to talk Brandon off the ledge before he really freaked out on camera. There were still ways to mitigate the cost of the roof.

"No, I still want to do the hardwood."

"Brandon, come on. If you're going to freak out about the budget, you have to be willing to make compromises. We can make up most of the cost of the roof by doing carpet, painting the front door, and using cheaper pavers out front."

"I have to think about this. I don't really want to compromise on materials or design at this point. There's already so much we've compromised."

"I'm just saying, if you're freaking out about the budget, there are still some changes we can make. But it's your house."

"It's my house," Brandon snapped.

"My opinion doesn't matter," Travis said. "I'm just here to put your plans into action."

Brandon grimaced. "Fine. Let me make this decision. Go ahead and contact roofers, get some bids in. I'll figure out what to do with the rest of the house. We can't put flooring in here until the leak is resolved anyway."

"Right."

Brandon stormed out of the room.

"This is good stuff," said Erik.

Once the cameras were off, Travis rolled his eyes. He wondered if he should go after Brandon or let him stew. Probably the latter. He needed to calm down before Travis pushed him any further. Travis took a deep breath. "Well, guess we gotta get to work fixing all this," he said to no one in particular.

BRANDON'S ANGER didn't dissipate much over the course of the day. Part of the issue was that he had nowhere to direct it. He couldn't be mad at Travis per se, since it wasn't Travis's fault the roof had a hole, although he was still mad no one caught it. He was a little irritated Travis had tried to reconcile the budget, but of course, that was his job.

Actually, what really stuck in his craw was that he'd been fantasizing about him and Travis living here together, and now he had to face a dilemma: do what was right for the project, which meant adhering to the budget to maximize profit, or do what was right for himself, which was making this house everything he imagined it could be. And he didn't know what would be best.

If he bought the house, did he want to live here without Travis? Because he wasn't at all sure Travis would say yes if Brandon asked him to move in. Brandon wasn't even sure they were ready for a step like that. He liked the image of them living here, but they'd only been seeing each other a few weeks, and in secret at that. And if they were both paranoid about getting caught, surely moving into the first house they renovated together would tip people off that something was going on between them. This idea of moving into this house was such a ridiculous fantasy, Brandon was mad at himself for getting emotionally invested in it.

Brandon was taking out his anger by banging floorboards into place on the first floor. There was something satisfying about the bounce of a rubber mallet off the edge of the board when it slid into place.

Travis walked into the room. "If you bang on those any harder you'll chip the sides."

Brandon sighed and stood up. "Did you need something?"

Travis held up his hands. "No. I was just coming in to tell you that the camera crew wrapped for the day. I guess Erik got all the footage of you whacking at flooring that he wanted."

He'd gotten plenty of footage of Brandon and Travis bickering all day too. Brandon was fretting about his dilemma so much that he was taking it out on everyone, and Travis most of all.

Couldn't he see how great they'd be together? Couldn't he see what potential this house had? No, of course not, because Brandon had never brought it up and they were having their romance in secret. And all of that was on Brandon.

So maybe the person Brandon was most angry at was himself.

He wanted to throw his rubber mallet at the newly painted wall, but he placed it on the floor instead.

The day crew was working on the bathrooms upstairs. All of the flooring and tiles, except for the backordered kitchen backsplash tiles, had been delivered the day before. Brandon had volunteered to do these floors because he thought getting his hands on a project would help him feel better, but being alone in the room had left him mulling over his thoughts.

Travis lingered.

"Is there more?"

"I'm debating about whether to apologize."

"For what?"

"Well, that's just it. My instinct is to apologize for pissing you off earlier, but I don't think I really did anything wrong. We told you about the roof leak as soon as we discovered it, but it was out of our control."

"I still don't understand why no one noticed it. You, Ismael, and the inspector we hired all agreed that the roof was sound."

"We were wrong. My working theory is that what we saw today is a new leak through a roof that was already compromised because it's old. We thought replacing the roof was one of those cans we could kick down the road in order to keep the budget intact, but we were wrong about that. It happens."

Brandon nodded because Travis was right, but that didn't soothe him at all. "What the hell am I supposed to do now? We're over budget. Depending on when we can get the roofer here, we may go over schedule. My profit margin is diminishing by the day, and this is starting to look like an increasingly stupid investment. So now I'm left wondering if I should just do the minimum to get the house done and sold, take what I can for it, or to stick with my vision."

"I can't make that decision for you."

"Why can't you?" Brandon snapped. "Sorry. I didn't mean it that way. Just… what would you do if you were in my shoes?"

Travis shook his head. "I don't know."

"Come on. You have opinions about everything."

"It's an absurd amount of money, Brandon. I don't even know how to process it. If money was no object, I'd stick to the original design and fix the roof. But you're worried about profits, so money *is* an issue.

So I'd evaluate which things will affect the value of the house. Most of the compromises I've suggested will save you money without really compromising anything. Well, maybe the floor, but some buyers actually like carpet."

"And if this was your house? Your dream house."

Travis rubbed his head. He looked exhausted. "I wouldn't put in carpet."

Brandon sighed.

"I'm not in your shoes. It's not my money. It has to be your call. I can't be your substitute Kayla."

That remark hit Brandon like a gut punch. "What the hell is that supposed to mean?"

"Okay, first of all, keep your voice down."

Brandon pressed his lips together. Of course. The house was still full of people.

"Second," said Travis, "you told me yourself that you work better when you have someone to bounce ideas off of. I get that, but that's not my role here. I'm not your cohost. I'm just the project manager."

"Come on, Travis. You're not *just* the project manager."

"So in what capacity am I acting now? You asked my opinion, I gave it to you. But am I the project manager or the guy you've been hooking up with?"

"Come on. You know you're more than that." Travis had to have felt how things were between them lately. Maybe they hadn't been together very long, but they had a good thing. Didn't they?

"I also can't be the one you pin everything on. My experience is in fixing houses, not selling them. If I give you a bad opinion, will you resent me? Because you know more about this shit than I do. Or are you just going to get angry and yell at me when you can't make your own decisions?"

"Trav, I…." But Brandon had no idea what to say.

"I'm not *trying* to be difficult. But the lines are getting blurry here. I'm having a hard time sorting out how I'm supposed to behave around you, and if it's different when the cameras are on us or when other people are around. And I'm starting to think it definitely is different in ways I'm not totally comfortable with."

"What are you saying?" Although Brandon already knew. He'd felt the same strain.

"Nothing," said Travis softly, stepping closer to Brandon. "There's no easy answer here. If we keep pretending that nothing happens after hours, we have to compartmentalize better during the day. And I gotta say, that feels a lot like going back in the closet."

"I'm sorry."

"This isn't the place to hash all this out." Travis took a step away. "I just think we need to think some things through."

"Yeah." But Brandon didn't like the sound of that. Did Travis want to break up? Brandon hadn't seen that coming. They'd argued today, but things had felt so good between them lately. Did Travis not understand that Brandon would live his life out in the open, in the light of day, for the first time in his life, if only he could? He wanted that so fucking badly, but given his position, it wasn't an option. Failure was not an option. If anyone found out about their affair, the show would get canceled.

He never should have taken this job. He'd quit tomorrow if it was the only thing he could do to keep Travis.

They stood there staring at each other for a moment.

"I should go check on the bathrooms," Travis said.

Brandon nodded and knelt back on the floor, ready to pound some more boards into place.

Erik walked into the room then. "Crew's gone for the day," he said. "I'm gonna head out too. You guys good? I heard the yelling."

"Yeah," said Brandon. "Difference of opinion."

Travis paused in the kitchen doorway and watched Erik leave. Then he sighed and left the room.

Chapter Seventeen

Brandon wasn't particularly looking forward to the fight with Travis that he knew was coming. Travis had followed Brandon home but had been acting surly all evening. They'd had a dinner of miscellaneous leftovers from Brandon's fridge mostly in silence.

As Travis gathered up the dishes and put them in the sink, Brandon said, "What would you have me do?"

"About?"

"Us, Travis. What should we do about us? Because here's what I know—I like spending time with you. I can see us having a relationship for a long time. I feel things for you I've never felt for anybody. But I don't think keeping things secret is really working. But what alternative do we have? Say we go public? Then my show gets canceled."

"Why do you think the show would get canceled?"

"The Restoration Channel is very heterosexual."

"Is it? Because I've seen episodes of other shows in which there are same-sex couples who are clients. That show with the brothers who make over houses? They renovated a house for a gay couple on an episode I saw just last week."

"Since when do you watch the Restoration Channel?"

Travis shrugged. "I can't sleep sometimes, and they reair all their prime-time shows at weird times of the morning."

"You know that we've spent nearly every night together since we started sleeping together?"

"You sleep really deeply."

Brandon sighed and rubbed his forehead. This wasn't getting them anywhere. "So, what? We go public and brace ourselves for the consequences? I think it will be bad, Travis."

"Maybe you're overestimating their homophobia. That show that got canceled, the one with the gay couple? That was Garrett Harwood's predecessor's decision, wasn't it? Maybe Harwood isn't so close-minded."

Brandon looked at Travis. Was he serious? "Well, is that what you want? To go public? Because I can already see the tabloid headlines."

Travis sat back down in the chair, hard. "You think our relationship would hit the tabloids? Are you really that famous?"

"My divorce was all over them. It's not fun having your dirty laundry aired like that. Even if the truth is not what people think. Some of those reporters are piranhas."

Travis looked startled. This was clearly not an idea that had entered his mind. "Oh God. That would be a scandal, wouldn't it? If we go public, we go *public*."

"Damned if you do, damned if you don't."

"What a goddamn mess." Travis put his face in his hands.

Brandon didn't know what choice, if any, they had. When they'd first started hooking up, it had been fun and sexy, but now Brandon was planning a future for himself and Travis—even if Travis didn't know about that yet—and he didn't want to break up. But they were in a bind, weren't they?

Before he could say anything, his phone rang. Brandon picked it up and looked at the caller ID. "It's Virginia. I better take this."

"Sure."

Brandon answered the phone.

"Hi, Brandon, glad I caught you."

"Hello, Virginia. How are you?"

"I was wondering if I could see you in my office at Restoration HQ first thing in the morning."

Brandon already knew that something was wrong, and his first thought was that somehow word about him and Travis had gotten to Virginia. But how? Ismael? That seemed unlikely; Virginia and Ismael had barely ever spoken to each other.

Or… Erik had left after Travis and Brandon had argued, hadn't he? How long had Erik been listening before he'd walked into the living room earlier that evening?

Shit.

"I can do that," he said. "Can I have a hint about what we need to discuss?"

"I think it's better to talk about it in the office. I know you've got things to film at the house tomorrow. So let's say nine o'clock?"

"All right. I'll see you then."

When Brandon hung up, Travis was looking at him expectantly.

"Virginia wants me to come to the Restoration offices for a meeting tomorrow morning."

"Okay."

"She wouldn't say what it's about. There's an issue. And I think it's that she knows about us."

"How can she… oh no. Erik was probably eavesdropping today."

"That's my best guess." It was like the realization of all of Brandon's nightmares. "Holy shit. If she cancels the show…. I mean, I've invested so much money into this house already, so much time, and what was it all for?"

"Maybe it's about the Jessica Benton house."

Brandon had nearly forgotten about that. He'd met with Jessica the week before, and they'd had a nice talk about her vision for the house she'd just bought. Starting Monday, he and Travis would have to split their time between Jessica's house and the Argyle Road house, and some of the crew would be moving now that the bulk of the work was nearly done. Travis was scheduled to do an inspection and put together an estimate for the renovation with Jessica's input in a few days.

Was it possible that they'd gotten to a place where their relationship just wasn't tenable anymore? Because now Brandon needed the show almost as much as he needed Travis in his life, but both….

"It's probably not a good idea to make any decisions until you hear what Virginia has to say," said Travis.

TRAVIS FELT like that phone call had let him off the hook.

Because what did he really want here?

It was as if he'd been floating for the past few weeks. The time he'd spent with Brandon was great. He enjoyed fighting over house design. He loved chatting over takeout meals. He'd come to Brandon's tonight without even thinking about it much. They did have something real, but Travis was growing frustrated with the secrecy.

The secrecy might have been their best defense mechanism, though.

Travis hadn't thought about the tabloid aspect of it all. In the scheme of things, Brandon was niche famous. Restoration Channel viewers knew Brandon, but did anyone else? Did it matter? Tabloid writers probably knew who Travis was now, so if they got wind of the fact that he was with Brandon—this nice man who used to be married to a woman who broke his heart by cheating on him, and who had found solace in the arms of a man—there would be hell to pay.

He'd thought he could put all of this in different boxes. That he could do his job on set and be with Brandon after hours and it wouldn't matter. But now it mattered. The lines were blurry. Separating the arguments they had about roofs and paint from how he felt about Brandon was getting harder. He cared for Brandon, wanted things to work out, but this was fucking hard.

So what would happen if Virginia did find out? The network had made too much of a financial investment to just cancel the show, at least in Travis's mind. Travis had thought that just being a couple as they worked on these houses would be fun, would make everything easier, but somehow, despite the persistent, pesky presence of cameras like mosquitos on a hot day, he'd pushed the fact that they were about to be on television out of his mind. It hadn't occurred to him that being a couple at the house meant being a couple on the show. And anyone invested in Brandon's divorce would likely have a lot to say about the fact that Brandon was with a man now.

"You're right," Brandon said, scratching his chin. "She might just want to talk about Jessica Benton, although if that was the case, why couldn't she just tell me that over the phone?"

Brandon pushed away from the table and stood up. He paced back and forth across the kitchen. "If they cancel the show, well, we'll finish the house. I'll pay everyone's salaries, and then we'll sell the damn thing and be rid of it."

"That's generous of you."

"I thought I loved this house. But it's only brought me problems." Brandon stopped pacing and leaned against the counter. "That house, the first time I walked it, totally charmed me. And I'll admit, in my crazier moments, I think about buying out the Restoration Channel's share and keeping the house. But fuck… this house. Thousands of dollars in the hole, I might not make that money back, and now it might be for *nothing* because I was thinking with my dick instead of my head."

"Not for nothing, Brandon." Travis stood.

But wait, Brandon was thinking about keeping the house?

Travis pushed that aside. He'd deal with it later. He walked toward Brandon. "Not for nothing. We did have some fun, didn't we? And we met each other. That never would have happened if it hadn't been for the show."

"What are you saying?"

"I know we started off with just a physical thing because we were attracted to each other. I understand, even, that part of why we argued so much in the beginning of the project was because we were both sexually frustrated. But the more time we spend together, the more I kinda like you."

Brandon smiled. "I kinda like you too."

Travis didn't want to break up—that was the bottom line. It would be taking the easy way out. They end things now, go back to just being work colleagues, and Travis got to keep his job. Brandon could go into the meeting with Virginia, tell her there was nothing between him and Travis, and he wouldn't be lying. But was that what Travis wanted?

No. They were too enmeshed. He didn't think it would be possible to just go back to working as though there was nothing between them. And Travis wanted to work with Brandon and be with him. They were good together.

Travis stepped closer to Brandon. "I've never been the best at expressing my feelings."

"You express a lot."

"About tiles and flooring, sure. About anything deeper than that? About what's in my heart? I have a hard time even thinking about that sometimes. But the truth is that you got under my skin. I didn't even think hard about coming home with you tonight because I want to spend as much time with you as possible. And I want for us to be able to have a fucking conversation at the house without feeling paranoid that we're about to be discovered. But shit, I don't need anyone digging into my personal life."

"You were right. Let's not make any decisions until I know what Virginia has to say."

"Brandon, hear what I'm telling you. I don't like doing this, so you may never hear it again."

There was that stupid little half smile on Brandon's face, the expression he made when he knew he had one over on Travis. Travis wanted to kiss that expression off Brandon's face.

Which told him a lot about how he felt.

"We can't just go back to how it was," Travis said. "I am feeling some things for you. I want for us to be together, but… I think this is about to get a whole lot more challenging."

Brandon nodded. "I don't want to think about it."

"Then let's not think about it."

Brandon looked up and met Travis's gaze.

Travis stood. He held out his hand. When Brandon took it, Travis helped him up and led him to the bedroom. They would forget about everything tonight except each other, if Travis had anything to say about it. They'd make love—as gross as Travis felt about that phrase, it was the best description of what he knew was about to happen—and lose themselves in each other. They'd worry about the rest of it when they woke up.

They'd been together long enough that Travis knew Brandon's body. He knew the shape of it, the contours of it, the way Brandon smelled, the noises he made. He got Brandon out of his clothes quickly and wriggled out of his own, until it was just the two of them, naked, on the bed.

Travis licked Brandon's neck, loving the rough texture of day-old beard and the salty taste of Brandon's skin. Then he trailed kisses along Brandon's shoulder to his armpit. Brandon wore some kind of woodsy/minty deodorant, but Travis would have much preferred him to go without. Travis loved the scent of sweaty man, probably some kind of locker room impression from his formative years as a gay teenager at a public high school in Queens, but he loved Brandon's weird affectations too. Brandon wasn't a cologne wearer, but he seemed to like aftershaves and lotions with aggressively masculine scents.

Travis trailed kisses along the center of Brandon's chest, which was like a blank canvas—no scars or tattoos, just a little dusting of hair that was a shade darker than the blondish hair on his head. Brandon's gym-sculpted body was something to behold, strong and masculine, with defined pecs and a six-pack. Travis ran his tongue over the bumps and grooves of Brandon's torso, and Brandon hissed in response. Then he groaned as Travis's body brushed over his hard cock. Travis smiled to himself, satisfied that he was making Brandon *feel*.

Brandon shifted his hips up. "God, suck me."

But Travis enjoyed torturing Brandon too much. He pressed his face into the space between Brandon's cock and the top of his thigh and inhaled. *This* was where Brandon smelled the most like himself. No minty soap or woodsy deodorant here, just sweaty man, and Travis reveled in it. He licked Brandon's skin, then turned his head and darted his tongue out to trace the side of Brandon's cock.

"Oh my God," Brandon grunted. "Stop teasing."

Travis propped himself up with a hand on either side of Brandon's hips. "Did you want something?"

"You bastard."

Travis laughed. Then he dove and swallowed Brandon's cock. Brandon moaned.

There wasn't enough space to do this well on the bed, so Travis knelt at the foot of it and yanked Brandon's body to the edge so his feet dangled on either side of Travis. Then Travis got back to work, worshipping Brandon's cock, touching it reverentially, kissing and licking it as though it would help him find religion.

"That's too good," Brandon said. "Get back up here."

But Travis kept at it until he could sense Brandon was getting very close. He reluctantly leaned away and crawled up on the bed beside Brandon. But before he could settle, Brandon practically jumped at him and took Travis's cock into his mouth.

"Jesus," said Travis.

"I'll make you see Jesus."

Travis wanted to laugh, but his body wouldn't form anything but a grunt as his cock was enveloped in the wet heat of Brandon's mouth. Brandon rubbed Travis's balls with the heel of his hand and started probing behind them with his fingers. Travis thrust forward, loving this attention, wanting more of it.

But he wanted Brandon too, so he shifted his weight so that Brandon still had access to the goods but Travis could continue to touch and taste Brandon's cock. This 69 position was suddenly the best of everything. Travis inhaled Brandon's sweaty scent and licked and stroked that big cock, loving the feel and taste of it, while Brandon made him feel like his whole body was pulsing. It was overwhelming, it was amazing, and it was about to get messy.

Brandon was really fucking good at sucking cock for a guy who had been in the closet until recently. Good Lord.

Travis thrust his hips, trying to encourage Brandon to speed up, and Travis rubbed Brandon harder, stroking that big cock with gusto. Brandon mumbled some blasphemies and started stroking Travis hard and a bit roughly, exactly the way Travis liked it.

"I'm gonna come on your face," Travis threatened, because suddenly he was *right there*.

"I'll come on yours first," Brandon said breathlessly.

Brandon won the race, coming with a long moan and pumping into Travis's mouth. Travis took it all, letting the metallic taste sit on his tongue before swallowing. But he could barely do that, because his body was falling apart, every bit of pleasure pooling near his cock, and then suddenly Brandon's mouth covered him again and he was coming.

He came back to himself slowly and realized he was staring at Brandon's hairy thighs. Laughing softly, Travis shifted around again so that he could lay his head on a pillow.

"I feel sometimes," Brandon said, "that sex with you is like the sex I should have been having in my twenties. It's intense, sometimes it's fast, and I always go off like a rocket."

"I've got skills."

Brandon smiled and ran a hand down Travis's chest. "You do." Brandon closed his eyes for a long moment. He looked content and satisfied. When he opened his eyes again, he met Travis's gaze. "I forgot all about drywall and paint for a minute there."

"When I can get it up again, I'll have to fuck you silly. It's not enough for you to forget drywall—I want you to forget your name."

Brandon laughed. "I bet you could do it." He sighed. "I have to pee, but my body is made of Jell-O."

Travis rolled onto his side and put an arm around Brandon. "Don't get up just yet." He kissed Brandon softly, a deep sleepiness and contentment starting to settle into his body. "Maybe we can get up tomorrow and everything will be the same."

"I don't think we'll be that lucky, but I'm willing to go along with it for now.

"Good." Travis yawned. He lifted his arm. "You can get up now. I'm gonna go to sleep."

"Is that how it is?"

"You may feel like you're in your twenties when we're having sex, but I'm definitely in my thirties, and I need some recovery time. I might as well get some shut-eye while my body recharges. That way, when we both wake up at three because we're worried about tomorrow, I can roll you over and—"

"I get it." Brandon got out of bed, laughing.

Chapter Eighteen

BRANDON'S HEART was in his throat. It took everything he had in him not to vomit on the elevator up to the Restoration Channel offices.

That morning, Travis had kissed him and told him everything would work out, but that was clearly a lie. And then Travis had gone off to work on the house and here Brandon was, losing his shit in an elevator.

The receptionist hopped out of her chair when Brandon walked up to the front desk. "Ms. Frank is expecting you, Brandon," she said. "I can call you Brandon, right? You just seem so down-to-earth on TV."

"Yeah, that's fine. Which office is Virginia's again?"

"I'm so excited about the new show. And I got to meet Jessica Benton the other day. She's *gorgeous*. You must be stoked to be working with her."

"I am." God, Brandon was nauseous. "Can I see Virginia now?"

"Oh, sure. I'll take you back."

Brandon followed the receptionist to Virginia's office. He knew it was melodramatic, but it felt like he was dead man walking.

Virginia was sitting at her desk when Brandon appeared in the doorway. She smiled brightly, which might or might not have been a good sign.

"Thanks, Hayley," she said. "Brandon, come in and close the door."

Shit.

The receptionist disappeared back down the hall, so Brandon shut the door and sat in one of the guest chairs.

"So, I received some news last night that was a bit surprising," Virginia said.

"Uh-huh."

"You all right, Brandon? You look like you're about to throw up."

"I've been better." Brandon grabbed a tissue from the box on Virginia's desk and wiped the sweat off his forehead. "It's bad news, isn't it?"

"No, I don't think so. I needed a little time to process it, but I have a great idea for how we should deal with it now."

"Okay." Brandon was dying. Why was she stalling?

"Let me cut to the chase. Erik called me last night to say he'd overheard a conversation between you and Travis that seemed to, er, strongly indicate that the two of you are… involved."

So they had been discovered. Brandon leaned forward and rested his head in his hands.

"I take it from your reaction that it's true. You and Travis are… doing something… together."

"Virginia, I'm so sorry. I—"

"Don't apologize. There's no law against it. Technically, Travis works for me, not for you." Virginia grabbed a notepad from the edge of her desk. "Tell me what's going on."

"I—" Brandon couldn't figure out what to say. Perhaps this was not the worst it could be. Virginia had a plan to deal with this, which implied the show wasn't canceled.

"You're not in trouble, I should state."

"I… I don't even know how to explain it. Travis is gay. Did you know that?"

"No, but I had a hunch. It's illegal for me to ask him, just as it's illegal for me to ask you. But two people who work for me having an affair with each other has the potential to affect the show I produce."

Brandon didn't know how much to confess. "I know. We weren't going to let it affect the show—not when we hadn't defined what was going on with us. You want to know what happened, honestly? Maybe two weeks into filming, we realized we were attracted to each other and we acted on it. Is it a capital-R relationship? I don't know. We've been discussing it but haven't decided anything for sure. We have feelings for each other. That's all I know. You satisfied now?"

Virginia grinned giddily, which was not the reaction Brandon expected.

"I will admit that having two people who work on the same show entangled romantically is not ideal if they did not have a previous relationship, because if you break up, that's bad news for my show. But if you *are* together, and it's working out, that's a different situation. We *love* couples, as you know."

"Are you kidding me right now?"

"Not at all."

Brandon couldn't make sense of this. "But I thought… that is, you don't have any gay hosts on any of your shows. Restoration Channel has always been pretty aggressively heterosexual. You canceled *Country Creatives* because the hosts were gay."

"*I* didn't cancel the show. My old boss did. Garrett Harwood is trying to change that. We've been testing out the audience by featuring gay couples on *Home Finders*. It hasn't affected ratings at all. I didn't think it would, not with our largely female demographic. Garrett and I have actually been in talks with this openly gay interior designer for a new show. He works with Oprah and has a line of home decorations for one of the big box stores. Nolan Hamlin. You know him?"

"Name is familiar."

"Well, cone of silence anyway, because that's not a done deal yet. He still hasn't signed the contract. But in the meantime, we have you."

"You don't… I mean, that's not really…."

"If Kayla hadn't so publicly cheated on you, I'd have a new theory about why your marriage ended."

Brandon didn't want to gossip. And although some of the tension had left his shoulders, his stomach still churned. He wanted to run out of here as fast as he could. "You said you had a plan for how to deal with this?"

"Oh! Yes. So, we've done some market research. We know our audience is largely female. We also know that our largely female audience is totally on board with having more gay men on the Restoration Channel. They like the idea of a gay man being their shopping buddy, even if it's for home goods."

Brandon bristled. "I'm a little offended by that."

"I'm not endorsing the opinion, just explaining what our research shows. I think there's also a bit of a stereotype about anyone involved in something like design. Even a few of our hosts who are most assuredly straight are assumed to be gay. The designer on *Down to the Studs*?"

"He's straight? Really?" Brandon had always thought that guy was deep in the closet.

"Banging his female assistant."

Brandon shook his head. "So what are you saying? That Travis and I should go public?"

"Here was my thought. You keep saying that you feel like you need a cohost, right? Well, what if Travis was your cohost? We could show you together the same way we would any other couple. We'd edit the pilot to show more of the two of you talking, or we could bring him in more gradually, eventually introducing him as your romantic partner as well as your partner in house flipping."

This… was not what Brandon had expected. Part of him loved the idea. But on the other hand…. "I'm not sure Travis would be on board for that. I'll have to talk to him."

"This could work out really well for all of us. I could sense the chemistry between the two of you immediately. I'm not really that surprised things turned out this way. And I think a show that features a gay couple could be something special."

"It also means more tabloid attention. If Travis and I go public with our relationship, which I'm not even sure we want to do at this point, all those trashy magazines that ran stories about me and Kayla will be *all over* this."

"All publicity is good publicity."

Brandon sighed and rubbed his head. "Come on, Virginia. This is my life. It's not *just* the TV show."

Virginia schooled her features. "I know that."

"Let me talk this over with Travis. Who else knows?"

"Erik, who I swore to secrecy, and me. That's it. I haven't even told Garrett."

"Okay." Lord, what a mess. Brandon couldn't predict Travis's reaction. Would Travis want to cohost? Unlikely. He seemed barely able to stand being on camera. "Is there any way we can go back to pretending you don't know about this?"

"Do you not want Travis to be your cohost?"

Well. Brandon did, actually. The two of them, as a couple, hosting a show and making over old houses in Brooklyn? That sounded pretty perfect, actually. But…. "I'm not the only variable in this equation. A lot depends on what Travis thinks. I'm surprised you didn't call us both down here."

Virginia shrugged. "You're the *star*."

It was his show, in other words. Something about her tone told Brandon that she assumed Travis would go along with it because Travis had to be into Brandon because he was famous. Of course, that was gross and, Brandon knew, not true.

"Let me talk to Travis, all right? I'll call you after we've had a chance to talk it over."

"Okay. Before we meet at Jessica Benton's place on Monday, all right? I want to make decisions before we start filming there. We can loop in Garrett for the final discussion."

"I can do that."

Because truth be told, Travis would either be on board or he'd tell Brandon to fuck off. And Travis breaking up with Brandon was not outside of the realm of possibility if all of this was not what he wanted. Travis didn't like bullshit and wouldn't put up with things that didn't make him happy. It was something that Brandon really admired about him.

Brandon left the Restoration offices twenty minutes later, wondering how the hell he'd gotten into this mess.

TRAVIS FOUND it suspicious that Brandon had been at the house for nearly five hours and Travis had only seen him in passing.

Clearly the show hadn't been canceled, but that might have been the only good news to come from Brandon's meeting with Virginia.

Erik wrapped a little early. On his way out, he walked through the kitchen, where Travis and Mike were screwing in the last of the upper cabinets. Erik said, "I'm gonna walk over to the Benton house and scope out the best places to put the cameras. I got some good footage of the cabinets going in here today already."

"Counters go in tomorrow," Mike said. "Hopefully before four o'clock, because my daughter has a recital and I promised I'd be there."

Right. People who weren't Travis had a life outside this house. Travis cleared his throat. "Stone's already cut, so I don't see that being a problem."

"Cool," said Erik. "I want film of the counters going in, so I'll be here in the morning. Later, guys."

Once everyone left the room, Travis touched a cabinet door. They were in the homestretch on this project, and Travis couldn't help but feel preemptively nostalgic. It seemed odd to him that a house he'd sunk so much of himself into, one that had so many memories of himself and Brandon embedded in it, would soon be sold to some family who had no idea that anything had ever happened here. It would just be a house.

A nice house. A clean slate in which to build something. It was sad, in a way, to be losing something that Travis had come to feel a great deal of fondness for, although he understood that this was how the industry worked. He just normally didn't feel this invested in his projects.

He opened a cabinet door, closed it, and tried to shake it off.

About five minutes after Travis heard the front door shut, Brandon finally appeared. At the same moment, Mike climbed down off the ladder. "And that's it for the cabinets."

"Looks good," said Brandon. "Did the backsplash tiles get delivered yet?"

"No," said Travis. "I called the store. They told me Monday."

"Okay. I want to put in the tile. That's a pretty easy thing Erik can film me doing."

"Sure."

Mike put his drill on a nearby sawhorse. "Is that it for today? I think Sandy's overseeing the last of the bathroom stuff, but we can't put in sinks or anything until the counters are done."

"Yeah, go home." Travis glanced at his watch. "Day crew's probably already gone."

"Ismael left a half hour ago," said Brandon.

"Cool," said Mike. "I'll go collect Sandy, then we'll see you boys tomorrow."

"Good night, Mike," said Travis.

When Mike left the room, Brandon said, "I guess we need to talk."

"I guess so."

Travis waited, expecting Brandon to say something, but he didn't speak until the front door opened and closed again, signaling that they were alone.

Brandon let out a long sigh. "I'll cut to the chase. Virginia knows. Erik overheard us talking last night and reported it to her."

Well, fuck. "Are we in trouble?"

"No. In fact, Virginia seemed almost giddy about it. Apparently they've already done all this market research that indicates that Restoration Channel's female viewership is generally okay with gay hosts, so management is actually looking for more. Virginia is already in talks with some openly gay Oprah-approved interior designer to host a new show." Brandon leaned against one of the newly installed cabinets.

"So… what. Does she want you to come out on the show?"

"Actually, her suggestion was for us to be cohosts. To recut the footage we have so far to make it look like the two of us bounce ideas off each other a lot."

Travis balked. "Are you kidding?"

"Serious as the roof leak."

"I can't be your cohost." Travis was mostly attracted to TV for the professional opportunity and the paycheck. He didn't aspire to fame. He definitely never wanted to see his own face on the cover of a tabloid.

"It's not a terrible idea. You and I team up and renovate houses. Not much changes except that you're on camera more."

Travis tried to imagine what that would look like. He couldn't quite picture it. "Brandon. I'm a general contractor. I never finished college. I've spent my entire adult life building things and repairing things and painting and laying flooring. I'm not charming like you are. I barely have any business being on television. How on earth can I be your cohost?"

"First of all, you have your own particular brand of charm. Second, how is this much different than what we're already doing? Well, you'd have to do some talking heads to the camera."

"What?"

"You know. Solo interviews where you address the camera directly. We have a spot to film those in the backyard. Otherwise, most of your job is just to manage the crew and argue with me about paint colors. And that is basically what's happening now."

"I don't know. I'm not sure I'm comfortable with that." Travis could barely tolerate the cameras in his peripheral vision as it was. He only managed by pretending the cameras weren't there. Could he address a camera directly and speak without sounding like an idiot? He wasn't so sure. "In the meantime, what happens? We go public as a couple? Even though we've only been dating for five minutes?"

"A month."

"A whole month. Jesus." This was insane. "Isn't that a lot of pressure on us? When we were just feeling each other out, it was fine. I like you, I enjoy being with you, but… I mean, hosting a show together, going public with our relationship? I haven't even told my mother I'm dating you, but you want me to tell the whole world?"

"I know it's a big ask."

"A big ask? This is huge! It's… I don't know, Brandon. It's too soon. I don't think we're ready for that. We're barely a couple. You want us to suddenly not only make a bigger commitment but do it on national television? I just don't know."

"I have to give Virginia an answer by Monday. If you say yes, she wants to change how we approach filming the show. Probably to give you more screen time."

God. This was too much. "That's the other thing. Is our relationship now subject to contract negotiations and filming schedules? I… I can't do this."

All of it was making Travis panic. He couldn't wrap his head around what Brandon was telling him.

"You don't want to at least go public on set? You said you don't want to be in the closet. Now we know you don't have to be. Your job and the show aren't in danger."

"Being able to be open with you and not worry all the time that we're about to be discovered would be nice, but if the cost is making our relationship fodder for gossip, I don't know if I'm okay with that."

"Travis, I—"

Travis held up his hand. "No, stop. I know where you're at with this. I can tell from the tone in your voice. I need some time to think now."

"Okay. You want to get dinner, or—"

"No. I'm going to go home. Don't follow me. I think I need some space to try to make this decision, to figure out how I really feel about all this."

Brandon's brow wrinkled and he opened and closed his mouth a few times, probably to lodge a protest, but then he pressed his lips together and nodded. "All right."

"I'm sorry, but… this is a big deal to me. This really changes everything between us. I need to think it through." There was a chasm of difference between two guys who were transitioning from casually seeing each other to maybe something more serious and a committed relationship displayed on TV for all the world to see. Wasn't that the whole gimmick with *Dream Home*? Brandon and Kayla had playacted at being a married couple for the cameras, and they'd provided lots of cutesy relationship moments for the show. Travis knew; he'd spent a few of the nights he and Brandon spent apart watching old episodes. Heck, the opening credits were a montage of cute photos of them as a couple, newlyweds in business together. The whole point of coming out to the crew would be to allow him and Brandon to have something real, but would being a cohost just pull Travis into Brandon's web of lies and subterfuge?

And was Brandon entertaining this idea because it was good for Brandon and Travis the couple, or because it was good for the show?

Brandon pushed off the cabinet and walked toward Travis. "I understand. But I'll miss you tonight."

"I'll miss you too."

Brandon kissed Travis. Perhaps it was a reminder that things between them were good. Travis believed Brandon cared about him. Warmth spread across Travis's chest, and his heart fluttered. Well, the unfortunate fact of things here was that Travis was already at least halfway in love with Brandon. That was why this decision was so agonizing. He couldn't just walk away. He didn't want to. Show be damned; Travis knew that if they couldn't find a way to make this work, that was the end of him and Brandon, and that was not what he wanted.

But could he stomach the alternatives?

He didn't know.

With one last lingering press of his lips against Brandon's, Travis sighed and stepped away. "Sleep well tonight. I'll see you in the morning." He summoned some cheer to pump his fist. "Gotta put in those counters."

"Yeah. Good night, Travis."

Travis nodded and left the house before he succumbed to his instinct to stay.

CHAPTER NINETEEN

BRANDON SLEPT horribly, but after the third cup of coffee, he was ready to face the day. He'd spent half the night imagining what it would be like to have Travis at his side just like the hetero couples on every other Restoration show. Maybe they'd start each episode talking to the camera about the house they'd chosen to work on, with their arms around each other. Or would they assess new houses together, Travis faithfully tallying up the expenses as they discovered each new issue with the cameras following them? They'd go shopping together, finding ways to compromise on their tastes to finish the houses in the ways they liked. It would be perfect.

Although Travis did have a point. They'd barely started dating. Putting the kind of pressure a whole television show's production team would exert on them to be happy would be almost as bad as the stress they'd felt keeping their relationship a secret.

If Travis said no, he'd be in his right, and Brandon would understand. But Brandon still hoped he'd say yes. They could figure out how to make it work. They could move into the Argyle Road house together. But if he said no, well, Brandon would just have to tell Virginia that. Maybe there could be a compromise, where Brandon and Travis could be a couple around the crew but off-camera.

Well, the hypothetical happy future was all in Brandon's dreams. The reality was more stark. Or, rather, reality was six strong men carrying a large slab of quartz into the kitchen and making Brandon doubt his design—it should have been marble, even if that would have been quite a bit more expensive—and laying it where the counter should go. Three of those men worked together to push the slab into place.

"Gorgeous," said Mike. "I like this quartz. I've never seen it quite this color before."

"Found it in this place in Red Hook," said Brandon. "I'll give you their info later."

"Cool. I never think to look in Brooklyn. I usually source material from Jersey. Less sales tax." Mike winked.

"Oh. Good to know."

"You fellas gonna yak all morning?" said Travis, his Queens accent a little more prominent than usual, probably because he was irritated. "We've still got the bathrooms to do."

"On it," said Mike, heading back out into the yard, where all the stone had been cut and was sitting, waiting to be carried inside and installed.

Brandon wanted to grab Travis and ask if he'd made any decisions, but he was conscious of the cameras, so he kept his hands to himself and followed the crew outside.

They spent the day finishing the counters and installing sinks and double-checking the plumbing. Ismael finished laying the tile on the floor in the kitchen and dining room. Brandon put up the wallpaper on the feature wall in the living room. At the end of the day, Brandon, Travis, Ismael, and Erik met in the living room.

"So," Travis said, his clipboard out. "The last remaining tasks are the kitchen backsplash, installing the kitchen appliances—those are supposed to be delivered on Monday when Brandon and I are at the other house, just a heads-up—finishing the tile in the master bathroom, installing the flooring on the second floor—Brandon still has to make a decision about that—and then the staircase and the fireplace. The night crew is working on those last two tonight." Travis pointed to the fireplace. "We picked out some nice slate tiles to go from floor to ceiling, and a reclaimed wood mantel that has gone missing."

"It's in the shed out back," said Ismael. "I'll grab it and bring it in before I go home."

"Cool. Anyone know of anything I left off the list?"

"Day crew is all exterior tomorrow," said Ismael. "It's supposed to be sunny, so I figured we'd paint. And the roofers are supposed to be here around eleven."

"Okay. Brandon, any thoughts on the floor upstairs?"

"Hardwood," Brandon said. He'd decided that if this was going to be his house, he'd want hardwood upstairs, not carpet.

"Fine. We have enough here? Do we need to order more?"

"There should be enough. I bought it before I knew about the roof. The money's already spent." Brandon rubbed his forehead, trying not to think about all the money he'd spent. "I'll come by Monday to do the backsplash tile and help install the appliances. We're supposed to meet with Jessica Benton, but I think I can be more useful over here while Travis does the inspection of the other property."

Travis nodded. "Fine. Okay. Anything else?" When no one said anything, Travis dropped his pen into an empty pocket of his tool belt. "Well, we're in the homestretch. See you all tomorrow."

Erik had already packed up for the day, so he waved and left. Ismael walked outside to grab his own stuff. Brandon turned to Travis, who was writing something on his clipboard. "You have enough time to think?"

"No." Travis kept writing without looking up. "And if you force me to decide right now, I don't think you would like my answer."

"Can we talk about it?"

Finally Travis stopped what he was doing and looked at Brandon. "I guess."

"My place, or…."

"Yeah. Let me just get my stuff."

TRAVIS HADN'T slept the night before. It turned out that when one spent nearly every night for a month with a man as large as Brandon Chase, one's bed actually felt absurdly empty without him in it.

And now here he was, eating pad thai at Brandon's kitchen island, trying to formulate a response to the question Brandon hadn't yet asked.

"I don't know what your experience has been," Brandon said, "and I don't have a ton of relationship experience, but I've found that in the past, I've kept quiet about some things as kind of a self-defense measure. You never know what the other person is thinking, you know? You don't want to say 'I love you' if you don't think that it's going to be returned."

Travis jerked his head up.

"To be clear," Brandon said, "I'm not saying that to you, just using it as an example."

The statement still didn't sit well with Travis. "Have you wanted to say it in the past? To other guys, I mean."

"Uh, well. Once. I dated an interior designer when I was in my early twenties. I'm not sure if that was really love, but the thought popped into my head a few times that I should tell him I loved him. But I didn't think he returned the sentiment. It turned out I was right, because he dumped me not long after that. But my point is, you know, in past relationships, I've held back."

Travis realized he was jealous that some man in Brandon's past had held on to his affections, even if just for a short time. Travis wanted that affection. Love he didn't know about just yet, but he was certainly very fond of Brandon.

And he was still talking. "But I've been very honest with you so far. And I think that if you and I are going to make a decision, we need to just put everything on the table. We can't worry about if the other person approves or not. So let's just be honest. I think that's the only way we'll get anywhere."

Travis nodded. That was fair. He still hadn't made anything like a decision, and he hated that he'd been put in this position. He wondered if they could go back to pretending they weren't a couple in public, if that was even what he wanted.

"I'll start, I guess," Brandon said. "I know we've just started 'dating,' if that's what this is." He gestured at the food on the table with his chopsticks. "And I understand all of the arguments against going public as a couple. Are we in love? I don't know. Could we get there? I think so, yeah. And honestly? I think doing the show together, with you, would be a hell of a lot of fun. I want to go public with our relationship because I'm tired of hiding. So I'm all in. If you say no, I'll understand and we'll work something out, but I want you to know that I really want for us to be a couple and do the show as cohosts."

Travis sat with that for a moment, stirring noodles around with his chopsticks. "I wish I had your confidence. But I don't feel like we're ready for all that. And honestly, being in the spotlight scares the hell out of me. I just want to fix houses. I don't mind being on TV, but I don't want to be famous. I took this job because I figured I'd hang out in the background and get some publicity for my solo business."

"You know that will happen anyway, right?"

"What?"

Brandon rolled his eyes. "You'll become famous, to a point. People will recognize you on the streets. Did you ever see that interior design show that was on the Restoration Channel when it first launched? *Room Swap* it was called. It was on more than a decade ago. It was that show where the neighbors swapped houses and decorated a room?"

"I didn't watch it, but I vaguely remember it."

"Well, that show was a massive hit. And do you know who the breakout star was? Not any of the designers. Not the host, whom no one has seen since the show went off the air. It was the foxy carpenter who got his own show on network television. And he does commercials and stuff now. *That* guy is famous."

Travis didn't like the sound of that. "I guess."

"Let me tell you something, Trav. You are incredibly sexy. I know you're a nice guy underneath all the muscles and tattoos and stubble, but you're gruff and direct enough that the women watching at home will think you're a bad boy. That shit sells. The viewers will love you. Teenage girls will put posters of you in their bedrooms."

Travis guffawed. What was even happening right now? "No. That would never happen."

"I want to put posters of you in my bedroom. You in just a T-shirt and those tight jeans you wear all the time, with the tool belt on your hips? Anyone attracted to men would have to be dead inside not to respond to that. Trust me when I tell you that you may not want the spotlight, but it will find you."

"But I don't have a tenth of your charm. You're a good host because you're not just handsome, you're also charismatic. You seem comfortable in front of a camera. Your teeth are white."

"My teeth are white?"

"You've got that… polish, I don't know." Travis took a deep breath. The idea that he might grab some attention despite not wanting it… that didn't sit well with him. He supposed he should have known better, and it was his own fault for agreeing to be on a television show. He knew he'd be on TV, but he figured he'd be one of those public figures that people sometimes recognized on the streets but couldn't place. In his previous apartment, he'd lived down the block from an actress who played a judge on *Law & Order*, and he always said hello when he passed her on the street because he thought they knew each other, but then it turned out that he only recognized her from watching reruns when he couldn't sleep. He imagined he'd be that level of famous.

But here Brandon was telling him it was all out of his hands.

"I just don't know," Travis said. "And this has nothing to do with us or how I feel about you. I'm second-guessing the show and being publicly out on it."

"You're not in the closet."

"No, and I don't give a shit who knows, but I'm not Mike and Sandy. I keep it separate from my professional life. I don't put little rainbows on my company T-shirts."

"I did notice that. In fact, I almost asked. Are they a couple?"

"No. Old Army buddies, but they're both married to other men."

Brandon tilted his head. "Huh. I mean, Sandy I kind of guessed because he flirts with me whenever I'm around, but Mike didn't ping my gaydar. He said he had a daughter, so I just assumed."

"His daughter is adopted."

"Ah. Well, it's not important."

"No, not to what we're discussing."

"So what are you saying?"

"I don't know. I don't know how to make this decision. It's not even the being out thing. Again, I don't care. It's more that I'd be in a relationship with you *in public*. That's the part I can't get past. I want to be able to tell you 'yes, let's do it,' but I don't feel confident that we can pull it off. And I'm worried that being so public will put weight on us that we don't know how to hold up. I care about you, I can see us staying together for the long haul, but through this? I just don't know."

"I have to give Virginia an answer."

Travis nodded. "But by Monday, right? So we have the weekend to think about it?"

"Yes. But do you think more time will really help?"

Travis thought about how empty his bed had felt the night before. "Maybe?" He sighed. "It's not fair."

"I know."

Brandon picked up a piece of pineapple with his chopsticks. Travis was surprised he could eat. Travis's stomach felt like it was inside out.

"Can I sleep on it, at least?" Travis said.

"Sure. And please know that I'm not trying to pressure you to decide one way or the other. If you want to tell Virginia to shove it and go back to pretending we're not together when the cameras are on, I can pitch that to Virginia. We can be open at the house, but not when the cameras are rolling. Does that feel like a reasonable compromise?"

"I mean, that's what would make me the most comfortable. We can revisit this in a month or so, depending on how filming is going, but I keep picturing us going public and there being too much pressure for us to stay together and be happy. I may not have a wealth of relationship experience, but I know things aren't rosy all the time, even when you're in love."

"I know. And I appreciate your honesty."

"I'll decide by Monday morning, I promise."

Brandon nodded. "I'd like to cohost the show with you because it would be fun. I'm not so much looking forward to the attention I'll get when it inevitably comes out that I'm gay. Part of me thinks it's better to just come out and control the narrative rather than waiting for someone to find out, but another part of me wants to kick the can down the road."

"No good answers here."

"No." Brandon smiled ruefully. He reached across the table and took Travis's hand.

Travis wove his fingers with Brandon's. He picked up their joined hands and kissed Brandon's knuckles.

Could they do this? Travis didn't know. But he was willing to try.

CHAPTER TWENTY

TRAVIS WOKE up Monday morning at Brandon's—where he now kept enough changes of clothes that he wouldn't have to go home in the morning—and his phone was buzzing.

"What the…?"

Brandon snored on, though he stirred when Travis sat up and grabbed his phone.

Email and text message notifications. A lot of them. Travis's stomach sank. Bad news. It had to be bad news.

It was.

It took Travis a minute to sort out what people were talking about, but it became clear soon enough that it was now public knowledge that Brandon Chase was having an affair with the male project manager on his new show, one Travis Rogers.

Travis kicked Brandon. "Get up."

Brandon came awake slowly. Then he blinked at Travis a few times. "Wha…?"

Travis hopped out of bed. He showed Brandon his phone screen, where messages continued to accumulate. "We've been discovered."

"Are you kidding?"

"No. The story hit some internet gossip site, and now everyone who has ever known me is emailing me to congratulate me on my now-public affair with a man everyone thought was heterosexual. My own sister is accusing me of turning you. Get the fuck out of bed. I have to go light some things on fire."

Brandon got up. He was still naked but didn't seem to notice. "Calm down. It can't be that bad."

"It's bad, Brandon. And there are a finite number of people who could have leaked this. All people I'll probably see today. You might have to hold me back, because I'm going to kill whoever did this."

"Okay, okay. Let me hop in the shower."

Travis's complete and utter rage did not wane on the way to the Benton house for their meetings with Jessica. He spent the whole subway ride seething while Brandon tried to talk him off the ledge. When they got off the train, they walked by a row of newspaper vending machines, and Travis half expected to see his own face on the cover of the *Post*. He supposed he wasn't that kind of famous yet, but this was no less unpleasant.

His private life, aired on the internet, without his consent. It was one thing if he and Brandon had control of the narrative, but for it to leak like this, before Travis had even completely decided that he wanted it to be public knowledge, was a violation. Anyone who didn't know he was gay sure as hell knew now. Anyone who might ever work with him in the future could find it out in a matter of seconds if they googled him. Viewers of the new show would watch Brandon and Travis talk about load-bearing walls and picture them fucking.

This was so bad.

Virginia was waiting for them at the house, and she was all smiles. "Hello, boys. I wondered if we could have a word before Jessica gets here."

"Was it you?" Travis asked.

Virginia didn't even bat an eyelash. "I need a decision, boys. Don't drag this out."

Travis's fury was like acid boiling in his belly. "It *was* you. I can't fucking believe this."

"Wait," said Brandon. "Let's be rational. What happened?"

"Isn't it clear?" Travis felt half-hysterical, but he couldn't believe this had happened. "Virginia leaked the fact that we're seeing each other to the press, thus taking the decision about what to do out of our hands. Because now the most intimate part of our lives is just out there in public. It doesn't matter if we wanted to keep it a secret. It doesn't matter that we never consented to letting that information be public. All that matters is that Virginia got the fucking hook for her fucking television show."

Brandon stared at Virginia. "Did you leak the information?"

Virginia shrugged. "I may have let it slip to a few strategically placed people. But I needed a decision out of you. And you'll thank me for this later. Neither of you are closeted, are you? Brandon was ready to go public. I figured Travis would be too."

"No," said Travis. He couldn't even see anything, he was so angry. "Fuck you, Virginia. I don't give a shit who knows I'm gay, but I *do* give a shit about being on a fucking gossip website."

"Well," said Virginia, not looking the least bit remorseful. "Cat's out of the bag now."

"Are you serious?" asked Brandon.

"Look, this way it's out in the open that you're a couple. We can recut the show to indicate that you're working on the houses together. That's how we'll present it. The audience will be thrilled to see a gay couple on television."

"You had *no right*!" Travis shouted. "We're not… I mean, Brandon and I are barely a couple. How can you…." Travis shook his head. He was all incoherent rage. "You should have let us decide so we could control the narrative. Now it's just… out there. You, Virginia, just outed Brandon to the whole fucking world. You don't know what his life is like. You don't know if his family or friends know. You have no clue what kind of fallout this will have. You just decided to put it out there because it's best for your bottom line. But this is tremendously unfair to us."

"Well, what's done is done. Jessica Benton will be here in about ten minutes."

But Travis couldn't even conceive of getting through a meeting with the cameras trained on them, or speaking to Virginia without wanting to punch a hole through a wall. "I can't do the meeting. I have to get out of here."

"Come on, Travis," said Virginia. "Let's discuss this."

"I'm out. I… I can't work with you. I have to think about whether I can even do this show now."

With one last long look at Brandon—and hoping like hell that Brandon understood—Travis stormed out of the house.

BY RIGHTS Brandon should have stormed out after Travis, but he couldn't quite force himself to do it. The meeting with Jessica Benton was too important.

And yet when Jessica herself walked into the house five minutes later, Brandon found himself saying, "Maybe we should postpone."

He was utterly starstruck, for one thing. They'd met once before, but Brandon couldn't get over the fact that this woman had been in a ton of movies he'd loved. Jessica had a girl-next-door charm to her, but even without her hair and makeup being done professionally, she was strikingly beautiful. Her strawberry blond hair was pulled up into a ponytail, and the simple gray sweater and jeans she was wearing were casual but expensive-looking.

"What's going on?" Jessica asked.

"We had a bit of a disagreement," Virginia said. "About one of the other houses. It's fine, nothing to worry about."

Brandon didn't want to start a fight with Virginia while Jessica was standing there, but he completely understood Travis's rage and didn't know how to process what Virginia had done. While Virginia and Jessica made small talk for a moment, Brandon pulled out his phone and texted Travis, *Where did u go?*

Not coming back was the reply.

Not asking u to. Where r u now so I can find u?

Brandon tried to tune back in to what Virginia and Jessica were talking about while he waited for the response. Jessica was starting to discuss her vision for the house, but Brandon already knew he wouldn't be able to have a rational conversation.

Travis might quit the show. He was angry enough that his quitting seemed likely, even. But Brandon couldn't do the show without Travis. There was just no way. They'd fixed the Argyle Road house together. It was *theirs*. And Brandon couldn't do this meeting without Travis because he didn't know enough about estimating the costs of repairs or even know with certainty whether things should be fixed. He couldn't identify load-bearing walls unless they were obvious. He couldn't say whether an HVAC system was in good repair or needed to be replaced. He had no way to know whether this would be a $50,000 job or a $250,000 job.

He cleared his throat. "I'm very interested to hear about your ideas for the house, Ms. Benton. But I think we should postpone this meeting until we can get Travis, our project manager, here. He's more knowledgeable about structural issues, so he'll be able to tell us what work must be done to the house before we can pretty it up."

Where the hell was Travis, and why wouldn't he tell Brandon where he was? Did he think Brandon was somehow complicit in this?

"Do you think we could get him over here now?" Jessica asked. "I've got another appointment this afternoon."

Brandon looked at Virginia. He tried to communicate telepathically that this was her fuckup and she had to fix it.

"I apologize, Ms. Benton, this was my fault," said Virginia.

"Please call me Jessica."

"Jessica. I'm so sorry, I screwed up the scheduling. We were all supposed to meet here this morning, but I miscommunicated with Travis. Let's do a quick walk-through of the house now so you can tell us what some of your ideas are, and Brandon can lend his expertise, and then we can meet again with Travis in a day or two."

"Production is going to start here this week, right?" Jessica asked. "We agreed to a pretty tight timeline. Six to eight weeks was what you said. I'm leaving for Prague to film a movie on June 1. I'd like to be done by then."

Brandon mentally counted. June 1 was a little over two months away.

"That should be doable," Brandon said.

"Good. Then let me tell you my ideas."

Brandon couldn't focus on Jessica at all. He managed to make himself say some things that she responded to positively, but mostly he thought about Travis, wondering why he hadn't responded to the text yet. Probably because he didn't want to be found.

They were partway through Jessica's explanation about what she wanted to see happen in the master bathroom—something about taking away a bedroom to make space for a bigger bathroom and a walk-in closet—when Brandon got a text from Ismael to say the kitchen backsplash tile was in and the crew was getting ready to install the kitchen appliances. Also, Ismael hadn't been able to get in touch with Travis.

Shit.

They got through the meeting. Brandon apologized that he couldn't be more helpful. "I like your design ideas, though, especially upstairs."

"Good," Jessica said. "Sorry, I'm such a fan of *Dream Home*. I've been wanting to flip a house since I started watching it regularly."

"You watched *Dream Home*?"

"Oh, yeah. That's why I called Restoration. The fact that they were able to get *you* to help out with this project is amazing. I was sorry to hear about what happened with Kayla, by the way."

"Oh."

"Anyway, please call me when we're ready to start filming here. I'd love to do the walk-through with Travis so he can help us with a renovation estimate. I've got a pretty healthy budget for this project, but it's not unlimited."

"Right."

After they shook hands and Jessica left, Brandon turned to Virginia. "How long before I signed on did you start talks with Jessica?"

Virginia at least had the good grace to look sheepish. "There are a handful of celebrities looking at houses in this neighborhood. This could be the next hot spot in Brooklyn."

"So you manipulated me into doing the show because you knew there were celebrities like Jessica who wanted to work with me, specifically. And then, as soon as you found out about me and Travis, you tried to manipulate us into being the happy gay couple you want to host one of your shows. Now it's all perfect. Except that I'm pretty sure you just violated my contract by leaking details about me and Travis to the press. Travis was still on the fence about committing to doing the show as a couple until we were on more stable ground, and now he definitely won't do it and will probably quit the show. So I hope you're fucking happy."

Brandon didn't wait for a response. He walked out of the house and headed for Argyle Road. On the way, he pulled out his phone and called Garrett Harwood.

CHAPTER TWENTY-ONE

WHEN HE stormed out of the house, Travis went home, not knowing where else to go. He turned off his phone, determined to ignore Brandon after he'd asked where Travis had gone. Travis didn't want to be found for a bit.

He was really tempted to walk away from all of it—to leave the house and the show and Brandon in the past, get a job somewhere else, forget any of this had ever happened. It was such a stupid idea, thinking he could be on TV.

But he was in love with Brandon and the house. The show he could take or leave. If he never had to see Virginia Frank again, it would be too soon. But he'd grown fond of the house on Argyle Road. He'd put a lot of himself into the project. And he was particularly fond of Brandon.

Brandon, who'd just stood there looking stunned when Travis had gone off on Virginia.

It wasn't in Brandon's nature to rock the boat, and Travis knew that, but he was still angry at everyone, and he had no outlet for that anger.

Where did Travis even stand with Brandon? What did he always say? *Failure is not an option.* Brandon was a man who had entered into a legal marriage with a woman he did not love in order to create the perfect false front for a TV show. This was a man who was so damaged by his father that he could not even contemplate failure.

So, yeah, Travis didn't care much about getting outed himself, although he cared a lot about Brandon, who hadn't so much as moved a toe out of the closet, getting outed, and he cared even more about not having any say in the matter. And he worried that Brandon, who was clearly willing to go to great lengths to secure his own success, his public image, and his television show, would choose the show over Travis. In fact, that was probably what would happen. If, by storming out, Travis had put the show in jeopardy, well, Brandon would choose the show.

He sat in his tiny studio apartment with the TV on for a while, but he didn't absorb anything he saw.

The world already knew about his and Brandon's relationship; Virginia was right that the cat was out of the bag. And Travis wanted to be with Brandon; people finding out wasn't a reason to leave. But maybe he shouldn't do the show anymore. He didn't like the idea of his life being so public. He knew that gay couples were still such a novelty to some people that they pictured what they did in bed instead of thinking about any other aspect of their relationship. Travis didn't want that kind of scrutiny.

He was contracted to film six episodes, though. He'd have to finish the job. Unless his temper tantrum that morning had gotten him fired. The Restoration Channel might actually be eager to let him out of his contract.

He let out a breath and shut off the TV. He turned his phone back on.

There were a half-dozen texts from Brandon, which he'd expected. A few missed calls too. There were three missed calls and a voicemail from Ismael, a missed call from a Manhattan number Travis didn't recognize—probably Garrett Harwood telling him his work for the network was done—and a handful of texts from friends who had seen the gossip sites.

There was one from Sandy: *So you WERE fucking him this whole time! I knew it!*

Travis sighed. He listened to his voicemail. Ismael said, "Hey, Trav. I know you have that other meeting today, but I just wanted to let you know we got the backsplash tiles in. The crew is putting in the appliances today. I'm not sure how we're installing the backsplash. Call me when you get a chance."

So Travis returned that call.

"Good news," said Ismael. "We got the appliances into the kitchen, no problem. Plumber came by and checked the dishwasher and everything. And Brandon's almost done putting in the backsplash tile. Erik filmed most of it, but there was some kind of hullabaloo around lunchtime."

So Brandon was at the house, working for the cameras. The show hadn't been canceled and Brandon was still on it. Did that say anything about the choice Brandon had made? Travis glanced at the wall clock. It was almost three. He'd been seething most of the day away. "Hullabaloo?"

"Yeah, Erik got a bunch of phone calls and we shut down production for about a half hour because he wanted to film the installation but had to talk to someone at Restoration corporate. I don't really know what happened. And Brandon was really upset when he got here, so I just assumed something bad happened at the other house. Did it?"

"Uh, I don't know. I went home sick. Feeling better now, though."

"Oh. Sorry to hear that. Anyway, no one will tell me anything, so I don't really know what's going on. But if it's related to the show production, that's not my job anyway. We're moving along with everything else."

"What have you got left to do today?"

"Well, Mike and Sandy did the tub in the master bathroom. I was gonna finish putting up that wallpaper in the family room, but Brandon told me to wait."

"They probably want to film that too."

"I figured. Rest of the crew is working on the exterior. We're trying to get the second coat done before we lose daylight."

"Excellent."

"And Brandon wants to show you the backsplash since you haven't seen the tile yet. It's kind of a bold choice, so I assume this is some TV thing where he calls you in so you can tell him how much you hate it."

Travis laughed. That seemed about right. If he was even welcome on the show. "He's my next phone call."

"Cool. You coming by tomorrow or…?"

"I don't know, actually. I think Brandon and Virginia probably had a conversation about the other house without me, but I don't know what the schedule is yet."

"Cool. Just let me know."

"I will. Thanks, Iz."

"No problema, boss."

When Ismael hung up, Travis held the phone to his chest for a moment. Then he called Brandon.

"Hi," Brandon said, sounding wary.

"I'm sorry for storming out and disappearing today," Travis said. "I'm home, by the way."

"I'm at Argyle Road. I have some news."

"I'm fired, aren't I?"

"What? No, of course you aren't fired. If they fired you, I'd quit the show. But… actually, it would be better if we talk in person. Can you come to the Argyle Road house?"

If they fired you, I'd quit the show. Travis closed his eyes and tried to feel that. "All right. Is Virginia there?"

"No. I'll send everyone home, even Erik. I want to show you something."

Travis took a deep breath and let it out. "No need to send Ismael's crew home early if they're still working. I just talked to Iz, he told me they're trying to finish the exterior paint before the sun sets. But I can't really deal with the cameras right now, so if Erik's gone, I won't be mad about it. Give me a little time to clean up. Then I'll get a cab. Be there in a half hour."

"Okay. See you soon."

ABOUT FIFTEEN minutes after he got off the phone with Travis, Brandon stood beside Erik as he packed up for the day.

"So what does this mean for the production?" Erik asked.

"Harwood didn't say exactly, just that we should keep shooting as if nothing happened."

"I hope you know how sorry I am. If I had known what Virginia would do, I never would have told her. We talk a few times a week so I can update her on the production when she's not here, and I told her about seeing you two together as a bit of set gossip. Like, ha ha, Travis and Brandon were acting rather close on set today, isn't that funny? I honestly had no idea you were gay or that the two of you were hooking up. I had a hunch, that's all. I never wanted to out you or get you in trouble with the network or anything."

"All right. I believe you. Travis may not trust you going forward, but given how everything has shaken out, I think your job is okay."

"Okay. So you're sending me away now because…."

"I want Travis to come by and look at the backsplash, but he doesn't want to deal with you or the cameras right now, which is fair under the circumstances. We can reshoot his reaction tomorrow if we think it would be good on camera."

"Is he that good of an actor?"

"If he hates it, we'll never hear the end of it."

Erik chuckled. "Fair enough." He zipped up his bag. "For what it's worth, I think you guys are good together. I like working with both of you. Travis never bullshits, which I appreciate."

Brandon nodded. He appreciated that too.

When Erik was gone, Brandon walked into the kitchen and tried to see it as Travis might. It was exactly what they'd discussed. They'd picked custom craftsman cabinets stained a dark color, rich brown with red undertones, not too dark. The brown on the backsplash tiles matched the color of the cabinets nearly exactly, and the teal popped against the wood. They'd put down medium-gray ceramic tiles that had some of the same undertones as the cabinets, which tied everything together. The off-white quartz counters broke up the colors and made the room look balanced.

It was perfect. Brandon loved this kitchen. Travis's instincts had been dead-on. And that was why Brandon needed him on the show.

Brandon needed him in his life.

He supposed the fact that Travis was willing to come over was a good sign.

Brandon heard the front door open a few minutes later. He headed in that direction and met Travis in the living room.

Travis looked tired. His hair was disheveled and his eyes were rimmed red.

"How much do you hate me?" Brandon asked.

"I don't hate you. I do hate Virginia. She'd better not be here."

"She's not. I, uh… I called Garrett Harwood after the meeting with Jessica Benton. Virginia's been fired."

Travis jerked his head up to look at Brandon. "You're kidding."

"Nope. I called Harwood to tell him what happened, and I ended up telling him everything. I figured if the tabloids have the story, he's heard by now anyway. So I told him about us, about Virginia finding out, and about her leaking the news to the press. I told him you were furious and that you were threatening to quit the show. And then I told him that if you quit, I was out too, so it was me or Virginia. I'm the cash cow, apparently, and Harwood picked me."

Travis's eyes were wide. "You got her fired?"

"So, fun story. I told all this to Harwood, and you know what he told me? He's also gay. And he sees himself as an Andy Cohen type. He wants to do more where he's on TV as a host and runs these specials where he gets people from all the different network shows to do a project together—to show that we're all part of one big family. Which I guess is neither here nor there, but I told him I'd be game for that sort of thing. Harwood has no issue with us as a couple, and he gave me permission to run the show however I saw fit until we could hire a new producer."

"But he just… fired Virginia?"

"Everything you said this morning about us being the ones who should decide when to come out was correct. Harwood understood that."

Travis nodded. He still looked unsure.

Brandon paused to listen. Mike and Sandy had left after overseeing the last of the plumbing-related tasks, and Ismael and the rest of his crew were all outside doing exterior work. No one was inside the house. "Look, here's the deal. I want to keep this job. The meeting with Jessica Benton this morning was awkward and I had trouble focusing, but I could tell she had good instincts. I think that house will be a hell of a lot of fun to work on. And I want to do the project with you, because you're knowledgeable and we work together well. And I want you in my life because I care about you and being with you makes me happy."

Travis covered his mouth with his hand and wiped it away slowly. "So what now?"

"Well, that depends on you."

Travis nodded. "What do you want to happen?"

Brandon didn't want to push Travis too hard yet. "You come back to work tomorrow. We can finish this house and start production at the Benton house. It's gorgeous, by the way. Beat all to hell, in horrible shape, but I think we could do a really elegant design there—something a little softer than what we did here. And I want you and Jessica to help with the design. I want you to have whatever role on the show you're most comfortable with. I want us to work together to hire a new producer to replace Virginia, someone we both like."

Travis nodded slowly.

"And," Brandon said, "I want you to come home with me tonight. I want you to be with me because we care about each other and make each other happy. I want to work with you at home and on set and in all the places in between. I want to make love to you every night and I want to fight about paint colors and wallpaper and tiles with you and I want to make over houses with you for the foreseeable future. That's what I want."

Travis looked unconvinced. “Brandon, I—”

“Before you say anything, I want to show you something.”

“All right.”

Brandon took Travis’s hand and wove their fingers together. Then he led Travis into the kitchen.

Travis gasped. “Those tiles.”

“They’re perfect, aren’t they?” Brandon said. “I saw those tiles in the store and they looked just like what you described. Did I get it right?”

Travis blinked a few times. He looked around slowly, clearly taking in the whole picture because he hadn’t seen the kitchen put together yet. Then he looked at Brandon. “It is perfect. It’s exactly what I pictured.”

“I know tiles are a silly thing to get excited over, but—”

“No, Brandon. This is beautiful. I can’t believe you found tile exactly like what I saw in my head.”

“They cost a pretty penny, but they were 100 percent worth it to get that expression on your face.”

Travis lunged at Brandon and kissed him hard. Then he put his arms around Brandon and pressed his face into Brandon’s shoulder. Brandon almost didn’t know what to do with this rare show of emotion, but he rubbed Travis’s back and held him close.

“These last few days have been a trial,” Travis said. “All I want is to fix houses and be with you. The rest of it is bullshit. I don’t want to be famous, I don’t care about television. I just want… this.”

Brandon kissed the side of Travis’s head. “I wanted to surprise you.”

“It’s a good surprise.” Travis’s voice was watery. “But why did you do this? You could have picked a more generic tile. Something safer.”

Brandon considered that as he considered the man in his arms. Why had Brandon done this? Because he loved Travis.

The thought came to him unbidden. He hugged Travis close and reveled in the sensation of their bodies pressed together. Yes, he loved Travis. But he wasn’t sure that was what Travis wanted to hear right now. “I wanted to. I knew it would make you happy.”

Travis pulled away and looked up at Brandon. “That’s a stupid reason.”

Brandon smiled. “I know.”

The front door crashed open, and Travis pulled away.

“Hey, boss?” Ismael called. “You here? Thought I saw you come in.”

“Kitchen,” hollered Travis.

For Brandon, it felt like the bubble burst. He stepped aside and listened while Ismael gave Travis a report on everything they'd accomplished that day. When Travis dismissed Ismael for the day, he turned around and looked at Brandon.

"Your place or mine?"

Chapter Twenty-Two

THE PHRASE *I love you* felt like the carbonation in a soda inside of Brandon. If Travis shook up Brandon any more, it would just bubble up and overflow out of him.

He worried Travis wasn't ready to hear it, though he had some faith that Travis's feelings for him were deep and genuine. But Travis had been acting a little strange since the big reveal with the tile. Not mysteriously so; Brandon understood that Travis felt overwhelmed. This day had been full of just the sort of messy, emotional moments Travis seemed not to like.

But they were at Travis's apartment, a space he seemed to feel safe. Travis moved through it, picking up clothes off the floor in the bedroom area of the studio while Brandon sat on the bed and watched him.

"It doesn't bother me that your apartment is messy," Brandon said.

"It bothers me."

"I can take a page from your playbook. I thought we were here to have sex."

Travis stopped what he was doing and turned to Brandon. "Today has been a lot. Can you just… give me a minute?"

"All right."

Brandon liked that he could figure Travis out now. He recognized that Travis was cleaning up to avoid his messy emotions. That was fine; Brandon didn't want to talk about emotions anyway. Instead, he unbuttoned his shirt and threw it on the floor near Travis's feet.

Travis turned toward Brandon with a frown. "Really?"

Brandon whipped off his undershirt and tossed it at Travis's head. "Just trying to get the ball rolling."

Travis rolled his eyes, then picked up Brandon's discarded clothes and put them in his own hamper. That was fine; Brandon had a drawer in Travis's dresser now. Brandon viewed this as more evidence that he and Travis should just live together in the Argyle Road house already, but he didn't say anything.

Not yet.

Travis sighed. “You did some incredible things for me today.”

“I don’t need to talk about it. Unless you want to.”

“I don’t. Just… I felt like I needed to say that.”

“Travis, come here.”

Travis picked the last item of clothing off the floor—one of Travis’s sexier and more form-fitting T-shirts—and tossed it in the hamper. He walked over to the bed and dropped down beside Brandon. “I fucking hate this.”

“What do you hate?” But Brandon already knew.

“I feel like a complete mess inside. I was so furious this morning. Now I’m kind of resigned about what happened. It’s out there. My sister, who I haven’t talked to in, like, six weeks because she’s too busy with her kids in Chicago, called today to congratulate me on landing such a hot guy. Like, what even is that? I’ve got people I haven’t seen since I dropped out of college leaving me messages on Facebook like, ‘I didn’t even know you were gay.’ Like… thanks, bro. I can’t even tell if you’re joking there.” Travis rubbed his forehead. “But whatever. It’s out there. It’s done. And you know what? I kind of expected you to just go along to get along, to pick the show over me, but no, you went over Virginia’s head and got her fired.”

“What she did was wrong.” Brandon felt assured of that, at least. She’d outed them without their consent. Brandon had been mentally preparing himself for being gay publicly, but he’d wanted to do it in his own time, in a way that let him control the narrative. “And my social media has been far worse. I’m already famous, you know. People think this gives them license to write vile, homophobic things on my social media accounts. I’ve been called a faggot online about seven hundred times today, and that’s mild. One young man told me he hoped I got AIDS and died.”

Travis let out a long breath. “That’s… that’s hurtful.”

Brandon was trying to be circumspect about it. For every vile comment he’d received, he’d gotten ten supportive ones. But every negative comment made his pulse spike and his stomach churn and made him angry at Virginia all over again. But he had to deal with the hand he’d been dealt.

“Harwood wants to beef up security on the set,” said Brandon. “I’m sure most of the more violent comments are empty threats and everything will be fine, but I agreed that some extra security couldn’t hurt.”

"Okay. Jesus."

"My point is, I was just as furious as you. But I was so stunned by the news at first that I kind of shut down. I regret not yelling at Virginia right alongside you, but I did give Harwood an earful, and she's gone now. We'll pick a producer we trust for the show, and I mean *we*. I want you to have a say in these decisions, even if you don't accept the cohost position."

"Right. But you got that done. And then you… you put up those tiles. For me."

"It's a small thing, I know."

"It's a huge thing. That's what I'm trying to tell you. You listened and you deferred to my judgment and it came out beautifully. Like a dream kitchen. I love everything about it. And maybe it's dumb to feel so excited about a kitchen, but I do."

"I'm glad. I saw that tile at the store and I couldn't get over how perfect it was."

Travis looked up at the ceiling for a moment as if gathering his thoughts. Then he let out a breath. "I stormed out of that house today and I thought you would try to smooth everything over and sacrifice me for the sake of the show. But no, you stood up for me, for us, and you tried to fix the problem." Travis put his hands on Brandon's shoulders. "I thought it would be easiest to just walk away from all of this. I thought about that a lot this morning. But stuff like this just shows me that I can't possibly walk away from you."

That bubbly soda sensation hit Brandon again, so rather than say anything, he kissed Travis.

He could feel Travis's sigh of relief. Brandon knew Travis didn't want to talk about his emotions, just as surely as he knew that Travis felt them, so he knew that Travis had been touched by the gesture and surprised that Brandon had acted as he did today. Brandon was here because Travis wanted him here. And that was enough.

They lay down beside each other on the bed, and Travis peeled Brandon's clothes off, so Brandon returned the favor. When they were both naked, Brandon traced his finger over the tattoo on Travis's chest. "Tell me about this."

The design was a slightly abstract tiger on Travis's left pec. Brandon studied it for a moment and then looked at Travis's face. Travis had closed his eyes.

This was related to something important to Travis. Brandon hadn't meant to poke that. He'd been imagining Travis had played a sport for a team called the Tigers, or something like that. But there was clearly a story here. "If you don't want to—"

"No, it's okay." Travis placed his hand over Brandon's. "I guess you found another one of my secrets. I had a friend growing up. Greg. We were like brothers, completely inseparable. He always accepted me and whatever decisions I made, and I did the same for him. I've never known anyone who was so at ease with himself and not afraid of anything. He became a firefighter after we graduated. And, ah, when were about twenty-five, there was a fire, just a few blocks from my parents' house in Forest Hills. Greg saved a little girl who had been hiding in a closet. He got her out before a beam collapsed on him."

"Oh God."

"Maybe a week after the funeral, I was in a Chinese restaurant and, like, staring at the placemat with the Chinese zodiac on it. And it said that tigers are self-confident, competitive, and brave, which described Greg perfectly. So this tiger is for Greg, and it's near my heart." Travis closed his eyes. "I hate telling that story."

"I understand," said Brandon. Travis clearly felt things deeply but didn't like to talk about them. And he had depths Brandon hadn't realized. "I assume the hammers on your arm are for your profession."

"Yeah." Travis rubbed his eye. "God, I haven't talked about Greg in a while. More than ten years have gone by. I can go for weeks without thinking about him, but every now and then he just pops in there and surprises me. The whole point of the tattoo was so that I could keep his memory with me, but I… well." He took a deep breath. "The lesson I took from his death is that houses have to be safe. That house, the one Greg died in? There'd been a gas leak. The investigators managed to put together that something electronic had sparked and the gas that had been leaking into the kitchen caught fire. I try to think about that when I'm doing repairs on a house. It has to be safe above everything. The design stuff is nice, but if what's in the walls is dangerous, it's not worth anything."

Brandon nodded. "I appreciate that."

"Ugh, listen to me go on. I'm sorry."

"No. Never apologize for your feelings. It's like I understand something new about you now."

Travis sighed. "I loved him. Our relationship was purely platonic, but I was in love with him. I never told him."

"I'm so sorry."

"I mean, it's the past. I think he knew. We never talked about it. He was… flexible, sleeping with pretty much anyone who offered. I think he saw me as a brother, though, not a romantic possibility, and I was mostly okay with that. But it still hits me sometimes that we never got a chance. But then, maybe it doesn't matter. I don't think Greg was the one I was supposed to be with."

Brandon didn't want to press his luck by asking if Travis thought it might be him, so he let it go.

Travis groaned. "I hate this shit."

Brandon ran a hand over Travis's chest, up his neck, and into his hair. He hoped the gesture was comforting. "Thank you for telling me."

"You're going to pry all my secrets out of me, aren't you?"

Brandon laughed softly, because Travis looked so put out. "I mean… probably."

Travis sighed and pressed his face into Brandon's chest. "You will be the death of me."

"I suspect you will enjoy every minute of it."

"Hmph."

Travis kissed Brandon then, whether it was to end the conversation or out of a moment of genuine feeling, Brandon didn't know and didn't care, because they quickly sank into the kiss together. Warmth spread across his chest, and those words bubbled in his throat. He *knew* he was in love with this man. He'd never felt anything like this, but the feeling was forceful, unequivocal, hovering in the back of his mind. He loved Travis. And he'd do whatever he could to make Travis happy.

As things ramped up and Travis grew hard against Brandon's leg, Brandon considered reaching for the nightstand drawer, but he couldn't tear himself away from Travis. Being pressed against him was too good. Brandon kissed Travis, ran his hands over Travis's body, shifted his hips against Travis's. Travis moaned softly, reached between them, and wrapped his hand around both of their cocks. And this was good, intimate in an unexpected way, their bodies sliding against each other and connected in nearly every way possible.

Brandon loved Travis.

But Brandon didn't want to say *I love you* in the middle of sex, in case Travis thought it was some heat-of-the-moment thing and not Brandon's most heartfelt emotion, so he kissed Travis instead. And they kept kissing until the sensation became too much. Instinct or animal brain took over and Brandon forgot all about the abstract feelings and could only feel what was happening between them.

"So good," Travis murmured, a strong indication that he was about to lose it just as surely as Brandon was.

They came within seconds of each other, the vibrations of Travis's body triggering Brandon's orgasm, and it was messy but so, so amazing.

Brandon held Travis close as they came down together, and they stayed wrapped up in each other until it got itchy and uncomfortable, at which point Travis wordlessly got out of bed.

Brandon followed him to the bathroom, where they cleaned up, and Brandon couldn't look away from the tender expression on Travis's face.

"I care about you a lot, Travis. I want you to know that."

"I know. I obviously care about you too, or I wouldn't be this stupid and emotional. I blame you for making me feeling this way. It's awful."

Brandon laughed. "It's amazing. You're amazing."

Travis let Brandon kiss him but then pushed him away. "Knock it off. Let's just… go to bed. I can't take any more mushy feelings today."

"WHAT ABOUT this?" Travis said.

"Mmm?" Brandon rolled onto his side and looked at Travis sleepily. Travis was half sitting up, leaning against the pillows, totally unable to sleep. Brandon had been dozing for a few minutes, so Travis had been thinking about how he wanted to handle the show. He didn't want to quit. He liked the work, and he definitely liked the show's host. But his comfort with being on TV was limited. More than that, he was in this thing with Brandon for the long haul, and he suspected Brandon felt the same. They might as well make it official.

"I don't want to cohost. I don't want to talk directly to the cameras except maybe every once in a while. But I can take on a larger role on the show. We've already been outed, so let's be a couple, on and off the show. Acknowledge that we're a couple on the show and that we're working on the houses together, but it's still your show, primarily."

Brandon smiled and ran a hand down the side of Travis's face. "I can definitely do that. Maybe I can allude to our couple status in the opening credits voiceover. That way it's clear what role you play in my life."

Travis nodded. He slid down into the pillows until he was closer to horizontal. He'd half expected Brandon to protest, but the fact that Brandon was willing to do what Travis wanted said a lot.

Brandon propped himself up on his elbow. "So that's it? We're a couple now? On and off the show?"

"I guess so."

Brandon took Travis's hand. "I wanted to wait to tell you this until I thought you were ready, but what the hell?"

Well, that didn't sound good. "What is it?"

"Don't look so terrified. This is a good thing. I just want to say that I love you, Travis. I have fallen so far in love with you in the last six weeks, and it feels overwhelming and perfectly natural all at the same time."

Travis squeezed his hand. God, was this love? Was that what had made Brandon get Virginia fired and put up teal tiles in the kitchen? Everything that had happened today had shown Travis that Brandon loved him, and it was some balm for the burn of finding out that his private life was public now.

Because Travis loved Brandon too. It was why he couldn't walk away.

He kissed Brandon's knuckles. "Falling in love with you is definitely the strangest thing that has ever happened to me."

Brandon grinned. "You love me?"

"Of course I do, you idiot. I definitely wouldn't be here now if I didn't. Walking away, going underground, getting some other job, all of those things would be easier than doing this goddamned show, and yet I still want to do it because I know it would make you happy. And that is completely ridiculous to me. When did I become that guy?"

"You love me."

"Shut up."

Brandon pulled Travis into his arms and kissed the side of his face. "I love you. I won't give you some song and dance about how perfect we are for each other, because I don't even think we are, but I do know that being with you has made everything that has happened since we started filming the show a million times better. Loving you makes my life better."

Travis hugged Brandon back and took a deep breath. "Yeah. All that."

"I mean, because we probably aren't perfect. You're really gruff and bossy."

"Your taste is bland and you're wishy-washy about making decisions."

Brandon laughed. "And yet…."

"Those tiles. I'm still not over it."

"I can't wait to show you the Jessica Benton house. You'll have all kinds of crazy ideas for it. And I won't have to bring in Kayla this time, because you'll know exactly what should go there."

"I'm no designer."

"No, but you have good instincts, and you're smart, and I love you to distraction."

Travis sighed. "I love you too, okay?"

"And, look, Ismael told me today the crew is fine with us as a couple, and even Erik thinks we're cute together, although he also apologized about seven hundred times. Apparently he thought he was just gossiping with Virginia when he told her about us. Like, ha ha, wouldn't it be funny if the two most prominent people on the show were hooking up with each other? He didn't mean for it to become a thing." Brandon ran his hand through Travis's hair. "I know he's not your favorite person right now, but I don't think he deserves to be fired."

Travis sighed. Most of his anger had dissipated, although that made it spike a little. "If you trust him, it's all right."

"I do. And I don't want to change too much of the staff midstream unless we have to. Virginia did something terrible. I think Erik was mostly innocent. Virginia told me she'd keep quiet about things until we made a decision, but then she didn't."

"Okay. I promise not to punch him tomorrow."

"Good." Brandon pulled away and looked Travis in the eyes. "So we're good now?"

Travis couldn't keep the smile off his face. Brandon was so earnest sometimes. "Yeah. We're good. We'll figure out how to make the show work. Okay?"

"Okay. Good. I love you."

Even though Travis liked hearing the words, he said, "Okay, jeez, don't wear it out."

Brandon laughed and kissed Travis.

Chapter Twenty-Three

Travis was so tired he could feel it in his bones.

He'd spent the day demolishing the interior of Jessica Benton's house, but also letting her get her hands dirty. He wasn't surprised that she'd shown up for filming with her hair and makeup done. She seemed game to do some of the work herself, although she objected off-camera when he made her put her hair up and wear safety glasses. She did it, though, and whacked a few walls and cabinets with a sledgehammer.

Demo could be fun, but it was hard, physical work too, and Travis's body ached a little as Jessica bid him farewell for the day.

Brandon had been there in the morning so Erik could get some footage of him ripping out the old, outdated kitchen cabinets, but he'd since gone back to the Argyle Road house to do… something. Travis didn't know what; there wasn't much left to do there. They had some minor things to finish, but most of the work crew had already moved over to the Benton house. Travis had promised Brandon he'd walk over to Argyle Road when he finished up here to do some of those last minor things, but he regretted making that promise now. He was beat.

Still, he locked up the house for the day and walked the three blocks to the other house.

It had been a weird few days. Travis bounced between houses—something he suspected he'd have to get used to because Brandon already had an eye on a new project in the neighborhood—and they'd picked a new producer the day before, a woman who had worked on a show about flipping houses in Westchester County, just outside the city. She seemed to know her stuff and had no interest in exploiting Brandon and Travis's recent coupledom.

Things would work out. Travis believed that. But all he wanted was to curl up in bed and sleep for two days. Ideally with Brandon beside him, but he was so tired, even that was optional.

Travis let himself into the house. He didn't think anyone would be here. Erik, Ismael, and their respective staffs had all been at the Benton house most of the day and had gone home. Travis walked back to the kitchen, where he'd left the remaining pieces of hardware that had to be installed on the kitchen cabinets.

Then Brandon appeared.

And that did make Travis feel a little better.

"Hey," Brandon said. He walked over and gave Travis a quick peck on the lips.

"Hi. We're all wrapped up for the day at the other house."

"Good."

"Just you here?"

"Yeah. I've been waiting for you, actually. I installed all the hardware in the upstairs bathrooms."

"Okay. One less thing for me to do."

Travis picked up a drawer pull and took a screwdriver from his tool belt and started to screw it on one of the drawers.

"I want to talk to you about something," said Brandon.

Travis didn't look up from what he was doing. His suspicion was that this was going to be a heavy conversation. He didn't really have the energy for that, but he said, "Okay."

"So, I had a crazy idea."

Travis looked up at that. He fiddled with the drawer pull. It was secure. He grabbed another. "What is it?"

"You and I have put so much of ourselves into this house. I fell in love with it the first time I did a walk-through. In making my final decisions, I took your advice and I thought a lot about what *I* would like to see in the house, more than what buyers would like to see. I never think like that. I chose this tile…." Brandon touched the backsplash. "Not because I thought it added value to the house, but because I thought you would love it. And I've been slowly realizing that I kind of don't want to sell the house at all."

Travis finished securing the handle to the drawer and looked up. "What are you saying?"

"I'm saying that even though it's a stupid thing to do financially, I'm thinking very seriously about buying out Restoration's share of the house and moving into it myself."

Travis didn't know what to do with his hands. He put the screwdriver on the counter. "Are you kidding?"

"We've talked about houses. I know you understand the need for a space like this as much as anyone. I've never had a real home, but I want one more than I can even say. I rented my place in Brooklyn Heights because I didn't want to commit to anything until I figured out what I was doing next. Well, I'm doing this now. And I'm committed to you. Why not put down some roots? And I love this house. The kitchen, the bathrooms, the living spaces, the master suite upstairs, the design Kayla and I put together? All of it is perfect."

Travis's stomach flopped. He'd been feeling a little like he'd felt when he'd found out he'd lost the house the year before. He was overreacting, and he knew that, but it had started to almost feel like a betrayal for Brandon to sell this house. And now he was buying it? "I thought this place had become a money pit, that you'd have to sell it to recoup your investment."

"I'm starting to think of it as more of a long-term investment."

Travis stared at the counter. The weird thing was that he had started imagining what it would be like to live in this house too, something he never did on the job. A house was a project he usually felt emotionally disconnected from, a series of tasks to complete more than something he was making for himself. But here, he'd imagined cooking meals in this kitchen, lounging in the living room, reading a book in the family room, getting ready in the morning in the master bathroom.

And here was Brandon, taking that from him.

Not that he could afford to buy the house, even though the thought had passed through his brain a few times.

Travis rubbed his face, hoping his emotions didn't show, and said, "Why do you need to talk to me about it? It's your house, literally. Your money."

"Because I want you to live here with me."

Travis met his gaze, utterly shocked. "What?"

"This is *our* house, Travis. My owning it doesn't make sense without you in it."

"You want us to move in together? And live here?"

"It makes sense. I know, it's early, blah blah, but first of all, we love each other, and second of all, we spend nearly every night together anyway. Wouldn't it be easier to have all of our stuff together in one house?"

Maybe it really was that easy. Travis looked around the kitchen, and he could see Brandon sitting at the island in the morning while Travis whipped up some breakfast. Brandon would scroll through his email on his phone or flip through a newspaper, and they'd look at each other moonily when Travis handed him a cup of coffee. There were plenty of logical reasons against moving in together, but a lot of emotional reasons why it made sense.

"You're serious," Travis said.

"Very. Honestly, I've been thinking about it for weeks."

"And you can just do that? Buy the network's half of the investment?"

"I mean, I assume so. Kayla and I owned the houses on our old show. Restoration only fronted the money here as a way to incentivize me buying in. I'm sure I can come up with the money to buy them out. It might even make for a good premiere of the show. Brandon and Travis fix up a house, fall in love, and decide to move into it themselves. That's quite a story."

Travis laughed softly and shook his head. He couldn't wrap his head around any of this. He wanted the house, though, and he wanted to live here with Brandon, and the fact that it was even a possibility was such a miraculous surprise.

But he also knew how much of a financial burden this put on Brandon. Travis had that nest egg he'd socked away to buy the house he didn't get; it wasn't enough money to buy this house outright, but it was enough to buy out the Restoration Channel's share.

Could he do this? It was a bonkers idea. But he couldn't just walk away from this house, either. It had memories of Brandon embedded in it; selling the house to someone else would be heart-wrenching.

Because Brandon was right. This house was Brandon and Travis's.

What an unexpected turn his life had taken.

"Let's do it," Travis said.

"Yeah?"

"Yes. I want to live in this house with you."

Brandon whooped and grabbed Travis, pulling him into such a tight hug that his feet lifted off the floor. Travis laughed and tried to regain control of the situation. He hugged Brandon, but then he pulled away to arm's distance. He put a hand on Brandon's chest.

"But I have one condition."

BRANDON BRACED himself. "What's your condition?"

"Let *me* buy out the Restoration Channel. I have money set aside for my own house. That way you and I will each have a stake in the house."

Brandon's first instinct was to tell him no. He felt protective of the house and of Travis. He could buy this house, and he'd make his money back as soon as they sold their next house. He wanted to buy the house as a gift for Travis, as an investment in their future together.

This could also get them into a messy financial entanglement. Brandon knew that. Realistically, it was probably time to get accountants and lawyers involved, and they'd have to renegotiate Travis's contract with the network, and they'd have to work out how to split profits, if they actually needed to split them up, or….

But that was all stuff that could be worked out at a later date.

And Travis was saying he wanted to go in on this house with his own money.

"I see you hesitating, but I think it's what makes the most sense," Travis said. "And it means that if anything happens to us or the show or whatever, that I'm not relying on you financially. Because I won't abide by that. I know you're far more wealthy than I am, but I never want to be dependent on you in that way."

And Brandon got it then. "We should be on equal footing."

"Exactly. I know that things will get hairy when we move in together and we'll have to sort through finances and the show and all that, but… that kind of takes the romance out of things."

Brandon laughed. "Really? You're the unfailingly practical one."

"Maybe I have a romantic streak."

"I know you do." Brandon leaned over and kissed Travis. The kiss lingered and grew until Travis pushed Brandon into the island.

Brandon nudged Travis away before things got out of hand. "So, do I understand you right? Are we doing this?"

"Yes. Let's move into this godforsaken house."

Brandon looked around. Yeah. He felt good about this. "It's a great way to get our relationship off the ground. Going in together on a house, becoming partners in all kinds of ways. I think this is good. Very good."

"We can move my furniture in here, though, right? Because some of yours is ugly."

Brandon laughed. "I love you."

Travis rolled his eyes. But then he said, "I love you too."

EPILOGUE

IT HAD been Travis's idea to host the premiere party for the show at their house. Brandon suspected this was because he had no interest in spending a night in a public place and he'd have some control over the guest list. Also, having the party in Brooklyn meant most of the Restoration Channel executives that might have gone to a party at a bar or club or other event space decided to pass.

Travis was a genius.

Erik and a few of his crew members had come. Ismael and most of the work crew were there too. Kayla and Dave had flown out for the party, and Maribeth, the new producer, had arrived with her husband as well. Mike and Sandy had brought their families, including Mike's teenage daughter and Sandy's six-year-old son, who spent a good portion of the evening running laps around the living room. There were far too many people crammed into the room, too much movement, too much talking, but it was just the sort of happy chaos that belonged in a home, and Brandon loved it.

Travis had deemed catering too much of an expense, but he'd had a bunch of snack platters from a fancy grocery store near his parents' house in Queens delivered, and he'd stocked up the bar they'd put in the dining room. Various party guests had brought other snacks and booze, so the offerings were eclectic. It certainly wasn't cocktails and hors d'oeuvres at a high-end restaurant. It *was* very Travis.

The TV was mounted above the fireplace in the living room; Travis had ultimately had to hire a guy to fix the chimney and fireproof everything, but it was worth it to make the fireplace the centerpiece of the room. The mantel below the TV was otherwise unadorned—Travis had cut that piece of wood himself too. Around them were the walls they'd painted together, the floors Brandon and Ismael had installed, the furniture Kayla had helped Brandon pick out, and the bright teal rug Travis had found at some discount store.

It wasn't like a staged house out of a magazine, as all the other houses they'd flipped had been. It was their home, and it reflected their tastes. And Travis's, it turned out, veered toward the bold and bright in unexpected ways, especially since his wardrobe consisted of mostly black, gray, and navy work clothes.

Brandon already knew this pilot episode ended with Travis and Brandon walking the cameras through their finished house.

They had since flipped four houses and had just gotten an offer on the fifth, so they were basically one voiceover away from having their initial order of six episodes in the tank. The Jessica Benton project had ended up being a blast, especially when Jessica herself got involved in the design. She and Travis had similar taste, which kept the arguing on camera to a minimum. The narrative of that episode shook out to be Travis and Jessica teaming up against Brandon, who had the role of being budget-conscious when Jessica's design ideas got too pricey for the neighborhood. And sure, maybe a giant crystal chandelier in the master bedroom of your Beverly Hills mansion made sense, but in an old Tudor-style house in Brooklyn? No.

They'd worked on four other houses, all more traditional flips, including one old house that had been built to look like a pagoda. The Victorians who had built houses in the neighborhood had drawn from a ton of different inspirations, and Japanese art was trendy the year this house had been built. Travis had done a ton of research on Japanese design to help make the interior match the exterior, and it had been a unique house for sure.

But they'd sold all five houses for decent profits, which made up a little for the pile of money Brandon had spent fixing the house he sat in now.

He'd heard from his family in the interim too. Robert had grudgingly congratulated his success, although didn't seem eager to invite him back to dinner anytime soon. Luke had been more enthusiastic, and they'd been getting along lately. Brandon had considered inviting Luke to the premiere party, but he was in rehab, which was probably for the best.

And the show had been renewed. There were a finite number of houses in Victorian Flatbush that could be flipped, but Maribeth's idea was to start flipping houses in other Brooklyn neighborhoods. Brandon was starting to look for abandoned houses in nicer neighborhoods closer to downtown, but Travis thought it might be worthwhile to look in areas a bit farther out. Travis already had a lead on a place in Gravesend not far from Coney Island—a brick three-story duplex that would be really fun to renovate—just a few blocks south of L&B Spumoni Gardens, a legendary Brooklyn pizza place. They'd do the show together at least one more season; they'd gotten a twelve-episode order this time.

It had been a year since Brandon had signed on to do this show. What an amazing year it had been.

"Babe, it's starting!" Travis shouted from the living room.

Brandon finished mixing his drink and walked into the living room, where everyone was piled on seats or the floor. Every possible piece of seating was taken, but Travis gestured at the floor in front of his feet, so Brandon sat there, between Travis's legs. Travis ran a hand through Brandon's hair, probably without even realizing he was doing it, because Ismael gave him the hairy eyeball.

"Dude," said Ismael.

"What?" asked Travis. Then he took his hands away, so he must have realized what he was doing.

On screen, Brandon said in voiceover, *My name is Brandon Chase. I've been flipping houses for nearly ten years. Now, with the help of my romantic partner Travis, a licensed contractor, I'm flipping houses in Brooklyn, New York. We're taking on the worst homes in otherwise great neighborhoods. Victorian Flatbush is a world unto itself, a gorgeous neighborhood full of hundred-year-old mansions in a variety of architectural styles. We're finding the neglected ones and restoring them to their original glory.*

The voiceover played footage of Brandon and Travis at work together on several different houses. There was an image of Brandon bashing a cabinet door with a sledgehammer, Travis laying down hardwood floor in the Benton house, Travis and Brandon having a heated discussion while standing over counter and cabinet samples. Then the episode opened with the footage of Brandon and Travis doing the initial walk-through of this very house, with Travis finding lots of issues.

"Ah, the good old days," Travis said. "Before I really knew you."

"You love me," Brandon said.

"I do. It's annoying."

"Hush."

The episode was a highlight reel of the whole process of renovating the house: Travis finding the foundation issues in the basement, Travis picking fights with Brandon over the design, Ismael putting up drywall, Brandon and Kayla shopping, Brandon putting in floors, Mike and Sandy working on the kitchen and bathrooms, Ismael telling Brandon about the roof leak. They'd filmed Travis's reaction to the final kitchen unveiling—he still hadn't quite been over Brandon's choice of those tiles, so it was a convincing reveal—and then they'd had to film Brandon and Travis having a discussion about potentially keeping the house.

After that was footage of Brandon and Travis moving their furniture in so that there could be good before-and-after shots with furniture. Then there was one final shot of the house, over which the house's purchase price and Brandon's investment were shown. Normally this would be the part of the show where the math illustrated how much of a profit they'd made selling the house, but in this case, Brandon explained in voiceover that he and Travis loved the house so much, they couldn't let it go.

"What did you think?" Brandon asked everyone in the room, although really he was asking Travis, who had never seen himself on TV before.

"Good shot of the McPhee company T-shirts," said Mike.

"You know what? That was fun," said Ismael. "That roof leak was a doozy."

Brandon thought the show was good. Two months of footage edited down to about forty minutes—plus commercials—made the whole experience seem a little more intense. But the crazy thing to Brandon was that he could actually see himself falling in love with Travis on screen. He recognized how his own facial expressions changed around Travis as the show went on. And he noticed Travis's body language changing around him too, in subtle ways that probably only Brandon could see. It was such a strange document of their relationship, this forty-minute television show.

"It's very weird to see myself on television," said Travis. "Is my accent really that bad?"

"It is," said Brandon. "I like it."

"Good Lord. I sound like Bernie Sanders."

Brandon laughed. "You sound like you grew up in Queens. Which you did."

"I don't think I want to watch many more episodes."

Brandon laughed. "Don't sweat it. You look great on TV. Like a badass with a heart of gold."

"Shut up. You're biased."

"I think you both look great," said Kayla. "On TV, I mean. And you look like you actually still like me, which will hopefully keep people from egging my house."

"Egging? Really?" asked Travis.

"I mean, it's only happened twice, but the second time I heard a woman yell, 'Cheater!' from her car. That Brandon is actually gay obviously never entered her mind as the reason our marriage didn't work out."

"There was that story in *People* in which someone who doesn't even know Brandon posited that he just fell in love with me regardless of gender," Travis said. "It was fun to read that I'd led the poor man to the dark side."

"I wanted to be lured."

"It's not the dark side!" Travis threw his hands up.

Brandon laughed. He twisted his body so that he could put a hand on Travis's thigh and look up at him. "Trav, I would not have fallen in love with you if you were not a dude. How's that?"

"A little better." Travis crossed his arms.

Brandon loved when Travis was passionate about something like this. He patted Travis's thigh. Other than that, did you like the show?"

Travis stared at the television. "It was very strange. Two months of work boiled down to less than an hour."

"Yeah, you never get used to that," said Kayla.

"On the bright side, we live in this house now," said Brandon.

"That's true," said Travis. "It is a pretty awesome house."

"It's the best house."

"It's *our* house."

"God, you guys are lame," said Ismael.

Travis laughed. He pushed at Brandon's shoulders until Brandon moved out of his way, and then he stood up. "Well, eat up. There's plenty of food left. I want you all to finish off the trays and stuff and then get out so that I can continue pulling Brandon over to the dark side."

"Too late," said Brandon.

"Sex. 'The dark side' means sex, doesn't it?" said Ismael.

"Dirty, filthy, gay sex," said Travis, apparently no longer offended.

"Yuck," Ismael said, but he was laughing.

After the credits ended, an old episode of *Dream Home* came on TV. "Ugh, this garbage?" said Kayla.

Brandon laughed and led everyone back into the kitchen, and his guests chowed down on the food. While everyone was preoccupied with eating, Travis sauntered over and hooked an arm around Brandon's middle.

"Does that whole seeing-yourself-on-TV thing get any easier?" asked Travis.

"No. I always see every blemish on my face or weird squeak of my voice or unflattering pose as I'm putting in tile."

"So let's just not watch our show again ever."

Brandon chuckled. "That's fair. But you know what I couldn't stop thinking about when I watched the episode?"

"What?"

"It was like watching myself fall in love with you. Restoration Channel viewers will fall in love with you too, you know."

"Hopefully not in the same way."

"Well, no, probably not. I'm just saying, you look hot when you're working on a house."

"You're *really* biased. I look sweaty and tired."

"Well, I am biased, but you're also hot. And I love you."

"Okay, okay." Travis stepped away. "I love you too. But I'm serious about watching the show. You're hot too, but I see you in person all the time. I don't need to see you on TV."

"Okay, Trav. Okay."

"I'd like to see *more* of you." Travis waggled his eyebrows.

"Not with all these people here."

Travis winked and turned around. He clapped his hands twice. "Party's over, folks. Eat up and get out."

KATE MCMURRAY writes smart romantic fiction. She likes creating stories that are brainy, funny, and, of course, sexy with regular-guy characters and urban sensibilities. She advocates for romance stories by and for everyone. When she's not writing, she edits textbooks, watches baseball, plays violin, crafts things out of yarn, and wears a lot of cute dresses. She's active in Romance Writers of America, serving for two years on the board of Rainbow Romance Writers, the LGBT romance chapter, and three—including two as president—on the board of the New York City chapter. She lives in Brooklyn, NY, with two cats and too many books.

Website: www.katemcmurray.com
Twitter: @katemcmwriter
Facebook:www.facebook.com/katemcmurraywriter

KATE McMURRAY

RACE *for* REDEMPTION

Elite Athletes: Book 3

Sprinter Jason Jones Jr., known around the world as JJ, is America's hope to take the title of Fastest Man in the World, the champion of the Olympic 100-meter sprint. Two years before, a doping scandal brought his winning streak to a crashing end, and even though he's been cleared of wrongdoing, he's finding it hard to escape the damage to his reputation. At the Games in Madrid, no one believes he's innocent, and officials from the doping agency follow him everywhere.

It just fuels JJ's determination to show them he's clean and still the fastest man on earth.

If only he wasn't tempted by foxy hurdler Brandon Stanton, an engineering student and math prodigy who views each race like a complicated equation. His analytical approach helps him win races, and he wants to help JJ do the same. But JJ's been burned too many times before and doesn't trust anyone who has all the answers. No matter how sexy and charming JJ finds Brandon, the Olympics is no place for romance. Or is it?

KATE McMURRAY

STICK *the* LANDING

BOOK TWO

ELITE ATHLETES

"...a sweet and sexy love story nestled among a solid sports tale." —*Library Journal*

Elite Athletes: Book 2

Jake Mirakovitch might be the best gymnast in the world, but there's one big problem: he chokes in international competition. The least successful of a family of world-class gymnasts, he has struggled to shake off nerves in the past. This time he's determined to bring home the gold no matter what.

Retired figure skater Topher Caldwell wants a job as a commentator for the American network that covers the Olympics, and at the Summer Olympics in Madrid, he has a chance to prove himself with a few live features. He can't afford to stumble.

Olympic victories eluded Topher, so he knows about tripping when it really counts. When he interviews Jake, the two bond over the weight of all that pressure. The flamboyant reporter attracts the kind of attention Jake—stuck in a glass closet—doesn't want, but Jake can't stay away. Topher doesn't want to jeopardize his potential new job, and fooling around with a high-profile athlete seems like a surefire way to do just that. Yet Topher can't stay away either….

KATE McMURRAY

HERE COMES *the* FLOOD

Elite Athletes: Book 1

Two years ago, swimmer Isaac Flood hit rock bottom. His alcoholism caught up with him, landing him in jail with a DUI. After facing his demons in rehab, he's ready to get back in the pool. He stuns everyone at the US Olympic Trials, and now he's back at his fourth Olympics with something to prove.

Diver Tim Swan made headlines for snatching a surprise gold medal four years ago, and then making a viral coming-out video with his actor boyfriend, the subject of splashy tabloid headlines. Now his relationship is over and Tim just wants to focus on winning gold again, but reporters in Madrid threaten to overshadow Tim's skill on the platform.

When Isaac and Tim meet, they recognize each other as kindred spirits—they are both dodging media pressure while devoting their lives to the sports they love. As they get to know each other—and try to one-up each other with their respective medal counts—they realize they're becoming more than friends. But will the relationship burn bright for just sixteen days, or can it last past the Closing Ceremony?

THERE HAS TO BE A REASON

KATE McMURRAY

WMU: Book One

Dave is enjoying his junior year at a big New England university, even if none of his relationships have been especially satisfying. He plans to hang around with his best friend Joe and focus on his studies until he graduates, and then he'll figure out the rest.

Meeting Noel changes his plans.

Noel is strikingly beautiful and unlike anyone Dave knows. Something about Noel draws Dave to him—an attraction Dave doesn't feel ready to label. And even if he was, why would Noel be interested in Dave? And what about Joe? He hates Noel and everything he represents, and he might hate Dave if he finds out about Dave's secret desires. So Dave will have to keep those feelings hidden—along with his relationship with Noel.

But Noel has fought too hard for his identity to be Dave's dirty secret. Will Dave tell the truth and risk the life he's always known… or live a lie and risk losing the love of his life?

THE BOY NEXT DOOR

KATE McMURRAY

Life is full of surprises and, with luck, second chances.

After his father's death, Lowell leaves the big city to help his sick mother in the conservative small town where he grew up. He's shocked to find himself living next to none other than his childhood friend Jase. Lowell always had a crush on Jase, and the man has only gotten more attractive with age. Unfortunately Jase is straight, now divorced, and raising his six-year-old daughter. It's nice to reconnect, but Lowell doesn't see a chance for anything beyond friendship.

Until a night out together changes everything.

Jase can't fight his growing feelings for Lowell, and he doesn't want to give up the happy future they could have. But his ex-wife issues an ultimatum: he must keep his homosexuality secret or she'll revoke his custody of their daughter, Layla. Now Jase faces an impossible choice: Lowell and the love he's always wanted, or his daughter.

DREAMSPINNER
PRESS
dreamspinnerpress.com